THE Worm MAN

THE Worm MAN

A NOVEL

MARY FRANCES HILL

ARCHWAY PUBLISHING

Archway Publishing books may be ordered through booksellers or by contacting:

Archway Publishing
1663 Liberty Drive
Bloomington, IN 47403
www.archwaypublishing.com
844-669-3957

Because of the dynamic nature of the Internet, any web addresses or links contained in
this book may have changed since publication and may no longer be valid. The views
expressed in this work are solely those of the author and do not necessarily reflect the
views of the publisher, and the publisher hereby disclaims any responsibility for them.

This is a work of fiction. All of the characters, names, incidents, organizations, and dialogue
in this novel are either the products of the author's imagination or are used fictitiously.

Any people depicted in stock imagery provided by Getty Images are models,
and such images are being used for illustrative purposes only.
Certain stock imagery © Getty Images.

ISBN: 978-1-6657-2175-2 (sc)
ISBN: 978-1-6657-2176-9 (e)

Library of Congress Control Number: 2022906841

Print information available on the last page.

Archway Publishing rev. date: 06/03/2022

To my mother, who loved all books, but especially mysteries and thrillers.

Author's Note

This story, which is primarily set in Merrimack County, New Hampshire, was inspired by vacations spent in the lovely town of New London. Though the author describes local businesses, recreational sites and schools, these depictions come from her imagination and memories. Please read this with a flexible open mind. Enjoy.

Chapter 1

I tighten my grip on my portfolio case, say a quick prayer, and enter the Wyndham Gallery. As white walls and framed pops of color surround me, the door clanks shut, causing me to jump. *You can do this, Kate. You've got to do this. Once upon a time, you earned an art degree. Don't forget that.* Trembling, I tuck some hair into my bun, smooth my cotton tunic, and look up.

Evelyn Taylor, the gallery owner, is seated behind her desk. Her manicured fingers rest on her laptop keyboard. When I greet Evelyn, she nods. She knows me. My late husband, Glen, an architect, designed her building, not that this means anything.

In the past, whenever I've pitched her my work, she's always rejected it. I've simply brushed off her rebuffs. But today is different. To say I'm desperate is an understatement. Glen died of leukemia eleven months ago. His medical bills crushed me. I'm about to lose our New Hampshire farmhouse, his dream home. I have to pull in some cash. But this moment is about more than money. It's about me proving my worth as an artist, as a person. Since Glen's death, I've felt purposeless, lost.

As I approach her, Evelyn's gaze drifts to my portfolio case. She purses her lips. "Show's less than a week away, Kate. I'm no longer reviewing or accepting submissions."

I take in her sleek bob and designer pantsuit. "But it'll only take you a few minutes to look over my drawings."

Evelyn taps her Rolex. "I've got an appointment in Manchester. Gotta get rolling. Traffic on I-93 is a bitch these days."

"Please, Evelyn. Just take a peek." I gesture at the towering gallery walls, the steel beams, and the canned lighting. "Glen's firm did a nice job with your space."

She cocks her chin at the Mercedes in the lot. "I'll give you five minutes. But only because I'm not eager to climb into that hot car."

"You won't be disappointed."

I hand her my sketchbook. As she thumbs through it, sweet, innocent eyes gaze up from the pages. This makes total sense. I'm a third-grade teacher and love drawing kids, especially my students. I've filled my sketchbook with their curious, eager likenesses. I consider these drawings my best work. Evelyn squints at the images, and I hold my breath.

"Well, technically these really are quite good," she says. "This little girl with the white-blonde hair, you drew her a number of times."

"That's Cassie," I say. "Cassie was in my class two years ago. She's a sweetheart."

I smile. Teachers aren't supposed to have favorites, but I've got one. It's Cassie. Because I tutored Cassie in math after school, at the park and at our house, and Glen regularly drove her home, he got to know her too. He claimed the architect in him liked that she preferred watching *Tiny House Nation* and *The World's Most Extraordinary Homes* over playing with American Girl dolls. After our tutoring sessions, Glen and Cassie often designed and built doll and birdhouses in our barn. On occasion, they met at the lake and made sandcastles. Though their close relationship was unusual, I didn't question it. My late-term miscarriage prevented Glen from having the family he desired. If spending time with Cassie made him happy, who was I to judge? And Cassie's mom, Lauren, who'd just had a baby, seemed to appreciate Glen's help. It takes a village to raise a child. Isn't that what people say?

Evelyn shuts my sketchbook and gives it back to me. "Skill-wise, these drawings are excellent. But they're simply not provocative enough. Come back when you've got something special. Your work is strong, just not compelling. These won't sell."

My chest tightens. "But I sold seventy similar drawings at the PTA fundraiser carnival last spring. And those were just freehand drawings. I did them in five minutes while the students were posing, well, sort of. Half the kids were eating cotton candy while I was drawing them. The others were playing with their ticket stubs and twisting their glow-bead necklaces. I have a website," I add when Evelyn glances at the door. "People hire me to draw their children quite regularly, especially Merrimack County residents. Someone will buy these if you include them in your show. I guarantee it. Since I launched my site seven months ago, I've sold 180 plus portraits. The school parents and staff still rave about my carnival sketches."

Evelyn shrugs. "Of course, they do. Everyone loves pictures of their friends and family members, hence the popularity of Facebook and Instagram."

"But—"

"Like I said, your technique and your talent, they're undeniable. But I'm running a business here. I've got a reputation to uphold. I need pieces critics and art aficionados are going to notice. What I want are images that'll make industry people talk. Faces of sweet children, well, to put it bluntly, are boring. Too tame."

"Please—"

"I'm having another show in December. Come back then."

"But—"

"No, not this time."

As Evelyn grabs her keys off her desk, I slip my sketchbook back into my case. My hand shakes, the case falls to the floor, and a drawing slides out. Bloodred squiggles cover the page. Instinctively, I reach for the drawing.

Evelyn swats my hand away. "What's that?"

"Nothing," I tell her. "Absolutely nothing. Just something I scribbled. A doodle."

She plucks the drawing off the floor, studying it. When she grins, I recoil.

In the drawing, a four-fingered hand grips a bloody snowball. Pieces of red yarn and worms poke out of the snow mound. As a teen, back in New Jersey, I witnessed my best friend Whitney's abduction. Whitney was murdered five days after she was snatched. Her killer, the Worm Man, died before he was caught and arrested. What I'd drawn was her murderer's hand and his calling card, earthworms.

I stare at the hideous drawing and shiver. The night I created it, I wanted to rip it up. But I knew the piece was exceptional, worth money, so I tucked it into my portfolio case for safekeeping.

Evelyn fingers my gory drawing. "We'll do a series. We'll display six of those kid drawings: the overbite girl, the scooter kid, the boy with the dimples, the freckle-faced twins, the girl sucking her thumb, and that girl you drew a dozen times, the one with the white-blonde hair."

"Cassie," I say.

She nods. "We'll juxtapose the kid pics with this bloody one. The effect will be shocking. My take is forty percent. You price your pieces." She points at my snowball hand drawing. "What do you want to charge for this one?"

"It's isn't for sale," I snap. "I don't want it exhibited. It doesn't fit my brand. It's—"

"Perfect for my show. Look," Evelyn says when I bite my lip, "just so we're clear, I'm not interested in the others without this one. Alone, they're dull. This one completes the message." She jingles her keys. "It's all or nothing? What's it gonna be, Kate?"

I picture the stack of unpaid bills on my breakfast table and think about my farmhouse and the countless hours Glen spent refinishing the hardwoods, painting the trim and sills, and tiling the bathrooms. As Evelyn grabs her briefcase, I do the math in my head. *Three hundred dollars times seven minus Evelyn's forty percent equals one thousand two hundred and sixty dollars*, enough to cover a mortgage payment and make a dent in my property tax debt, but not so much that I'll turn off buyers.

"You've got a deal. Three hundred each." I hand her my sketchbook. "And thank you. I truly appreciate the opportunity."

Evelyn and I speak about mounting and framing the pieces and details pertaining to the upcoming show. She slips my horrific hand drawing and my sketchbook into her briefcase. We exit the gallery, and she climbs into her Mercedes. As she drives away, in my mind, I see my murdered childhood friend, Whitney Bay, eyes wide, arms flailing, and snowflakes hemorrhaging from her white-blonde hair.

I walk across the parking lot, and the sour taste of guilt fills my mouth. *What's wrong with you, Kate Boswell?* I think. *What kind of person profits from her childhood friend's murder? It's sick. Wrong!*

I vomit on the asphalt and retreat to my SUV. Weaving and swerving, I drive home to my farmhouse, where I check my window and door locks until my knuckles bleed.

* * *

Despite my initial freak-out in the galley parking lot, the week that follows my pitch to Evelyn passes quickly and uneventfully.

It's mid-August. I'm still on summer break from teaching. Hoping to gather information for next year's astronomy unit, I attend a lecture about the Milky Way in Concord. The next day, back at home, I clean out my SUV, do yoga, draw, and text my mother. I'm keeping tabs on her. My father suffered a fatal heart attack five years ago. I'm an only child and Mom's on a sightseeing tour, traveling through Europe. But though I'm busy and Mom's texts indicate that she's having the time of her life, I'm haunted by the bloody snowball hand drawing I gave Evelyn. Like a horror movie, scenes from Whitney's abduction replay in my mind.

* * *

I see Whitney walking beside me, kicking snow. In my memory, her lips move. "Straight up, now tell me!" she belts, mimicking the late 80's pop-star Paula Abdul.

"Do you really want to love me forever? oh, oh, oh," we sing in unison.

"So glad my mom's not here," Whitney mutters, rolling her eyes.

The teen me laughs as Whitney presses her fist against her lips and tilts her head back like she's guzzling a drink. *A dance move*, the teen me decides. Following her lead, I attempt a pirouette in the snow, throw my head back and mimic her guzzling motion.

I blink, and the scene changes. I see Whitney wiping snow off the park slide and climbing the slide ladder. I see a man with steely-grey eyes. He's staring at her. Whitney slides, and the man charges toward us and grabs her. As he slams her head against the metal slide base, her red mitten flies off. He scoops her up and carries her, running.

"Give her back!" the teen me shouts, chasing after them.

I blink again, and Whitney and I are in the back seat of an old Chevy sedan. She's limp, not moving. The man with the steely-grey eyes is in the front seat. A hatchet and bucket of worms are on the floor by my booted feet. When the man turns and grips the Chevy's headrest, the teen me grabs the hatchet and slams it down on his hand. As I bolt from the car, the man's bloody finger sails toward the windshield.

"You little bitch!" he snarls, "tell anyone, and I'll cut off yours! Don't think I'll forget you!"

I blink a third time, and I'm alone in the snowy park, no Whitney and no steely-grey-eyed man. I see the old Chevy fishtailing down the icy road.

* * *

Desperate to ward off these memories, I binge-watch Netflix, swim laps at Bucklin Beach, bake a batch of butter cookies, organize my linen closet, and sketch a sixth-grader from my church.

Before I know it, it's Saturday, the evening of Evelyn's show. I'm at the Wyndham Gallery, and the place is packed. My legs are yogurt. I want to bolt home and hide beneath my bedcovers. *It's just one night. Woman up. Sell your pieces,* I tell myself, hesitating in the doorway.

New London, population 4,397, doesn't have a movie theater, a mall, or a bowling alley. Residents participate in recreational activities at their churches or the schools or through the community sports programs. The Barn Playhouse, the library, and Colby Sawyer College provide cultural programs for the town. But regardless of the limited night scene, I'm surprised to see so many locals milling about. I didn't expect the press either. Three reporters, wearing press-credentialed lanyards, chat with Evelyn. I stare at the reporters and the crowd and my stomach dips.

I didn't invite anyone. Since Glen's death, I haven't wanted to socialize. People who haven't lost a spouse, think I should be over Glen's death by now. But I'm not, not even close. The only time the sad empty feeling dissipates is when I'm teaching or drawing. The stress of being without the man who was my everything continues to overwhelm me.

But tonight's anxiety isn't just about losing my better half. No one in New London knows I witnessed Whitney's abduction, and I'm determined to keep my secret under wraps. But the bloody snowball hand drawing makes me feel as if I'm outing myself. Even worse, I've got this sense that by exhibiting my image of the Worm Man's bloody hand, that I'm potentially resurrecting a monster. In other words, I'm taking that cursed Annabelle doll out of the cabinet, brushing dust off that Jumanji board and rolling the dice. Though it's completely illogical, I'm worried that something awful is going to happen because of my lack of respect for the Worm Man's evil. Okay, so I'm being ridiculous.

As my five fellow artists stand near their pieces, their nametags pinned to their blouses and lapels, I wave to Evelyn. I collect my nametag off her desk, and position myself near my work. Desperate for a distraction, I study the room.

Images of deformed nudes, the pope brandishing a sword, Iraqi soldiers, abstracts, and photographs of a burning teepee adorn the walls. As my fellow artists converse with their guests and smile, I make a beeline for the bar. I request a glass of pinot grigio and down it. As I grip my empty wineglass, Lauren Rossi, the mother of my favorite student Cassie, saunters over to my series. Lauren, a stay-at-home-mom, smiles at my piece of her daughter. As she points at my gruesome snowball drawing, three PTA moms surround her.

Lauren is poised, polished, blonde, and curvy. She's basically everything I'm not. Most women adore her. But there's something off between her and me. Even though I taught and tutored Cassie, and Cassie was Glen's little buddy, Lauren steers clear of me. Whenever we do interact, I find myself questioning the effectiveness of my deodorant.

As Lauren chats with the PTA moms, policeman Liam Messer, taps my arm. *Thank you, Jesus. It's someone I like, someone who genuinely likes me.* I can literally feel my muscles relaxing.

Liam's been good to me since Glen's death. He's kind, protective, patient, and rugby player hunky. Tonight, he's wearing khakis, a blue blazer, and loafers. He should look boring, too preppy. But he doesn't. Liam's a catch. Even since he moved here from Boston a few years ago, we've been running into each other at the local coffee shop, Grounds, and he regularly picks up his niece, Emma, from Kearsarge Elementary, where I work. Though were good friends, Liam's made it clear that he'd like us to be more. He's been asking me out, off and on, for the past six months. I'm super attracted to him. We've even kissed a few times. But though his lips are delicious and I can see myself having something solid and real with him, I'm simply not ready for a relationship with any man.

As I twist my wedding band, Liam gestures at my hideous snowball piece. "Love the kid pics, Kate. But what's with the bloody snowball?"

I force out a laugh. "I devoured a meatball sub, fell asleep, and dreamt about all of that."

Liam winks. "You mean you don't always dream about me?"

"I …"

Randi, my closest friend and a fellow third-grade teacher, elbows me. She grins at Liam. "My girl, Kate, here only fantasizes about George Clooney." Randi hugs me. "Good to see you out and about, Kate, but really, no personal invite? I had to find out about this shindig from Evelyn."

I shrug. "Sorry. You're absolutely right. I should have invited you. I've been holed up for so long. Since Glen … I've lost my people skills."

"They'll come back," Randi says, patting my wrist. "Give it time."

Randi has two sons, eight and five years old. "So how are Mikey and Justin?" I ask her.

Randi, who has the physique of a gymnast and the energy of an Olympian, tightens her shirtdress sash. "Crazy. They're at home, terrorizing their sitter."

As Randi and Liam talk, I scan the crowd. Lauren and the other PTA moms have migrated to the pope oil painting. Two of Glen's architect colleagues, Harris and Reese, are now staring at my drawings. Their voices float toward me.

"She's an aspiring portrait artist, correct?" Harris, Glen's partner, says, eyeing my pieces. "I assumed she'd draw Glen."

"If not Glen, then one of his buildings or their home. Glen loved that old farmhouse," Reese says to Harris.

I nod. Reese is correct. Glen did love our old farmhouse. And despite its age, my initial concerns about its isolation, and all of Glen's half-finished projects, the place is home to me too. I can't imagine living anywhere else, which is why I have to sell my drawings and get that money to pay my mortgage.

I frown at my grisly hand drawing. *Don't get any ideas. If you weren't so potentially valuable, I'd put you through a paper shredder. Just because I didn't destroy you before, doesn't mean I won't now. Don't tempt me.*

As I gaze at the ghastly piece, Randi tugs at my sleeve. "Kate, where'd you go? Evelyn just announced the featured artist award winner. It's you! Go!" Randi nudges me toward Evelyn. "She wants you to answer questions. You know, a Q & A with the patrons."

I look up. The guests, reporters, and featured artists are all staring at me. As they clap, I stumble over to Evelyn, who hands me a blue ribbon and a $500 check.

"The ribbon and the check are tokens, trinkets so you can remember this night. The real prize is the press you're gonna get," Evelyn says, smiling at me.

"And your gallery's gonna get," Harris shouts.

Evelyn laughs. "Well, I should reap some benefits for discovering her." She motions to my drawings. "Congratulations, Kate. Your collection, *Innocence vs. Evil: A Study in Contrasts,* is going to be featured in the Arts and Entertainment section of the *Boston Herald, The Globe,* and *The Concord Monitor,* and mentioned on my gallery's and *Art New England Magazine's* Instagram pages. I'm sure the coverage and articles will lead to big things." She motions to the crowd. "Does anyone have any questions for Kate?"

My knees weaken. The attendees' features blur.

A woman whom I recognize from my yoga class waves her hand. "The news is filled with reports about mass shootings, hate crimes, and war. Kate, did you draw the bloody hand drawing to symbolize the toll of protecting children in today's violent world?"

Before I can respond, Louise, one of the PTA moms, says, "I'm not sure about that. But I'm certain the snow symbolizes sadness, and the earthworms represent hope for the future. You know. 'Cause snowy winters are bleak, and worms help plants and life grow."

"Oh, and the red string means protection and good luck. Red strings are in trend. I wear one," Heather, another PTA mom, adds, motioning to a red string encircling her wrist.

"I ..." My lip quivers. I'm not prepared for this. It seems since Glen's death, I'm ill-prepared for life in general.

As I search for words, a grey-bearded man wearing a press badge clears his throat. "Folks, let's get real. Ms. Boswell didn't come here to teach Art Themes 101. I mean, come on. She doesn't lecture at Colby Sawyer College. The woman's a third-grade teacher for Christ sakes."

I lock eyes with the reporter. I know him, but from where? "Mr.?"

"Kingsley," the reporter says. "Tom Kingsley from *The Globe*."

I nod. "Mr. Kingsley is correct," I stammer. "As most of you know, I am a third-grade teacher." I swallow. "But I'm afraid you're all overthinking this. I wish I could tell you that I had an agenda, some sort of master plan, a specific message or theme I wanted to convey when I created my drawing. But I didn't. I simply put pencil to paper, and that bloody drawing on the wall over there came out."

I plaster on a smile. "But I'm glad my drawings have made you think. We all bring our unique experiences and perspectives to galleries. That's what makes shows like this so interesting. You've all inspired me. Thank you for that." I tap my forehead. "But based on your reactions, I'm thinking I might need therapy."

The crowd laughs. Kingsley raises his hand.

"Do you have something to add Mr. Kingsley?" Evelyn asks.

"Yes. I'd like to clarify my previous statement. When I said before that Kate was a third-grade teacher, I wasn't implying that she's not talented or is undeserving of her award. I simply meant that to understand her pieces, we need to focus on who she is as a person, her unique life experiences, her personal history." He gestures at me. "As a girl, Kate—"

The room spins. My heart drums. I know what's happening. It's happened to me a thousand times before. I'm having a full-on panic attack. Liam seems to sense I'm in trouble.

"A toast!" he shouts. "A toast to Kate Boswell, to the five other talented artists whose work adorns these walls, and to Evelyn Taylor for making this night happen."

"To great art!" Evelyn says.

"To great art!" everyone shouts.

Liam whispers in my ear, "Let's go somewhere quiet."

"Quiet sounds wonderful," I murmur.

As Liam guides me through the crowd and toward the back exit, I glance at Kingsley. An image of a cluttered New York City office and a younger, thinner, clean-shaven Kingsley pops into my head.

"That reporter interviewed me when I was living in New Jersey. He was writing a book about a childhood friend of mine," I say.

Liam huffs. "Something tells me he's working on a sequel."

Liam pulls me through the back exit. The door shuts. We're alone and surrounded by cars. It's a warm, humid evening. The sun is a sinking orb. The world seems different out here, calmer and safer. As cheerful voices seep through the gallery windows, my breaths come easier. The feeling of doom that threatened to paralyze me dissipates. Suddenly I'm disgusted with myself for bolting.

I motion to the gallery behind me. "Why am I hiding? Everyone's inside. I should go back in. What's wrong with me?"

"Don't be so hard on yourself," Liam says. "Tonight, would be a lot for anyone."

He squeezes my shoulder. His touch comforts me, feeling right. Still, I back away.

"Okay," I say, "so I didn't actually want to be here tonight. I don't like crowds, talking in front of groups, or selling myself. But I've dreamed of having success as an artist my entire life. And I was starting to enjoy myself. Being with you and seeing Randi, it was nice. And winning that award was so unexpected, so great. But—"

He nods. "It's hard. I get it. You wish Glen were here to celebrate with you. But I'm sure he'd want you to enjoy your success."

"He would."

Liam's voice tugs at me. "Kate, the sadness and the pain, you've got to let it go."

I shake my head. "You sound like that snow fairy from that Disney movie."

"Well, from what my niece tells me, Queen Elsa is pretty smart. Enjoy your moment. You deserve it. Have fun. Relax. You don't have to do anything special. Just be yourself. Nobody expects—"

I frown. "That reporter, Kingsley."

"Forget Kingsley. Guy's a jerk."

"But he—"

"We better go back inside." Liam glances at the door. "Your fans are waiting."

I reach for Liam's hand. "Thank you."

I spend the rest of the evening with Liam by my side, working the crowd and praying my award will lead to the sale of my drawings. Kingsley doesn't approach me, but I feel his eyes on me.

When the wall clock reads 11:00 p.m., Evelyn hands me a sold sticker. "Congratulations! Someone bought your entire series!"

My heart thuds. "What? The entire series? That's awesome! Who?"

Evelyn zips her lip with her finger. "The buyer wants to remain anonymous. Everything will be handled on Monday, as long as you're fine with the terms."

"Terms?"

"The price. The anonymity of the sale."

"So how much are we talking here?'

"Ten thousand."

"Ten grand!" I mouth. "But I set the price at three hundred dollars each."

Evelyn nods. "I know. The offer is shockingly high. Absurd! There was a bidding war. You broke a gallery record. The most anyone's ever paid for a series is three thousand." She grins at me. "Do I have an eye for talent or what?"

"But it's too much, way too much. It's insane. It doesn't make sense. The drawings of the children I understand. Their faces are precious, darling. But who would want to hang that bloody hand on their wall? The image is thought-provoking, yes. But—"

"Look," Evelyn says, "Whether the buyer simply loves your pieces and thinks you have talent, or they admire you personally, he or she wants you to have the money. I'd take it."

"But—"

Evelyn leans toward me. "Listen, Kate. New London is a small town. Everyone knew and loved Glen, he—"

I nod. "Yes. Of course. The price and the secrecy, is because of Glen. Whoever made the offer doesn't want to embarrass me. I accept the terms. Ten thousand is mind-blowing, exceeding all my expectations. And the anonymity, I'm good with it."

Evelyn points to the sold sticker in my grasp. "You're a terrific artist. You should feel proud." She grins. "Everyone has a dark side, Kate. Don't be afraid to tap into yours. Our aberrations make us interesting. They give us character. Think about it. I'll call you when everything is formalized with the sale, probably Monday. Does PayPal work for you?"

"Sure," I tell her. "Absolutely. Thanks for the opportunity."

I hurry off to tell Randi and Liam about the sale.

The rest of the night is a blur. Randi's realtor husband, Bill, arrives. And Liam, Randi, Bill, and I head to Peter Christians' Tavern for coffee and pie. Our fellow diners congratulate me. The waitresses make a list of the wealthy people who summer and ski in New London. They place bets and speculate about who the generous buyer might be. Everyone seems to be having fun, wagering and guessing, but I can't relax. I can't stop worrying about the buyer's secrecy and the crazy sale price. I keep picturing Whitney's limp body and the old Chevy fishtailing down that icy road.

The rain, which falls softly at first and later pounds the windows and roof of the restaurant, only exacerbates my unease. But it's the phone calls that disturb me the most. Somehow *The Globe* reporter, Kingsley, obtains my number. He leaves me six voicemails and texts me, wanting to talk about the Worm Man. His messages are pushy. I delete them.

Exhausted and craving peace, I say goodbye to Liam, Randi, and Bill and drive home.

As the rain slows to a drizzle, I dart up my porch steps. Once inside, I flip on my foyer light. As is my habit, I double-lock my doors and set my alarm. Yawning, I head to my bathroom and bathe. Still feeling jittery, I escape to my bed, skim a Pottery Barn catalog, and watch reruns of *The Office*. Finally, at 3:00 a.m., sleep comes. But it's a restless sleep, full of nightmares of that New Jersey playground slide, worms wiggling in snow, steely-grey eyes, and Whitney.

I wake eight hours later to daylight and the sound of my ringtone. I glance at my cell screen. *Kingsley.* Annoyed, I turn off my phone. I spend my Sunday morning weeding. When it starts to rain, I head indoors. I read a chapter of Lisa Duffy's novel, *The Salt House*, draw, and do laundry. Feeling lazy, I heat up a frozen lasagna dinner, watch CNN, and crash on the den couch, not bothering to turn off the TV or the lights. I don't turn on my phone again until Monday morning.

Two hours after I do so and as the television drones in the background, Evelyn calls to get my PayPal account information. She wants me to come down to the gallery to collect my copy of the bill of sale. *Thank God. I'll pay my mortgage and those property taxes tomorrow. Pay my gas/electric bill. Maybe even get my SUV serviced. Those damn brake pads need replacing.*

When our conversation ends, I scoop the TV remote up off the couch, intending to turn off the power, but the edge in the Channel Five reporter's voice grabs me.

"Ten-year-old New London resident, Cassie Rossi, disappeared yesterday afternoon while playing on her street. Cassie was wearing pink sneakers, pink shorts, and a white T-shirt. She stands four-foot-two, weighs sixty-four pounds, and has white-blonde hair. Cassie has blue eyes and a dimpled left cheek. Her parents stated that she was wearing a New London Rec backpack containing softball gear. She was carrying a golf umbrella, a red plastic sand shovel, and a bucket. Prior to her disappearance, she was spotted collecting worms in the rain on Pressey Court. If you've seen Cassie or have any information pertaining to her whereabouts, please contact the New London Police Department."

The reporter's face vanishes, and a Progressive Insurance commercial appears on the screen.

Collecting worms. I drop my TV remote. The AA batteries spill out and roll under the couch.

Chapter 2

*F*orty-five minutes have passed since I plucked the under-the-couch dust bunnies off my TV remote batteries. I'm sitting cross-legged on my foyer floor. A notebook rests on my lap. My gut tells me to hightail to the police station, but logic holds me back.

After Whitney's murder, the cops linked her killer to two other victims: a girl in the Poconos and a thirteen-year-old from Hamilton, New Jersey. Forensics matched fingerprints left at the Hamilton abduction scene to those obtained from a transient carpenter, parolee James Hoover. Because Hoover left a fistful of worms with each of his victims' bodies, the press dubbed him "the Worm Man." After the Hamilton murder, the cops tracked Hoover to a homeless shelter in Trenton. But before the authorities could grab him, Hoover fled. Despite a slew of tips from the public and extensive media attention, he vanished—not a peep, no other victims, no sightings, no leads, nothing.

Then out of the blue a decade later, Hoover's New Jersey childhood shore home burned to the ground. Fire investigators determined that a lit cigarette was the cause of the accidental blaze. A single body was discovered amidst the ashes. The news media and cops stated that the victim's DNA matched Hoover's.

I know the Worm Man, AKA James Hoover, is dead. Even so, most days I still feel as if I'm walking a tightrope. Today I'm teetering, about to fall. The vertigo isn't new. Whenever I hear about a child going missing in the Lakes Region, I go to pieces. Twice after reviewing the details of a case, I considered going to the authorities, but didn't.

But now I ponder. *You can't run down to that station and tell them you think Hoover has Cassie. The cops will think you're crazy. Ghosts don't kidnap little girls. You'd just be wasting their time. Besides, you could get in legal trouble. It's called obstruction of justice, something like that.*

I dig my nails into the floorboards beneath me. Other than my parents, my therapist, and the cops, Glen was the only person I confided in about Whitney's abduction. I told him how I climbed into Hoover's old Chevy, how I panicked and failed to pull Whitney out. Glen swore he could handle my Worm Man baggage— my nightmares, my PTSD panic attacks, and my OCD door lock obsession. But I could tell my secret weighed on him. At times, he bore it like a trooper. But then something would shift. He'd distance himself. And the alone-ness would swallow me. Sharing survivor's guilt has a cost, a hefty one.

My thoughts tumble. *Stay put, Kate. You know Hoover's dead. He burned to death. He's gone. But the timing,* I counter, *you can't overlook the timing.*

Using my pen, I make a list.

1. Cassie disappeared after your drawing of Hoover's hand with the missing finger was exhibited.
2. You exhibited a drawing of Cassie. Hoover clearly knows what she looks like.
3. Cassie is your favorite student. You tutored her at the park. It's possible he saw you together. If Hoover wanted to hurt you, he'd grab her.
4. Cassie vanished while collecting worms in the rain. Earthworms are the Worm Man's calling card.
5. An anonymous buyer paid a stupid amount for your drawing.

Oh, just go, I tell myself. *Talk to Liam. You know you'll be useless until you do.*

I spring to my feet and jam the list and pen into my pocket. Trembling, I slip out the door, climb into my SUV, and take the dirt road fronting my house to Main Street. But instead of easing into the Wyndham lot, I drive another half-mile, pull into the police lot, and enter the red brick station house through the lobby. I recognize the woman behind the reception desk, Lori Kent. Lori's son was in Randi's class four years ago. As I near her, Lori stands.

"I need to speak to Officer Messer," I say.

Lori gestures to the corridor behind her. "The guys are pretty swamped back there. What's this about, Kate?"

I swallow. "Cassie Rossi."

Lori motions for me to follow. She's moving fast, and I'm in a daze. I trail her down a narrow hallway, past a conference room, and head to the third door on the right, an interrogation room.

"Have a seat." Lori points to a chair. "Someone will be with you shortly. Do you want something to drink? Coffee? Water?"

"No thanks. I'm good."

Beneath my dress, my legs shake. Lori hovers. She plays with her watchband. "It's horrible about Cassie. When your kid's missing, it's so scary. I lost Ryan at the Lebanon Mall once when he was a toddler. I thought I'd go crazy."

I press my knees together and hope Lori doesn't notice them bouncing. "How is Ryan?"

Lori's face brightens. "Doing better with his math. He's playing hockey. Joined the Boy Scouts."

I picture her ruddy-cheeked boy. "He's a great kid."

As Lori's heels clack down the hall, I take in my surroundings. A rectangular table faces a one-way mirror. Beige walls descend from a popcorn ceiling. A single window peers out at a lot filled with patrol cars. I hone in on the nearest patrol car and focus on the steel mesh cage and bulletproof glass separating the perp area from the front seat.

My thoughts swirl. *This is absurd, Kate. What are you doing here? Liam's gonna think you're nuts. He's clearly busy. He doesn't need your drama.*

I stand, but before I can get to the door, a bald, fifty-something, medium-built man with hazel eyes struts into the room. "FBI Special Agent Kroy Leeds," he says, shaking my hand. "You must be Kate Boswell."

"I am. Nothing personal, but I was hoping to speak with Officer Liam Messer."

Leeds nods. "I understand. But this is a tender-years situation. The missing girl is under the age of thirteen. That makes it my case, though I believe the chief has asked Officer Messer to assist me." He gestures at the hallway. "Lori said you know something about Cassie Rossi's disappearance?"

"Maybe. I don't know … I …" Leeds seems approachable enough, like he could be someone's uncle, a history teacher, or middle-rate Jeopardy contestant. Even so, my stomach knots. "The truth is, I probably shouldn't be bothering you," I say. "But, you see, I teach at Kearsarge Elementary School, here in New London. Cassie Rossi was in my third-grade class two years ago. Like a lot of people in town, I care about her."

My heart thuds. I picture the Worm Man carrying Whitney's limp body and charging toward his Chevy. "This is tough for me," I say. "I don't talk about this often. Actually, I never do. Mostly, I try to forget it ever happened." I stare at the floor tiles, one's broken and another's scuffed. I hear the words coming out of me, but it's like someone else is saying them. "I witnessed the abduction of my best friend, Whitney Bay, when I was thirteen, back in Lawrenceville, New Jersey. The—"

"Worm Man's first victim. I know the case." Leeds' eyes widen. "So, you're the young girl who was with Whitney that day?"

"I am."

Leeds scratches his chin, seeming to study me. "Coincidently, I just had a long conversation about Hoover with that reporter from *The Globe*, Tom Kingsley. He rattled on and on about that lowlife. That *Globe* guy wrote a book about Hoover. More than likely, he's relaunching it. Perhaps he's writing another one. His motivation's obvious. But I'd like to hear from you. Rarely do two citizens point the finger at the same dead suspect. I assume you're going to tell me that James Hoover, AKA the Worm Man, is very much alive."

I shrug. "Hoover grabbing Cassie is just a feeling."

Leeds retrieves a pen and a small memo book from his briefcase. "I've got a few minutes. Let's go with the theory that forensics got it wrong, that the body in that Jersey shore house wasn't Hoover's." He eyeballs me. "What makes you think the Worm Man's got Cassie?"

"Because I exhibited a drawing of Cassie at the Wyndham Gallery two nights ago, and Cassie was out in the rain collecting worms when she vanished."

Leeds frowns. "But the Worm Man's MO is burying worms with his victims' dismembered bodies and tossing worms on their assault sites. He did that with all three of his victims. Grabbing a victim who's in the act of collecting worms is—"

"Apples and oranges," I say.

Leeds points to two chairs. We sit. He looks at me. "Do you mind if I record you?"

"Go ahead."

He grabs a tape recorder on the table and presses the green button. "Let's start from the beginning. When did you first think James Hoover took Cassie?"

"When I saw the news report two hours ago. When the reporter mentioned worms and Cassie's bucket." I scratch at my cuticle. "I'm sorry. I shouldn't be here. I know Hoover's dead. But every time there's an Amber Alert or a kidnapping in the Lakes Region, I'm certain he's to blame. I make a list and lay out both the logic behind my theory and the clues that negate my belief. In the past, I've kept quiet and stayed home."

Leeds speaks slowly. "So why are you here now?"

"Because I told the Worm Man's secret. Well, not verbally, but I revealed it just the same and to a crowd of people. And now Cassie's gone."

Leeds' brows arch. He motions to the recorder. "What secret?"

"I … I …"

I haven't spoken the words aloud, not to anyone, ever. Though I described Whitney's abduction to Glen, my parents, and the authorities, I held back the part about hacking off Hoover's finger. Revealing this is huge to me.

"If you don't feel comfortable saying it out loud, write it down." Leeds pushes his memo book and pen toward me.

You don't have to tell him if you don't want to, the teen me inside my head whispers. But I do. If I don't speak and James Hoover is actually alive and he truly has Cassie, she might never be found. She'll die, just like Whitney and Hoover's two other victims, and it'll be my fault.

I fan my fingers. They shake seizure-like. "He's missing a finger, his right, hand pointer. I severed it with a hatchet. I climbed into his car to help Whitney. The hatchet was on the floor. Just lying there." I shake my head. "I used to think Hoover was really stupid. I mean, what killer leaves a hatchet within his victim's reach? But Hoover wasn't dumb. He was bold, confident actually. He didn't care if he got a little bloody. He liked the mess, the violence, and the possibility that we'd use the hatchet on him. His victims fighting back was part of his game, the killing. Anyhow, I grabbed that hatchet and swung. Hoover's finger flew off. I didn't tell the cops. I've never told anyone, well, except now you."

I look directly at Leeds. I need him to pay attention. "I drew Hoover's hand with the missing finger, and the drawing was exhibited at the Wyndham Gallery last Saturday. Patrons and press filled the place. Three papers published an image of the drawing. I won an award. I'm being featured on several media sites."

Leeds nods, as if digesting this. "So, you think James Hoover saw the drawing and grabbed Cassie to get even with you for spilling his secret?"

"I don't know. Maybe. I just needed to tell someone. That's all. I needed to put it out there. And I've done that. So ..."

Leeds taps the table. "Let's go over this again. You kept James Hoover's secret for thirty years. That's a hell of a long time. You were married and had close friends. I imagine you've undergone therapy given what you went through."

In my mind, I see the Carrier Clinic, the mental health facility where I was hospitalized prior to moving to New London. "Yes."

"And you never told anyone about Hoover's missing finger? Not your therapist or your parents? Not your college roommate? A priest? Your husband?"

"Not a soul," I murmur.

Leeds seems to consider this. "Did Hoover threaten to kill you or your family members if you talked?"

"No. He didn't say that. But he said he'd cut off my fingers if I told anyone. He said he'd never forget me."

"But he never said he'd take another girl?"

"No, but that doesn't mean he ..." I shiver. "Look, my students are important to me. I don't have children of my own, and my husband is deceased. So, if James Hoover wanted to punish me, taking a child from my school would make sense, especially Cassie." I peer at my nails. They're short, chewed-up, and worn down because I mess with them.

I exhale. "Of all the students I've taught—and I've been teaching ten years now, since I left New Jersey—so there are a lot of them. Hands down, she's my favorite. My husband adored her too."

Leeds frowns. "Why? What's so special about Cassie?"

I smile. "She's smart, creative, and empathetic beyond her years."

"Empathetic? That's not a word people usually associate with a ten-year-old."

"You're right." I attempt to explain. "Cassie has ADHD, attention deficit hyperactivity disorder. She talks during class and has trouble staying in her seat. She has to work hard to get passing grades. But her struggles have made her more perceptive, kinder, and wiser. She's an old soul."

"You've spent time with her outside the classroom?"

"I have. My late husband did too." I motion to the window, at the bright August sun in the sky beyond the pane. "We're taking a break for the summer. But for the past two years, during the school year, after school, I tutored Cassie in math in the park and at my home. My husband, Glen used to drive Cassie back to the Rossi's house after our sessions. Lauren's infant son, Ian, was napping, you see."

"Schleping someone else's kid across town. Sounds like an inconvenience for your late husband," Leeds says.

"It wasn't like that. Cassie's a unique girl. Glen and Cassie shared a passion for building things. They clicked. But the truth is, he drove her for me. Cassie's mother Lauren—I assume you've met her—has a strong personality. Glen offered to play chauffer so I wouldn't have to deal with her." I look down. "Glen passed away last year. He had leukemia." I grip my chair arms. "Anyhow, there's something else you should know. It pertains to the gallery show."

Leeds leans toward me. "I'm listening."

"Not only did I exhibit my drawing of Hoover's finger, but someone bought the piece for an insane amount of money, and they did it anonymously. Actually, they bought my entire series."

Leeds' eyes widen. "How much are we talking here?"

"Ten grand."

He whistles.

"I don't know how someone in hiding could get their hands on that kind of money. But I'm terrified that Hoover bought the series to mess with me." My voice quivers. "Do you think he's alive? Do you think Hoover's got Cassie?"

Leeds' brows knit. "Honestly, after thirty years, Hoover seeking revenge on a girl who witnessed one of his abductions is unlikely. No one's seen or heard from him since he was declared dead a decade ago. If he fooled us and is actually alive, that means he's been off the grid since the house fire. Do you understand what that means?"

"Not really."

"Well, to put it simply, that kind of lifestyle in today's world takes commitment. No ATMs. No cell phones. Can't buy a house or cash a paycheck. Can't form close friendships. No using the interstate. A lot of moving from midsized city to midsized city. You get the picture." Leeds shakes his head. "Anyhow, my point is, if Hoover did all of that for ten years, I doubt he'd throw it all away to make good on a threat to a teen. Don't take this the wrong way, but if he's duped us and he's alive, he probably doesn't even remember you."

"You're right. I'm being silly. Sorry for wasting your time." I glance at the door. "I have to be somewhere. Excuse me."

"Ms. Boswell, wait! We're not ..."

I dart out of the interrogation room, stumble through the lobby, and bolt onto the sidewalk. When I hear a door slam, I turn, half-expecting to see Leeds or Lori on the steps behind me. When neither materializes, I walk briskly down Main Street, toward Evelyn's gallery.

I pass a bookstore, a pottery shop, a Dunkin' Donuts, and a café. A bicyclist zips past. A squirrel scurries up an oak, all normal stuff. Nothing is even remotely scary. Nothing indicates that the Worm Man is breathing and stalking me. *You did it. You told him. It's over,* I chant. By the time I see the Wyndham, I'm feeling better and calmer, but still rattled.

Just thank Evelyn and go. Keep the conversation casual. Whatever you do, don't talk about Cassie. Get that bill of sale invoice and go. I'm determined to stick to this plan. But the moment I enter the gallery, Evelyn, who's staring at her iPad, slides off her high stool.

She frowns at me. "I can't stop listening to those news reports." She gestures to the floor. "That little girl's mother was standing right there. Christ, she hadn't a clue as to what lay ahead. She was oblivious, laughing with her friends, drinking wine. It's terrible and shocking."

I take in Evelyn's paleness. "Are you alright? You seem …"

"Unglued? I am. And I shouldn't be. I don't even know the girl." She points at me. "This is all your fault."

My heart thuds. "Mine?"

Evelyn nods. "That sketchbook you showed me was filled with images of that missing kid. I can't get her damned face out of my head." She motions to her iPad. "I put the money in your PayPal account." She hands me my bill of sale invoice, and I tuck it in my purse.

"Thanks." I picture the Worm Man. I see him shoving Whitney's face against the snowy park slide and yanking her white-blonde hair. The image blurs, and in my mind, I see Cassie, the same white-blonde hair and same pale-blue eyes.

"Evelyn," I say, "I have to know who purchased my drawings."

Evelyn's shakes her head. "You know I can't tell you that, Kate."

I touch her arm. "Please. I won't harass the buyer."

"Sorry. But I signed a contract, what in essence was an NDA. I can't—"

"But …"

As her lips part, the door swings open, and Liam enters the gallery looking handsome in his uniform. Though our eyes lock, he speaks to Evelyn instead of me. "I'll handle Kate," he says, nodding.

"Thanks," Evelyn mouths.

Before I can stop him, Liam steers me outside. "Let's snag a table at the Pizza Chef," he says, guiding me across the parking lot and onto the sidewalk. "We can grab a bite to eat and chat."

"Wait. Whoa," I say, wiggling from his grasp. "Why do you keep swooping in and dragging me away?"

"Because I'm worried about you." We pass a pedestrian. His voice quiets. "Listen, I just spoke with Agent Leeds. Kate, you could have told me about Whitney Bay, about your connection to the Worm Man. I would have …"

I glance around. "Please don't mention my history with that monster to anyone."

"I get it. It's intense. But your secret's safe with me."

I glare at Liam. I feel naked, exposed, and for some reason, this makes me angry. "Evelyn was about to give me a name, you know. Before you zoomed in, she was going to tell me who bought my drawing." Feeling a need to justify my visit to the police station, I add, "Look, I know Hoover's dead, but I can't stop thinking about the timing of the gallery show, Cassie's abduction, and the anonymous purchase. It's such a ridiculously high purchase price."

"That anonymous purchase has nothing to do with what happened to Cassie."

I stop in my tracks. "Wait! What? You know who bought my drawings?"

He nods. "The buyer's completely uninvolved. Trust me. You don't need a name."

"Of course, I do."

I dart across Main Street, down Squires Lane and onto Barrett Road. Liam trails me. Barrett's a quiet road dotted with houses, without joggers, dog walkers, or lawn crews.

"I thought we were going to Pizza Chef," he says.

"I'm not hungry."

We walk by a Greek revival, a Cape, and a colonial with a red barn.

I gesture at the barn. "Cassie could be in there right now, tied up in a horse stall or hidden in some hayloft." My eyes mist. When the tears fall, I can't make them stop.

Liam touches my lip. I'm sure he's going to tell me to be quiet, to get a grip. But as I search for words to sway him, to get him to tell me who bought my drawings, he kisses me firmly.

"You're a passionate woman," he says, peering into my eyes. "I love that about you. Passionate people like you deserve to lead unencumbered lives. That's why I bought your drawings."

His kiss me makes me heady, like I'm soaring and the world and all of its badness are miles below and can't reach me. Still, when he leans in to kiss me again, I push him away.

"I'm sorry," he says, putting up his hands. "You're not ready for us ... for this. I get that. I got carried away. I won't kiss you again until you say it's okay."

My cheeks burn. "The kiss was great, amazing actually." I attempt to explain. "It's ... You don't think I can support myself."

Liam's eyes widen. "Of course, I do. That's not it at all. Randi told me about your debt, Glen's medical bills, the mortgage payments and the back taxes you owe. I knew you wouldn't have accepted the money if I'd offered it to you."

I stand taller. "That's right. I most definitely would not have accepted it." I shake my head. "You do know Evelyn gets a forty percent commission?"

"I don't care. You got the recognition you deserve. You should know that my bid wasn't the only bid, just the highest. And I would have told you eventually."

"When?"

"After you paid your bills and the weight of your money stress was off you. After you'd sold a few more drawings and weren't so invested emotionally in these particular pieces." He glances at the barn. His forehead creases. "But I see now why that bloody hand drawing is different, why you're sensitive about it. But regardless of the rather disturbing subject matter, it's a good investment for me. Evelyn convinced me of this. So, this is a win for me too."

I lean against a split rail fence. Two goats behind it bleat, pushing their noses against my arm. I don't like taking money from anyone, especially a man. Being independent is important to me. But I have to be practical too. I need the money badly.

"I'll accept the money," I say. "But only as a loan. I'm going to pay you back. I swear it."

"I don't doubt that you will."

We start to walk again, in rhythm this time.

"Where'd you get it?" I ask. "A cop's salary isn't usually—"

"I inherited some lakefront land in Springfield and sold it about a month ago."

"Well, thanks. Thanks for buying my drawings. By the way, where are they?"

"Those lovely drawings of your students are hanging in my guest room." He chuckles. "And that bloody snowball hand drawing is in my coat closet, covered with a sheet."

"As it should be. I wouldn't hang it over my mantle either." He grips my hand. His fingers interlock with mine. This time I don't pull away. "I can't believe Cassie's missing," I say. "I probably shouldn't get involved, being that I was her teacher and tutor, and because of what happened to Whitney. I'm too close, too emotional. But I want to help. What should I do?"

"Your boss, Principal Jane North, is organizing a search party. Everyone's meeting this afternoon at three o'clock by the bandstand. You should participate. Look for Cassie. If we're lucky, someone from the group finds her."

I squeeze his hand. "A search party. I'm there."

Chapter 3

I park my SUV beside Randi's minivan in the church lot and scan the village green.

The search party crowd, which consists of about sixty residents, fills the grass butting up to Main Street. Positioned a Frisbee toss away from the bandstand, Liam and Leeds appear to be keeping their distance from the crowd. My guess is they're studying the search party participants.

I catch Liam's eye and sign up for Randi's group. Upon joining the other searchers, I immediately notice Cassie's mom, Lauren Rossi.

Lauren is standing on the bandstand, her hands pressed together, as if in prayer. Her white-blonde hair hangs loose and past her shoulders. Pink matte lipstick adorns her lips. Although she has to be in crisis mode, her joggers and matching sweatshirt look stylish. I shut my eyes and cross my fingers. *Hang in there, Lauren. You got this.*

Though I'm not a Lauren fan, it doesn't mean I don't feel for her. I watched Whitney's parents fall apart after her murder. My miscarriage devastated both Glen and me. Losing a child, I don't wish that on anyone, which is why I came, even though being here is tough for me. If we don't find Cassie or some clue to her whereabouts, I don't know what I'll do.

As I shift my weight from side to side, the search organizer, Jane North, my boss, the elementary school principal, whistles and quiets the searchers. Jane, a tall, thin woman with cropped white hair, joins Lauren on the bandstand stage. She points to the clipboard circulating through the crowd.

Her voice, replete with its New Hampshire accent and avoidance of the letter R, carries across the green. "Everyone, if you haven't already done so, please print your name on the sign-in sheet. Note the color of the star on the line by your name, and join the group associated with your star color. Each group has a leader. And each group will be assigned an area. We're going to form six groups of ten. You'll walk across your area in a line, shoulder-distance apart, and at the same pace. If you find something of note, don't touch it. Take a pic on your phone." She waves a tiny red landscaping flag. "Put a flag near the evidence. If it seems urgent, call the number on your group map ASAP. One more thing." Jane drapes her arm over Lauren's shoulder. "Lauren, Cassie's mother, would like to speak."

Lauren stares owl-like at the crowd. Despite the gravity of the situation, her eyes are dry. I'm not surprised. Keeping a brave face is typical of Lauren. Even after she fractured her ankle skating at Cassie's eighth birthday, she remained with the guests, served cake, and recorded who gave what gift. She didn't head to the ER until after she'd plucked all the confetti off the ice.

"My husband and I, we love Cassie with all our hearts," Lauren says, her voice raw with emotion. "Cassie's little brother, Ian, keeps asking about his sister. Not knowing where she is, well, it's unbearable. We want her back. We just want to hold her." She motions to the crowd. "Thank you all for coming, for caring."

As Lauren shudders, Dr. Oscar Rossi, Lauren's husband/Cassie's dad, darts up the bandstand steps. Lauren and Oscar hug. Oscar, a dark-haired man with an olive complexion, is a dentist.

"Wow," Randi says, scuttling up beside me. "That was painful to watch. If Mikey or Justin …" Her eyes moist, Randi says, "We've got the area by the elementary school."

I frown at Randi. "The school? That's no good. Let's switch with the park group."

Randi tilts her head and looks at me. "Why? Cause you tutored Cassie at the park?"

"Yes. But it's more than that," I say. "It's a gut thing. Cassie's not going to be near the school. She doesn't like school. School's hard for her. She wouldn't go there in the summer, not in a million years. Searching the school grounds is pointless. We have to do the park!"

Randi touches my arm. "Kate, you're scaring me. Maybe you shouldn't do this, given how close you are to Cassie."

"No. It's fine. I'm fine," I say, my face warming. "It's just that I've watched a zillion *America's Most Wanted* and *In Pursuit* episodes. Predators take kids from parks. The elementary school is in a neighborhood surrounded by houses. Someone would have heard or seen something if whatever happened, happened there. And like I said, Cassie doesn't even like school, so she wouldn't go there. Searching it is a waste of time."

"Point taken. I'll switch with the park group." Randi's brows knit. "But I don't see why it matters. It's all going to get down in the end." She squints at me. "You sure you're okay? You seem …"

"I just want to find her. That's all."

Randi taps my hand. "I know you do. We all do."

As Randi leaves to talk to the park group leader, I scan the crowd. I know most of the searchers. They're parents from my elementary school, Cassie's neighbors, and parishioners from my church. There are more women than men. But a few unfamiliar males mingle with the town residents. One stocky grey-haired man stands out. My heart thudding, I retrieve the birdwatching binoculars I packed from my bag and study his hands. The man's fingers are intact. *Of course, he's got all his fingers,* I think to myself. *The Worm Man's dead. What are you thinking?*

As I slip my binoculars back into my purse, Randi returns and says, "We're doing the park. Let's find the rest of our group and get started."

Our group, the yellow group, consists of two PTA moms whose daughters play on Cassie's softball team; Joyce Hadley, whose grandson was in Cassie's second-grade class; a deacon from the Baptist church; two of Cassie's neighbors who live on Pressey Court; Marge the school nurse; Randi; me; and Glen's partner Harris, from the architectural firm. Harris is the reason we moved to New Hampshire. He bought the firm in New London and convinced Glen to join him. I'm surprised to see Harris out of his office. He's single and in his mid-forties. *Perhaps he knows Lauren through one of the many organizations she heads, or maybe Oscar is his dentist,* I reason.

Harris nods at me. We didn't speak at the gallery. Other than hello, and necessary financial conversations about Glen's stake in the architectural firm, we haven't spoken since Glen's funeral. We haven't had a reason to. Glen was the link between us.

As we march down Main Street and hit Parkside Road, Harris keeps his hands in his jean pockets. Since the sidewalk on Parkside is narrow, like a class on a field trip, we move in single file. Harris walks in front of me, his shoulders slightly hunched. Feeling oddly disoriented, I stare at his shiny bald spot, following it like a flashlight beam. Though there are ten of us and we all know one another, we don't speak. Chatting seems disrespectful, like texting at a funeral. When we reach the gravel entrance road leading to the park itself, Randi, who's at the head of the line, stops.

"The park's closed to the public today," she says. "So, we can take our time and not worry about disturbing any sports practices or picnics. Let's form our line here on this road. We'll move past the shuffleboard area, the parking lot, the tennis courts, and the playground equipment and onto the fields. The park fans out at the fields, you know, where they normally have the hockey rink in the winter. We'll do one straight swoop. Then we'll move to another portion of the grid and keep altering our course until we've covered the entire park. Any questions?"

"Nope," Joyce Hadley says.

"Seems pretty simple," Harris adds.

The rest of us are dead quiet. I'm guessing that, like me, my fellow searchers are both terrified and desperate to find Cassie. My parents didn't allow me to participate in the search for Whitney. What I'm doing now feels both surreal and long overdue.

We reorganize our line and move. I'm beside Randi now, closest to the pines. Gravel crunches beneath my shoes. Beside me, Randi coughs. One of the PTA moms takes a pic of an empty beer can.

Joyce Hadley fans herself with a golf hat. "Should never have worn perfume," she mumbles. "Stupid bugs can't get enough of me."

As I step onto the sports field, Charlie Tucker, the deacon from the Baptist church, sneezes. Marge, the school nurse, who's walking beside him, trips and falls.

"Didn't mean to scare you, Marge," Charlie says, pulling Marge to her feet.

A branch snaps.

"Cassie!" Marge shouts at the top of her lungs.

"Cassie Lynn!" one of the PTA moms yodels.

Please, Cassie. Please answer! I silently plead.

As an image of Whitney, lying doll-like in the back of Hoover's Chevy, fills my mind, Harris points to what appears to be a piece of clothing in the grass. "What's that?" he asks.

My eyes shoot to the ground. The thing in question is bright red and made of mesh. As Harris hurries toward the mesh thing and kneels beside it, I hold my breath.

"It's a soccer goalie pinny. It's not important," he proclaims.

"We can't assume that," Marge says, catching up to him.

As she takes a pic of the vest and puts a flag beside it, a monarch butterfly flutters above the grass. Marge's Kodak moment triggers something in me, a memory. I picture Cassie twirling across this very field, her girl arms outstretched, a multiplication flashcard in her hand. *I'm flying. Look at me. I'm a butterfly*, the Cassie in my mind shouts. The image fades, and Harris and Marge rejoin the group.

We cross the field, turn, and shift our line. This allows us to search the other side of the field, the playground area, and the parking lot. Randi finds a quarter. One of the PTA moms steps in dog poop. Off in the distance, a lawn mower roars, all things I can deal with. Nothing sends me into a panic or causes me to question what we're doing here. But then we near the playground equipment, Marge's designated area.

My body stiffens. I peer back at the flag Marge placed beside the red vest. It's already lying on the ground.

I don't care what Marge or anyone else thinks. I don't give a rat's ass about breaking the search rules. I jump out of line, hop onto the slide ladder, and, using the handrails, climb to the plastic covering the chute.

"What's Kate doing?" Marge yelps. "Randi, Kate's out of order. The slide's in my zone. She needs to go back to her space."

"Get off the slide, Kate!" Randi shouts. "Marge is right. The slide isn't in your zone. Come on," she scolds as I scramble higher. "You're making me look bad. I'm going to have to give you detention. Quit it, Kate. Whatcha doing up there? Get down."

Waving off Randi's words, I peer into the plastic tube-like covering shielding the chute. My heart thuds. "Something's inside," I yell down. "A pink sneaker, I think."

Randi's voice floats up to me. "Here, let me give you a flag. Put the flag in the tube, Kate."

Below me, Harris retrieves his cell from his jean pocket and says, "I'll call the number on the sheet."

As he punches numbers into his cell and speaks to the recipient of his call, I study the pink sneaker. It isn't protocol, but following rules isn't going to get me anywhere. Besides, I don't trust the FBI. They didn't rescue Whitney. I grab the pink low-top Converse. The name Cassie is printed in block letters on the toe. As I stare numbly at the canvas shoe in my grasp, fear paralyzes me. My body won't let me climb down the slide ladder.

Randi motions to the sneaker. "Drop it, Kate," she coaxes, as if I'm a puppy.

"Give her the shoe," Harris says. "The authorities need the shoe, Kate. It's evidence. We need to take a photo of it. Kate? Hey. You okay?"

"I—"

Muffled voices waft up to me. Beneath me, the slide ladder shakes. I hear the clank of climbing. Then Harris grabs me from behind. He guides me down to the ground. Out of the corner of my eye, I see Joyce Hadley sink onto a swing seat.

Joyce says, "Kids don't just leave one shoe. They leave two, not one. Leaving one behind means Cassie was in a hurry. The shoe fell off her foot, and she didn't have time to go back and get it. Or she was too scared to."

"Or she forgot it," a PTA mom says.

I want to scream. The cheery note in the PTA mom's voice is beyond annoying.

"She didn't forget it," Marge says. "It rained Sunday. There were puddles on the ground. You don't forget that you're missing a shoe if you're walking around in puddles."

Randi points to the wood chips beside my feet. "Kate, put the sneaker down. We'll flag it and tell the FBI guy, Leeds, you touched it accidentally."

Dazed, I release the shoe. It lands on the wood chips, flipping over. Something dark red, probably blood, mars the sole.

I scream, "No! No! No!"

Harris bear-hugs me.

"Breathe," Randi commands. "Breathe, Kate. Breathe."

As I sway, Harris pats my back. Behind me, I hear footfalls.

"Everything alright here?"

I push Harris off me and turn. Leeds is staring at me. In his gloved hand, he's holding a clear evidence bag. Leeds plucks Cassie's pink sneaker off the ground and drops the shoe into his bag.

"What are you doing with that?" I yell, lunging for the shoe. "That's Cassie's favorite sneaker!"

"Kate, why don't you and I take a little break," Randi says, holding me back.

As the other searchers stare at me, Randi drags me across the field and toward Parkside Road. Even though Leeds and the pink sneaker in his bag get smaller and smaller and ultimately disappear from my view, I keep turning around.

"It's just a shoe. You're gonna see her again," Randi says, nudging me onward and toward town. "Kids disappear every day and 97.8 percent of them are found. The vast majority are perfectly fine. I know. I Googled it yesterday."

I hone in on the figure in the diamond crosswalk sign. "But what if Cassie's part of the 2.2 percent?"

"She's not. Don't even go there. Think positive."

She grabs my hand, leads me across Main Street, over the grass, and to the bandstand. As the other searchers head into the adjacent parking lot, climb into their vehicles and drive away, Randi and I sit on the stage, shoulder to shoulder. The sun is warm, but not intense. But there's a glare, and Randi keeps squinting at the clouds framing Mount Kearsarge. When a gnat lands on my cheek, I squish it with my fingertip, and feel the dampness of a tear on my face.

"You should come back to my house with me," Randi says, her voice scratchy and rough. "This is too much for you. You shouldn't be alone. You're still reeling from Glen."

Glen—I have to tell him! My knees shaking, I stand. "I want to go to the cemetery to visit Glen's grave."

Randi's lips part.

"I'll be okay," I say, avoiding her eyes. "Really."

"But you're upset. You shouldn't be driving."

"I'm good now," I tell her. "The walking helped. You sitting with me helped. It was just a momentary breakdown. I'm fine." I hold my palms out flat. "See. I'm only trembling a little."

As she trails me, arguing with me, I hurry to the parking lot and climb into my SUV.

"I'm okay," I tell her, as she reaches for my door handle and eyes my keys like I've been drinking. "I swear it. Go pick up Mikey and Justin. I can drive myself. I promise."

"No. You just..."

"I can."

As my motor rumbles, she frowns and steps away from my front fender.

I watch her watch me as I drive out of the parking lot and onto Main Street. When I hit South Pleasant Street, I turn. Disoriented, I drive a mile down the quiet single lane road, past homes, the Public Works building, and Lyon Brook Trail, to the town cemetery on Old Main Street. I park beside a spruce and walk toward the graves. From what I can tell, I'm alone, though I could be mistaken. At times, visitors park on nearby streets.

As the scents of pine needles and freshly cut grass fill my nostrils, I follow the familiar pebbled path to Glen's headstone. I think about the afternoon Glen and Cassie met. It was two Octobers ago.

* * *

Cassie and I were sitting on my living room rug, working on multiplication problems. It was the first day she'd come to my home for tutoring, before Glen started his painting and flooring projects, before Cassie and I escaped temporarily to the park.

"What's nine times seven?" I asked her.

Cassie tugged a strand of her white-blonde hair. "Nine times seven?"

The front door swung open and Glen appeared beneath the doorframe. When Cassie sprang to her sneakered feet, I figured she was tired of memorizing and wanted a distraction.

She waved and Glen's eyes brightened. "Well, hello, young lady."

"Hey," Cassie said back. Her cheek dimple deepened.

"This is Cassie," I said.

"He knows," Cassie said as if she were a social media star, an influencer. She made a sour face and pointed her thumbs at the floor. "We're doing times tables. Yuck!"

Glen laughed and loosened his tie. "Why's that's a bad thing? I love multiplication. I do math all day long. Can't get enough of it."

"What's nine times seven?" Cassie shouted.

Glen grinned. "Sixty-three."

"Glen," I scolded, my heart secretly swelling with love for him. "Don't give her the answer."

"Why not? She'll remember it." He pointed at Cassie. "Quick! Nine times seven?"

"Sixty-three!" she shot back, giggling.

* * *

A car door slams behind me, bringing me back to the present, to the cemetery. I turn and spot a grey Volvo heading up Old Main Street. I'm not sure. The sun's glare, the distance to the street, and the vehicle's movement obscure my perception, but I think the Volvo driver is Lauren Rossi.

No way. Can't be her. Why would she be here? She has to be out of her mind with worry, I reason. But then I remember that Lauren's family has lived in New London for generations. *Lauren's likely got relatives and friends buried here,* I decide. *Perhaps like me, she comes here when she's upset. She probably talks to a deceased loved one, a grandmother or a favorite aunt.*

The Volvo disappears around the bend. I study Glen's headstone. The stone is covered with leaves, which is normal. I have to clean it off each time I visit. But what isn't normal, what I don't expect, are the fresh daisies. A dozen of them lay on the marble slab. I finger one of the stems. It's damp, like someone just yanked it out of a water-filled vase.

My eyes shift back to the street. *Nah. Wasn't Lauren. Doesn't matter the timing, today's horrific circumstances ... why would she leave Glen flowers anytime? Sure, Cassie adored him, and Lauren and Glen chatted from time-to-time, but still.*

Harris, I decide. *It had to be Harris. More than likely, he scooted by here after the search.* I glance at the daisies. *Oh, who cares who left the flowers? They're beautiful, lovely. But the grave …*

Leaving the daisies be, I brush the dead leaves off Glen's grave. As the sun's rays warm my spine, a rare calm envelops me. It's almost as if Glen's here, pressing against me, embracing me. As I kneel, a bead of perspiration slides down my cheek.

Cassie mattered to Glen. Since his death, I've kept an eye on her, but from a distance. I still tutored her when school was in session. But unlike when Glen was alive, I didn't encourage her to linger. Cassie reminds me of Glen, so I pushed her away. Oscar, who stepped into Glen's role as Cassie's driver, always picked Cassie up promptly at 4:30 pm. If he were alive, Glen would tell me to cut myself a break. He would say that I'm handling his death as best I can. But now that Cassie's missing, I feel as if I've failed him. I have to tell him.

"Cassie's missing," I whisper. "It's horrible, unfathomable. What's worse is that I have this crazy feeling that James Hoover grabbed her because of me. I know what you're thinking. He's dead. I'm being paranoid. It's all in my mind, like before, like back in New Jersey, like at the Carrier Clinic. But Glen, there's something you need to know."

As the wind gusts off Mount Kearsarge, I tell Glen about James Hoover's missing finger, how I severed it, about my gory snowball hand drawing, and the gallery show. "So, you see, it's different this time. They had a search. I found Cassie's sneaker. I think there was blood on the toe. It was awful, truly awful. The authorities are working the case. But they're not taking my Worm Man theory seriously. Who knows? Maybe they're right to ignore it. What should I do?"

It's not as if I expect to hear Glen's voice. But I'm hoping something will steer me in the right direction. I hold my breath, wait, and shut my eyes. When my cell dings, signaling a text, I retrieve my phone from my purse and glance at the screen. The texter is Kingsley, *The Globe* reporter from the gallery show.

Can you meet me at noon tomorrow? It's important.

I jam my phone back into my bag and stomp up the path. I'm on edge, about to lose it. I don't need some aggressive reporter harassing me. Shaking, I climb into my SUV.

As air blows through my lowered windows, I take the backroads home. Like I do often when I'm alone, I picture Glen's tall lanky basketball body, that smile that entranced me our sophomore year at NYU, and those long arms that clung to me first in my dorm room, then in our Fort Lee, New Jersey apartment, and later in our New Hampshire farmhouse, always with rolled-up oxford shirtsleeves. It's been less than a year since I lost Glen, but his voice no longer comes to me as easily as it once did. Though hearing it now causes a tightness in the back of my throat, I evoke it anyway.

They'll find her. They'll find Cassie Lynn, the Glen in my mind assures me.

I ease onto the dirt road leading to my farmhouse, pass Gene's, my neighbor's orchard and cornfields, park, and take my porch steps inside. Standing in the foyer, I peer into the entryway mirror. I'm sweaty and dirty from the search. Despite my efforts to discourage them, mosquito bites dot my arm.

Who knows what was in that park? What I traipsed through? Poison ivy? Poison oak? I climb the staircase to the second story and opt for a shower, a cold one this time. As water pounds my spine, I check myself for ticks. I don't see any, just a few scratches on my wrist. I turn off the shower and step onto the bathmat. After wrapping myself in a towel, I catch a glimpse of my thin frame in the vanity mirror. Spaghetti-strap tan lines stretch over my shoulders. I find a bra, panties, a T-shirt, and shorts and put them on. I move past my bed and slip into my flip-flops.

It's as I step toward the open bedside window that I hear the song. At first, I think I'm imagining it. It's starts that softly. But then the verse blasts, "Straight up, now tell me. Do you really want to love me forever?"

I stifle a scream. *Paula Abdul's song! Whitney's song!*

My eyes shoot to the open window. Outside, I see trees, my birdbath, and my clothesline. As I dart across the room, the floor creaks beneath me and the familiar notes quiet to elevator music level. This should make me feel better, but it doesn't. The Paula Abdul verse has meaning, regardless of its volume.

The Worm Man's alive! He's here, and he's come for me! My heart pounding, I grab my purse off the bedside chair. Inside the bag, I keep pepper spray, my cell, and a tactile knife. Clutching my knife, I tiptoe to the first floor, nudge open the back door, and squint into the sunlit yard. Something white moves in my peripheral view.

I freeze. The wind gusts, and the white thing, a clothesline sheet, flaps.

Cautiously, as the late 80's pop tune plays, I step off the landing and slink through my yard. A jay shrieks. Grass blades prick my ankles. Then, as the afternoon sun pummels me, the Paula Abdul song suddenly ceases. The silence is almost painful, shards of glass in my ears.

I shout into the trees, "Leave! I've got a weapon. I called the cops. They're on their way."

I brace myself for a response but get nothing. I squint into the forest. Sunlight doesn't permeate the thick pines beyond my yard. This means if I keep going, I'll be entering an evergreen cave of sorts. I finger my cell and consider truly calling the cops. But Leeds' words, *Don't take this the wrong way. But he probably doesn't even remember you*, propel me into the trees. Pines and oaks crowd me. The temperature drops. The world around me darkens. As a chipmunk scurries over a log, something tugs at my T-shirt. I bolt into the clearing.

"This is my property!" I yell. "Get off!"

But I'm alone. I know this with 99 percent certainty. But someone was here. A blanket is stretched out on the ground. I see cigarette butts, beer bottles, a condom wrapper, and flattened weeds. I can see my bedroom window too. It sits clear as day, above the tree line. I kick the condom wrapper and imagine the Worm Man doing unspeakable things to Cassie, violating her while tormenting me with Whitney's favorite song. It's all too much, too awful to bear alone. I have to call Liam.

"He was here!" I blurt out when he answers. "He was outside my window."

"Kate? What are you talking about? Who was there?" I hear the tick of Liam's turn signal. He's driving.

"James Hoover, the Worm Man."

Liam doesn't even try to tell me that Hoover's dead. I'm clearly panicking. He knows better than to reason with me. "Where are you?"

"In the clearing, the one behind my property."

I hear the squeal of tires and picture him doing a quick U-turn. "You sure he's gone?"

"Think so."

"I'm going to stay on the line so I know you're safe. I'm two miles away," he tells me. "I'm by the post office. Do you have something you can use as a weapon?"

"A knife. Pepper spray."

"Good. I'm turning onto your road now. I can see Gene's apple trees and the fields."

As Liam drives and points out landmarks, gripping my knife, I stare at the trees and listen for sounds, for movement. When I hear a car door slam, I jump.

"I'm here," Liam says. "I'm at your place. Hold tight. I'll be at the clearing in a minute."

Rubbing the goosepimples on my forearms, I count and pace. When I reach a hundred, footsteps sound, and Liam appears. I run to him, bury my face in his linebacker chest, and drop my phone and knife in my purse.

"The Worm Man. The Worm Man," I murmur, clinging to him. Liam's arms are pillars around me.

He releases me too soon. His gaze drifts to the blanket, the beer cans, the cigarette butts, and the condom wrapper. "Looks like kids have been using your woods as a hangout."

"No. No, it wasn't kids," I say, though Glen caught Colby Sawyer students in the clearing a half-dozen times. He shooed them away and yelled at them. Once he confiscated their weed. "It was definitely not kids. It was the Worm Man." I'm shivering now, swaying.

Liam steadies me. "Kate, help me understand. What did you see that convinced you that the Worm Man was here?"

"I didn't see. I heard this song playing. Paula Abdul. 'Straight Up.'"

He frowns. "I'm not following you."

"It's an old song from the late 80's. Whitney was obsessed with it. She drove her mom crazy singing it. We were singing it that morning at the playground when Hoover grabbed her."

"Well, more than likely someone else loves it too, a high school kid who's into 80's pop music, thinks it's retro." He motions to the beer cans. "So, it's a good party tune?"

"It is. But what are the chances?" I say, shaking my head. "Cassie going missing while collecting worms and me hearing the song Whitney and I sang that morning? There's too many coincidences."

"Coincidences happen all the time. They only seem telling when you're looking for them." Liam touches my wrist. "Were you looking?"

I think about the cemetery and how I was looking for a sign from Glen. "Sort of." I frown. "But why were they listening to it over and over again?"

He shrugs. "It's catchy. You just told me you and Whitney kept singing it."

"We did, but ..."

Liam drapes his arm over my shoulder. "Let's drive down the service road behind your property and make sure no one's there. We'll check your house too. Make sure the locks and windows are secure and your alarm system is working. Sound good?"

I nod, and we walk. I say, "No one else knew about that song, what it meant to Whitney and me. I don't know how to explain it, but he's back."

"I'll look into it," he says when my lip quivers. "I promise. I'll talk to Leeds. I'll tell him what you heard and what we found in the clearing. More than likely Leeds will send his forensic team over to collect evidence. That guy dots all his Is and crosses all his Ts. I'm glad you called me," he says when we reach my driveway. "I like that you feel you can rely on me. You can, you know, rely on me for anything. Nothing's off-limits." He motions to the field. "Come on. Let's check out your property."

We climb into his patrol car and bounce down the dirt road that parallels the cornfield beside Gene's apple trees—no tire tracks, no stoned teens, and no Hoover. It's just waist-high corn. But in my mind, this means nothing.

Liam parks in the driveway beside my Subaru. Then we inspect the exterior of my house. We spot raccoon prints on the sill and a cracked windowpane in the den, but no obvious signs of a human intruder. But the lack of evidence doesn't alter my perception. James Hoover was in those trees just beyond my property line. He was playing that Paula Abdul song, taunting me. I sense his presence in the air. I feel his evil closing in on me, just like I did that snowy morning at the park playground with Whitney.

After Liam checks the lock on my cellar door, we return to my driveway. He fingers his car keys and motions to the road. "I've got to head to the rec fields now. A couple of soccer practices going on. Because of Cassie's disappearance, the parents want a police presence. But I'll be close by. Promise. I wouldn't leave if I thought you were in any danger. I swear it."

But—"

"I know you're worried. Given your history with the Worm Man, I get why you'd be concerned. But the guy's dead, Kate. Don't forget that. More than likely, it was kids partying. That clearing's a classic hangout spot." He waves his phone. "Call me if you need me. I can be back here in a flash."

He climbs into his patrol car. I watch him back out of my driveway. When his patrol car disappears down the dirt road, I slide my cell out of my pocket and reread the text from *The Globe* reporter, Kingsley.

Can u meet me at noon tomorrow? It's important.

After hearing the Paula Abdul song, I'm now positive that the Worm Man is alive. I don't know how James Hoover fooled the feds and the cops, or where he's been for the past ten years, but I'm certain he grabbed Cassie.

Curling my fingers, I dig my nails into my palms. Liam isn't taking my Worm Man fears seriously, and I doubt Leeds will make the forensic investigation of my clearing a priority. Not that I blame Liam and Leeds for blowing off my concerns. If I hadn't dealt with the Worm Man personally, I'd underestimate him too.

I stare at the trees. Time matters when kids are abducted. I know this better than anyone. I can't wait for Liam and Leeds to come around to my way of thinking.

I text Kingsley back, **Yes, I'll meet you on Main Street, at Tucker's**.

* * *

Concerned about another impromptu concert, I pack a duffle bag and spend the night at Randi's house. I sleep in her guest room/playroom surrounded by Legos, plastic dinosaurs, wooden train tracks, and superhero figures. Covered in a Snoopy comforter, I dream that Batman and Robin battle the Worm Man. In my dream, the Worm Man steals the Batmobile and runs over the Dynamic Duo.

Chapter 4

*T*he DNA collected off the sneaker I found on the park slide matches the DNA obtained from the hair follicle sample the FBI took from Cassie's brush.

I know this because Kingsley just told me. He has an in at the police station and is good at digging, which is why I texted him back despite my desire to keep my connection to James Hoover, AKA the Worm Man, quiet. I've been panicking ever since I heard the Paula Abdul song. I've got this irrational fear that Cassie is bleeding out.

Kingsley and I are seated at Tucker's, a causal café on Main Street. Tucker's serves salads, sandwiches, soup, and Arnold Palmers. It isn't private, far from it. As residents use the sidewalk several yards away from our patio table, Kingsley watches them. He leans toward them as they speak. He takes in their movements and mannerisms. Kingsley isn't merely a journalist/self-published author. He's an observer, a student of human behavior.

The truth is, I'm not entirely comfortable being here with Kingsley. I normally steer clear of reporters. But on occasion, a journalist corners me. It's usually a recent college grad wanting a fresh angle on the overpublicized Worm Man story. The last cub reporter wanted to interview me for her podcast. In this respect, Kingsley is different from the others. He's a journeyman and not searching for a unique perspective. I know from having been interviewed by him ten years ago, that in his mind, there's only one way to view the Worm Man—as a monster. On this, we agree. But that doesn't mean that Kingsley being a reporter, doesn't give me pause. But bottom line, I need him. I need his investigative skills, his vast Worm Man knowledge, and his contacts. I can't find the Worm Man and Cassie without him.

"I've been waiting for you to contact me," Kingsley says, when the waitress leaves after refilling his drink. "Ever since Cassie Rossi disappeared, I knew you would."

He sounds eager, almost giddy. But I don't let his insensitivity to the situation bother me. Some people get off on violence and crime. Kingsley is obviously one of those people.

I ball up my napkin. "Look, I need your help. I know you talked to Leeds, and that you told him you thought Hoover was alive and that he snatched Cassie. I believe Hoover's living and breathing too. I'm positive that he has Cassie. I want to find him. And, well, you're a Worm Man expert."

Kingsley peers at me through smudged bifocal lenses. His grey beard needs grooming. "And you're not?"

"I ..."

What I don't want Kingsley to know is this— James Hoover's documented death didn't change how I operate. I think about the Worm Man daily. I have since Whitney's abduction. I don't make any significant life decisions without factoring Hoover in. I study him, read articles about his MO, and watch TV shows portraying his crimes and victims. But my obsession isn't a choice. It was thrust upon me. But Kingsley appears to enjoy researching the sicko, in the same way that some retirees delight in taking cruises or millennial foodies relish the experience of preparing and eating meals. Kingsley's interest in the Worm Man is a hobby on steroids, one that seems to dictate who and what he is. In that sense, I can relate to him. Though I see myself as a widow, a daughter, an artist, and a teacher, first and foremost, I'm the best friend of a murder victim.

"You're right. I'm a Worm Man expert too," I say in a quiet voice. "It's just not something I'm proud to admit or want anyone to know about. As you know, I work at an elementary school, and my side business is drawing children. I could lose both jobs if … and they're not just jobs to me. I love what I do. I live for my students, my art." I exhale. "If people associate me with someone as dangerous as the Worm Man, I'm done, not just my career. My life's over."

A young couple with a poodle, scurries by, their arms linked. The man whispers into the woman's ear. She giggles.

Kingsley eyes the couple and faces me. "You've got a lot on the line. I get it. Look," he says when I fidget. "I won't mention your connection to that devil to anyone. I shouldn't have said what I said at the gallery. I'm sorry. I won't write or talk about you either. You're off limits. Pinky swear."

I laugh. "Pinky swear? That's the assurance you're giving me?"

"Look. I'll admit. I went a little crazy with the texts, the phone calls. Truth is, I'm writing for Arts and Leisure now, mostly fluff pieces. So, when I smelt a real story, I went overboard. But I promise you, this. What's happening here…" He gestures at the table. "Is strictly about finding Hoover and the girl. What you tell me stays between us. It's off the record."

"Thank you," I say. "Thank you for not making me into a story. I'm glad we're on the same page."

We shake hands. I start to relax, to feel okay about opening up. He sips his Pepsi and seems to study me.

I glance down. I'm wearing a sundress, a pink one. The bright shade matches Cassie's sneaker, the Converse from the slide.

I say, "It's because you've never met Hoover. That's why you're into him. To you, he's a character, a villain from a superhero movie. But to me, he's flesh and blood."

Kinsley winks. "I'm emotionally detached. But that doesn't mean I don't want to get him as badly as you do. Hell, I probably want him more."

"Good," I say. "Because something happened yesterday. I wasn't sure if Hoover was alive when Cassie first disappeared, but I'm certain now."

Kingsley's eyes widen. "Out with it!"

I tell him about hearing the Paula Abdul song in the clearing, the same song Whitney and I sang before her abduction. "No one else knew Whitney and I were singing it that morning. So, it had to be him. Hoover's toying with me." I make a tight fist. "I'm going to find that psycho and Cassie. But I can't do it alone."

"What about your man, Liam Messer, the cop? You two seem cozy."

My face burns. "We are. But I don't want Liam jeopardizing his career, his position on the force, or his relationship with Leeds for me. Being selected to work closely with Leeds is a big deal for Liam professionally. Liam wants to be a detective. He's already completed his training courses, and he's taking his exam at the academy next April."

"Plus, Liam doesn't believe the monster's walking and kicking, does he?"

"He doesn't," I admit.

Kingsley bites into his burger. "So that leaves me. You're stuck with good ole' Dan Rather." He grins. A piece of lettuce clings to his tooth. He pries it loose with his fingernail. "You knew him before he grabbed your friend. You met him." It's a statement, not a question. Kingsley knows the details surrounding Whitney's abduction. They were in his book. But he seems to want to revisit the subject. More than likely, he's wondering if he missed something pertinent when he interviewed me a decade ago.

"James Hoover wasn't a family friend, not even an acquaintance," I say. "But the cops said he'd been living in the area, in Ewing." I play with my Caesar salad. "Whitney and I used to go to the Mercer County Public Library every Tuesday at four. We went even if we'd already finished our homework, just to talk and read magazines. Whitney liked that it was quiet. I think she needed the break. Whitney's mom was pretty intense. Mrs. Bay made her take all sorts of lessons: ballet, piano, and Mandarin.

Anyhow, we always sat in the same place, at a round table in the children's section. It was by the adult magazine reading area. Whenever Whitney and I were there, James Hoover was in a chair reading this woodworking magazine. Apparently, he was a carpenter." I shake my head. "I didn't realize I knew him that day in the park. But a decade after Whitney's murder, during a therapy session, the library memory surfaced. Hoover looked different, clean-shaven, at the library, not unkempt and dirty. When he grabbed Whitney, I thought he was a stranger. And he was, but not completely."

Kingsley takes a bite of his burger. "Did he ever talk to you at the library?"

"Not to me. But he spoke to Whitney. She usually got there before me. Whenever I showed up, they'd stop chatting and he'd start reading. But I always had the sense that he was listening and watching us. He used to smile at her. We planned our outing to the park at the library. I believe that's how he knew we'd be there."

I frown. Hearing the Paula Abdul song was my aha moment. But why is

Kingsley so sure that Hoover faked his death? I have to know. "So, what makes you think Hoover didn't burn in that shore house?"

"Not what. Who. Emily Rose."

"I don't—"

"Emily Rose was James Hoover's neighbor. She lived beside the Hoover's New Jersey family shore house, the one that burned. She claimed she saw Hoover a week after the fire that supposedly killed him. She told the feds that she caught him hiding in her basement and that he bolted when she called 911. She was in her mid-eighties and had just been diagnosed with early-stage Alzheimer's when the feds questioned her. That's why they dismissed her statement. But when I interviewed her, yeah, she drifted in and out, but when it came to the basement incident and Hoover, she seemed on point. Her story never changed."

"Really? This is the first time I'm hearing about this Emily Rose. I've seen a slew of crime shows on Hoover. The cops and feds never mentioned her either."

"Like I said, she's got Alzheimer's. That makes her an unreliable witness." He shakes his head. "It's sad. Emily's disease has progressed since I last spoke with her. She's in a nursing home now." He sprinkles salt on his fries. "So, what's your plan? How are we going to find Hoover and Cassie?"

"By following up on sightings," I say. "Sight is my strongest sense," I add, touching my temple. "I believe it's that way for a lot of people. If Hoover is in the area, someone has definitely seen him. I saw him grab Whitney." I shudder. "She was a hundred and five pounds. He scooped her up like she was nothing. Cassie isn't going anywhere he doesn't want her to go. He's the one in charge. If we find him, we find Cassie."

"Makes sense," Kingsley says, nodding. "But don't forget Hoover's older now. He's in his mid-fifties. He's likely not as strong, not as quick as you remember."

"True. But if he's still working manual labor, doing carpentry, like he's done in the past, he'll be in shape."

Kingsley fingers some grey hairs in his beard. "Good point. Plus, age does provide some advantages."

I frown. "Like what?"

"Older adults blend better. People don't notice them. They dismiss them. They consider them irrelevant, not a threat." Kingsley taps his chest. "Big mistake. Let me tell you."

I smile. "So, what was the last tip you got pertaining to Hoover's whereabouts?"

"Blueberries."

"Ahh?"

"I heard through a source that a man who matched Hoover's description was working the blueberry fields up in Maine. That was two months ago. My source said Hoover was living in an RV outside of Waterboro, at a grower's farm.

I went to Waterboro, talked to the grower, showed him a picture of Hoover, and explained why I needed to locate him. The grower swore he wasn't there."

"And you believed him?"

"Not completely. But I questioned the field workers. I even talked to their kids. Kids tend to be honest. They all backed up the grower's claim. Though most were illegals, Guatemalans and Filipinos, so it could be they were scared to talk." Kingsley gulps his Pepsi. "I went to Christian school, the whole nine yards. The grower, the owner of the blueberry farm, is a minister. Name's Reverend Shasta. Guy's a saint. He looks after all the seasonal migrant workers. He runs a camp and teaches the migrant children while the parents are working the fields. The reverend's an upstanding guy. But like I said, I had this sense he was keeping something from me."

"No other leads since?"

"None. I have a website, and I'm active on social media. People write to me from all over the country. My *Globe* coworkers keep their ears open for me too. If he is alive, Hoover's controlled his impulses. He hasn't grabbed a girl in ten years. At least, not that we know of until …"

I stare at the sidewalk. A group of teenage girls hurries by. Dressed in cutoff shorts and tank tops, they chat and clutch their cell phones. One of them is blonde, white-blonde, like Cassie and Whitney.

I say, "We need to go back to Waterboro to talk to Reverend Shasta."

"You think Cassie's disappearance will motivate him to talk?"

"Maybe." I hesitate, bite my lip. Though it's the second telling, the account of the finger severing sticks in my throat. "Plus, when you were there before you didn't know that James Hoover was missing a finger," I say. "I wait for Kingsley's reaction. When he merely nods, I frown. "You know about the missing finger?"

"Of course. I heard you hacked it off. I also heard you contaminated the evidence obtained from the ground search." He leans toward me. "Why'd you grab the kid's sneaker?"

I shrug. "It was a reflex. I guess I don't trust the authorities."

Kingsley chuckles. "No judgment here. I would have been all over that kid's shoe."

The waitress gives us our bill. We pay for our lunches, and Kingsley and I go our separate ways to get organized for the trip to Waterboro. He needs to check in with the paper, and I want to call Liam. Liam texted me. He asked me how I was holding up and if I wanted dinner. Liam doesn't answer when I phone him from my SUV, so I leave him a voicemail and decline his dinner invitation. I tell him I have to go to the teacher's supply store in Portland to prepare for the upcoming school year.

I never lie to Liam. I don't lie in general. But I don't want him to worry about me or call me back and tell me not to go looking for Hoover. I don't want him to say, "Going to Maine with some overzealous reporter who interviewed you once, a decade ago, is nuts, potentially even dangerous. Why would you even trust him? He's got an agenda. Besides, Hoover's clearly dead."

But what Liam doesn't understand is this— I have to take a chance on Kingsley. Kingsley's the only one who believes my Worm Man resurrection theory, and Cassie's been missing for two days.

I tap my dashboard twice for luck. Then I fill up my Subaru with gas, drive home, slip a cardigan and bottled water into my over-sized handbag, and read my emails. On impulse, I grab my sketchbook, the one filled with drawings of my students.

* * *

An hour after leaving Kingsley at the cafe, I pick him up in front of the Fairway Motel, where he's staying. Kingsley barrels bearlike to my SUV and collapses onto the passenger seat, and we head up I-89. We take the interstate southeast, veer onto Highway 202 East, toward Portland and the coast. I adjust my sunglasses and the air vent. As the sun's rays bounce off my windshield, the road curves. It's a perfect day for sightseeing, an ideal day for blueberry picking.

"So Reverend Shasta owns a blueberry farm," I say, wanting to learn more about the man I'm about to meet.

"He does," Kingsley says. "He inherited it from his grandfather before he became a minister. Reverend Shasta preaches at the Old Corner Church on Federal Street in Waterboro. The farm is his way of serving the community. Like I said at lunch, Shasta employs migrants. And he's got this camp thing. While the pickers work the fields, the reverend teaches and entertains their kids. He helps his workers with all sorts of things— health-care issues, legal problems, and citizenship concerns. He feeds the workers and their families too. He lets them stay in cottages and RVs on his property. Although most migrant workers travel up to the barrens in Washington County, Reverend Shasta's crew returns to work his York County farm summer after summer." Kingsley crosses himself. "I haven't stepped foot in a church since my nephew's baptism. That was eight years ago. But even I can tell that what he's got going on at that farm is special."

I nod. "I imagine he sells jam, muffins, and pies."

Kingsley pats his belly. "Yup. The farm's got a little store. The blueberry pies they sell there are out of this world. Did you know that ninety percent of the US blueberry production comes from Maine, mostly from the barrens up in Washington County? They harvest low-lying bushes up there. Reverend Shasta grows highbush berries. I wrote an article on the industry several months ago."

We leave the granite state and enter York County, Maine. We pass lakes, campgrounds, farms, and roadside motels. In total, we drive two hours. As puffy white clouds form in the sky, we cross a covered bridge and turn onto a dirt road that snakes through trees and farmland. I squint at the cornfields, and my heart pounds. *Is Cassie lying injured, hidden by the tall stalks? Is she trapped, bound and tied, in some abandoned well, or held captive in an old outbuilding cold, hungry, and bleeding?*

"The farm's down there, two miles on your left," Kingsley says, his voice jarring me out of my head and back to the road. "It's a big place. You'll be surprised when you see it."

Kingsley yawns and sits up straighter. The road shifts. The Subaru bounces and rattles. Potholes jar us. When I don't see a sign for the farm, I wonder if my GPS, or Kingsley, has taken me off course. But then we hug a tight curve, and the forest opens into fields. I gasp. The rows of blueberry bushes stretch for acres. Workers, mostly Hispanics sporting hats, grip baskets and work bushes the height of basketball hoops. Some stand on ladders.

Kingsley gestures to a white farmhouse adjacent to the fields. "That's Reverend Shasta's place. He teaches Bible study classes there. There's a massive dining hall inside." He motions to a red barn. "The rec room is in that barn. It's pretty decked out—TV, ping pong tables, and a pool table too. You see those cottages near that pond?"

I nod and drive slowly. "Is that where the workers and their families sleep?"

"You got it." Kingsley points to a motorhome. "And that RV behind the cottages. If he's here. That's where our man, Hoover, likely resides."

I eyeball the RV, an old Winnebago, and my stomach knots. It terrifies me to think of James Hoover potentially living in that camper, just yards away from the cottages where families with children live, so near to the house where the minister holds his Bible study classes and sings hymns with his students.

"Let's talk to Reverend Shasta. Find that monster. Thinking about him being right there ..." I squeeze my steering wheel. "Well, frankly, it scares me."

As Kingsley lowers his window, I park in front of the reverend's farmhouse, on the grass beside a white van. The farmhouse door swings open, and kids scamper down the porch steps. Their brown faces gleam in the sunshine. The boys wear shorts and T-shirts. The girls sport colorful cotton dresses. I ascertain that they're between the ages of five and seventeen. Still singing, the campers plop onto folding chairs shaded by a large maple tree. Their chairs face a blackboard. As Kingsley and I climb out of my Subaru, the campers wave.

"What a friend we have in Jesus," they sing.

When the farmhouse door opens again, the kids quiet, and a white-haired man in a clerical-collar steps onto the porch.

"Reverend Shasta?" I ask.

Kingsley nods. "The one and only."

As Kingsley salutes him, the reverend grins. "Tom Kingsley! So glad to see you! To what do I owe this unexpected but blessed visit?" He smiles at me. "And who is your lovely companion?"

Kingsley touches my shoulder. "Reverend, this is Kate Boswell. She's a new friend." He motions to the campers. "Sorry to intrude again. But I have more questions."

The reverend nods. "Well, I can't say I've got any more answers."

"It's important," I say. "A little girl from New London has gone missing."

"In that case …" The reverend gestures to a pretty teen with a long braid. "Maria, would you mind starting the lesson today? We're studying forgiveness. The verse is Matthew 6:12–15."

Maria heads to the blackboard. As she reads the Bible verse, Kingsley and I ascend the porch steps. The reverend ushers us through a foyer and into a parlor. He gestures to a seating area.

"Maria's a wonderful young lady," he says, glancing out the window. "She's been coming here since she was seven. She wants to be a nurse. My farm awards three college scholarships each year. She's slated to receive one."

As I sit in an upholstered chair, Kingsley claims a bench facing the fireplace. I glance around. The room is formal but well-used. Lace curtains frame picture windows. A Persian rug adorns wood floors.

I fixate on a knot in the wood and fidget. I was sure I'd know if the Worm Man was recently here. In much the same way one smells cat odor in clean vacuumed rooms, I thought Hoover's evil would linger, that I'd sense his presence. But I get nothing. I'm at a loss.

As windchimes twinkle somewhere outside, I speak to the reverend. "Kingsley told me about all the good work you do here: feeding families, giving the parents jobs and housing, and educating the children."

Reverend Shasta sits on a sofa across from my chair. "They're all such deserving folks. I only wish I could do more. The picking season is short here, July through September. I close up my farm in October. My workers spend their winters elsewhere. Most head to Florida or Texas."

As I clutch the chair seat beneath me, Kingsley clears his throat. "You're a busy man, Reverend. I'll get straight to the point. We have reason to believe that James Hoover, the serial killer I spoke to you about back in June, is alive and working here at your farm. We're afraid he grabbed that missing New London girl, the one on all the newscasts. Like I said last time we spoke, Hoover would be using an alias. Hank Martin, Mark Ross, and Fred Howell perhaps. Given the circumstances, with the local girl missing and all, I wanted you to look at his photo again." Kingsley shows the minister an age-progressed picture of Hoover.

Reverend Shasta shakes his head. "I wish I could help you, Tom. But, like I told you before, the man you call James Hoover isn't here. He never was here."

"You're certain?" I ask.

"Well, I can't be entirely sure," Reverend Shasta says. "I employ hundreds of workers annually. Though I'd love to keep one crew for the entire season, the truth is, my workers come and go. Some work for a month, others a week or two, some just a couple of days."

Kingsley nods. "I get it. It's chaotic. Still, you told me when we spoke before that you had a lot of repeaters. And I could be wrong, but it seems as if you know your employees pretty well. They live here. You eat meals with them. You pray with them. I'm guessing that a grey-eyed Caucasian would stand out amongst this crowd."

The reverend shrugs. "You'd be surprised. We get our fair share of down-and-out Mainers here. Poverty doesn't discriminate. Neither does God. Neither do I. I don't see skin color. I see souls."

"Perhaps," Kingsley says. "But you dig deep. You pay attention. You and I have only met once before. And I feel as if you know me." Kingsley chuckles. "Granted I'm a memorable fella, but still ..."

The reverend laughs. "We don't get many reporters visiting our farm."

I retrieve my sketchbook from my bag, flip to a drawing of Cassie, and hand the sketchbook to Reverend Shasta. "This is the missing girl. Her name is Cassie Rossi. She's ten years old. I teach third grade. Cassie was in my class two years ago."

The reverend looks at the image. "She's a lovely girl."

I nod. "And smart, creative too. She loves designing and building bird, doll, and treehouses. She's a budding architect."

The reverend's brows arch.

"She's a gem. Talented," I say, my eyes misting.

Reverend Shasta returns my sketchbook. He grabs a box of tissues off the end table and passes it to me. "And you're here because you care about her. Because you care about all your students, as do I."

Above us the ceiling fan whirls. Kingsley speaks, "Reverend, we're also here because new evidence has come to light. We've learned that James Hoover is missing a finger. Now, you can't tell me you wouldn't remember a picker with a missing finger."

I fan out my fingers. "Right hand, pointer finger."

Reverend Shasta frowns. "Sorry, but I've never hired a picker with a missing finger. That would be a rarity." He motions to the wall clock. "I'm sorry. I know you drove all the way up here. But I've got a sermon to prepare, and Maria, bless her heart, shouldn't have to cover for me. She's a bit under the weather today. But she's like that, you know. Puts others before herself." His eyes shift to the window, to Maria, who's standing beneath the oak. He fingers the cross necklace dangling from his neck. His lips move as if he's silently praying.

It's a hunch, but I go with it. A decade of dealing with playground squabbles has taught me to trust my instincts. "James Hoover threatened to hurt Maria. That's why you're not talking. You're protecting her."

The minister stiffens.

"I'm right," I say. "You're protecting Maria."

Reverend Shasta faces me. His lip quivers. "Maria's like a daughter to me.

But it's not just Maria I'm worried about." He gestures to a photo of his farm on the mantle. "This place is everything to me. If the workers don't feel safe here, they're not going to come back with their families. Staying here, even briefly, is a respite for so many of them, a lifesaver."

My gaze flies to the window, and to the workers beneath the bushes. "Is he here now?"

"No. Of course not," the reverend stammers. "I couldn't let a man like that stay." He speaks to Kingsley. "The day you talked to me, the minute you walked out that door, I questioned Roger. Roger Stone was the name he'd given me. I dragged the fella into this very room, and we had ourselves a frank discussion. I told him I was going to drive him to the police station and that he needed to turn himself him. He said he wanted to pray before he left. I gave my nightly sermon and left him alone with the Lord. When I returned, he was gone. But before he fled, he left a message on my chalkboard." Reverend Shasta points to the window, to the chalkboard beneath the oak tree. "'If you talk, Maria dies.' That's what he wrote."

"Did anyone else see it?" Kingsley asks.

"No, heavens no. I erased it before the kids and their parents could spot it. I didn't want to unnerve them. I was too afraid to tell the police. I couldn't take the risk." He claws at his collar. "It's not that I don't care. I do. The truth is, I can't sleep. I can't eat. I've been having nightmares ever since Stone left. I'm terrified he's going to return and hurt Maria or another camper." Tears fill the reverend's eyes. He trembles. "I should have done more. I should have turned Stone in, and now this girl from New London is missing. It's all my fault. If I could go back in time and fix it, I would."

I speak softly. "It's okay."

He looks into my eyes. "I want to help the missing girl, your former student, Kate. I just don't know how. Roger Stone, James Hoover, the Worm Man, whoever he is … is gone. He's not here anymore. What can I do? I have no idea where he is."

"Can you remember anything, something he said even in passing, that might give us a clue as to his whereabouts?" Kingsley asks. "Did he mention any family members? Friends?"

The reverend seems to think. "I heard him speaking to someone on the phone. I believe it was his brother."

"Samuel?" Kingsley says. "Samuel is James' younger brother."

"Yes, Samuel. That's the name I heard." Reverend Shasta nods.

Kingsley frowns. "Anything else stand out?"

Reverend Shasta shakes his head, no. "He was only here a couple of weeks."

"Come on, Rev. This is important," Kingsley snaps back. "Think."

Shasta gestures to the window again, this time at the buildings beyond the driveway. "There was an incident in the rec room. Someone was smoking a cigarette. Stone had some sort of asthma attack. He had to breathe into a paper bag to keep from passing out, nearly turned blue. The next morning, Dr. Watson, the physician who treats my employees, wrote him a prescription for an oral steroid."

Kingsley faces Shasta. "Reverend, do you have Dr. Watson's phone number? Perhaps the doc made note of Hoover's pharmacy. I realize there are HIPAA laws. But if the doc understands what we're dealing with here, he might be willing to talk."

"Of course. Follow me to my office. We can call him from there." Reverend Shasta motions to me. "Kate?"

I clutch my sketchbook. "I'll meet you outside. I want to sit. The heat and the drive, I'm a bit queasy."

Kingsley and the minister disappear down the hallway, and I head to the front porch. As Maria's voice fills the air, I sink onto a rocking chair. With shaky hands, I open my sketchbook and draw. As a breeze blows, tugging at my hair, an image of Maria—upturned nose, long single braid, and broad forehead—forms on the page. Just like the pretty Hispanic girl teaching the campers beneath the tree, the Maria in my drawing wears sandals and a cotton dress. A charm bracelet encircles her wrist.

When I finish my drawing, the door opens, and Kingsley and the reverend step onto the porch. I give the reverend my sketch of Maria. "For you."

He hugs me. "It's lovely. I'll cherish it."

As the reverend and the campers wave, Kingsley and I head back to my Subaru.

I make air quotes as we climb onto our seats. "So did Roger give the name of his pharmacy?"

Kingsley nods. "He did. The Warner Pharmacy."

A wave of unease clips my bones. "Christ, Warner is twenty minutes from New London."

Chapter 5

*A*s the sun flickers through the pine branches, Kingsley and I take the windy dirt road back to Highway 202. By the time we reach Highway 89, the sky is dark. I drive with my headlights on. Though it's past dinnertime, we don't stop to eat. I'm emotionally drained and would prefer silence, but Kingsley wants to talk.

"I can't believe that monster was at Shasta's farm when I was there," he rants. "I drilled Shasta that day too. I questioned his workers hard and scoured that property. I even climbed one of those rickety ladders. Christ, I made Shasta unlock that Winnebago so I could check it, and I still missed the louse."

"Don't beat yourself up. Hindsight is 2020. If Hoover heard you were there and asking around about him, he probably hid."

"Yeah, but I should have looked harder. I knew the reverend wasn't being upfront with me. I sensed it. What's killing me, is the guy's still holding back." Kingsley punches my glove compartment. "You don't let a serial killer go like that, especially if he threatens to hurt someone you love, especially when the creep's murdered three girls. What is Shasta thinking? Hoover's going to kill again. That's a given."

I play devil's advocate. "Could be the reverend truly believes in forgiveness and redemption."

Kingsley shakes his head. "Maybe, but he also likely believes in the devil, and the Worm Man is the devil incarnate."

I grip my steering wheel. "Hoover's gone. He's not at the farm anymore. We can't go back in time. We can only move forward. We know Hoover was there in June, the same day you were, and that Shasta kept quiet about it. The question is, what's the reverend hiding now? What isn't he telling us now?"

"Hell, if I know. But I'm damn sure gonna figure it out."

As Kingsley checks his texts, fiddles with the radio, and searches for news on Cassie on his cell Wi-Fi, raindrops hit my windshield. The rain stirs up a memory. My thoughts drift back to another rainy night, back to Cassie and Glen.

* * *

Several months before Glen's leukemia diagnosis, he and I headed to Bucklin Beach for an early evening swim. Glen wanted to get out of our stuffy farmhouse. He didn't care about the drizzle in the air.

"Get off that couch, Lazy Bones. Let's go to the lake," he said, tickling me.

His enthusiasm got to me. I dropped the novel I was reading, stifled a yawn, and rose.

Like most couples, Glen and I had ups and downs. My panic attacks and hospitalization prior to our move to New Hampshire were tough on me. And the long hours and the stress of running his firm took a toll on Glen. But the summer before he got sick, things were good between us. My miscarriage the previous summer and the mutual grief it caused us, seemed to bring us closer. That June, the spontaneity that had eluded us since our move to New England returned.

We slipped on our bathing suits, grabbed towels from the dryer, and hopped into Glen's truck. The vinyl seat stuck to my bare back and thighs. Beside me in the driver's seat, Glen sang Eddie Rabbitt's "I Love a Rainy Night."

The drive to the lake took all but five minutes. We parked in the empty lot and tossed our towels and Glen's truck keys onto the covered picnic table. Laughing, we darted through the raindrops and toward the lake. Glen did a cannonball off the farthest wooden floating raft, and I swam breaststroke. For twenty minutes, we relaxed in the chest-high water as rain spritzed our faces and shoulders. I felt happy and content, complete.

As we swam back toward the sand, Cassie and Lauren Rossi scampered past the lifeguard stand. They were alone, which was unusual. Lauren normally came with a group of stay-at-home PTA moms, who in turn brought their kids. Lauren rarely went anywhere without Cassie's baby brother, Ian. That summer, she was still breastfeeding.

As we trudged through the shallows, Lauren tugged at her tankini top. She hadn't lost her pregnancy weight from having Ian. Cassie wore a pink one-piece. Her damp white-blonde hair hung loose in ringlets and made me think of the Broadway show *Annie*.

As Lauren placed her towel on the table beside our belongings, Cassie pointed to Glen. She made a beeline for him, giggling and stumbling. I elbowed Glen. I wasn't bothered by her show of favoritism. He was her fellow architect. I was merely her old third-grade teacher, her math tutor.

I smiled and watched Cassie charge into the lake, splashing and waving her arms wildly. She halted several yards away from us. As raindrops dimpled the lake's surface, she pointed at a red plastic bucket and shovel on the sand.

"Mr. Boswell, I brought my tools. Wanna build?"

"Absolutely!" Glen motioned to a spot on the beach beside the lifeguard stand. "I'll meet you at the building site."

Oblivious to the rain, Glen and Cassie spent the next hour making a castle and moat. Meanwhile, Lauren and I sat at the covered picnic table in silence. Though I attempted to converse, she folded her arms across her chest and kept her gaze glued to her daughter.

"Why doesn't Lauren like me?" I asked Glen later that night as we relaxed on our screened porch and sipped wine from coffee mugs. "Wait. I know why she hates me," I said, poking him with the red plastic shovel Cassie had left behind. I'd grabbed it, intending to return it to Lauren. I grinned at Glen. "It's because of you."

Glen jumped and spilled his wine.

"Lauren's jealous," I teased, laughing. "She thinks Cassie likes you better than her because Cassie left you her shovel."

Glen blotted up his spill with his napkin. "Yeah," he said, not looking at me. "Lauren's pissed because Cassie told her I make better turrets than Lauren does."

* * *

The rain intensifies when Kingsley and I reach his New London motel.

Before he climbs out of my SUV, Kingsley says, "I'll go to the pharmacy in Warner tomorrow, see if the pharmacist and the cashiers can tell me anything about the customer who picked up James Hoover's, AKA. Roger Stone's prescription... if it was actually James, or someone helping him. If we're lucky, the management might be willing to share their security tape. I'll call you afterwards, and we'll take it from there."

"Sounds good. Hey, thanks," I say, "Thanks for your help."

Kingsley grins. "No problem." He hurries into his room.

As rain pounds my windshield, I head back to my farmhouse. I'm eager to get inside. My clothes are damp, my driving leg is cramped, and my back aches.

"Warm bath. Warm bath," I mutter, cruising by Gene's orchard.

But as I pull into my driveway, my headlights illuminate the US government plates of a sedan blocking my detached garage.

My heart skips two beats. "Oh, no. Not Cassie." Ripping my keys out of my ignition, I leap out of my Subaru and into the storm. The wind gusts, the driver-side door of the government sedan swings opens, and Leeds exits the vehicle. "Any news about Cassie?" I say, rushing toward him.

Rain pelts Leeds' face. He shakes his head and zips his windbreaker. "No. But we need to talk."

"Of course."

I want to tell Leeds about Roger Stone, AKA James Hoover, the Worm Man, being at Reverend Shasta's Waterboro farm and potentially in Warner, but something about Leeds' demeanor silences me. Shivering, I grab my sketchpad and purse off the passenger seat, shut my SUV door, and we duck beneath the porch overhang.

Without looking at his wristwatch, Leeds says, "It's getting late. Where've you been?" He stomps on my landing mat.

"Waterboro, Maine," I tell him, opening my door and stepping in the foyer.

Leeds trails me inside. Like a stray cat, he weaves, circles, and invades my space. Oddly, he seems more menacing in my cozy entryway than he did yesterday morning at the stark stationhouse. I glance at Leeds' badge and the gun in his holster. I feel jittery, weak-kneed, and vulnerable. A panic attack seems imminent.

"I need to eat," I say, hoping food will calm me. "Do you want something? A salad? A sandwich? Soup?" I finger my cell. "Did you call? I didn't know you were waiting for me."

"I didn't call. I ate earlier. No food for me," he says. "But I'll take a Coke if you've got one. I could use the caffeine."

I gesture to the coatrack. As Leeds removes his jacket and hangs it on a hook, I tighten the sash of my cardigan and drop my purse and keys on the foyer table. Water from my ballet flats puddles on the hardwoods.

I turn on the lights while moving toward the back of the house. "My kitchen's this way."

As rain thrashes the roof, Leeds follows me down the hall, past the dining and living rooms, and into the kitchen.

"Nice place," he mumbles.

"Thanks. It's comfortable," I tell him.

Though I motion to a chair, Leeds leans against the counter. As his eyes drift to the dirty breakfast dishes in my sink, I grab cold cuts from the fridge. Leeds taps his foot.

Wishing he would take charge and start the conversation, I ramble, "My late husband, Glen, picked out this house because of its character. You know, the crown molding, the glass doorknobs, the nooks and crannies." I point to the windowpane above the sink. "Glen loved that stained glass. He loved the oak banister in the foyer too, the way it curves into a ball. Would you believe we actually have a fallout shelter in our basement? They're not uncommon in New Hampshire. We use ours as a wine cellar."

I get bread from the pantry, spread mayonnaise on the slices, and add turkey. After putting my plate on the table, I locate two sodas in the fridge, hand one to Leeds, and sit at the breakfast table. Leeds remains standing.

"So, what's going on?" I ask.

"Nothing," he says, tracing the grout between my counter tiles. "That's the problem. My divers have combed the lakes. We've canvased the town and hiked Mount Kearsarge. We haven't found Cassie, and the clock is ticking. From what we can tell, she's not in Little or Big Lake Sunapee, on the conservation land, or in any of the seasonal cabins by the ski slopes."

"Have you looked into the possibility that James Hoover is alive and that he's holding her?"

"I'm sorry, Kate. But no evidence supports that theory."

I frown. "Not true. Did Officer Messer tell you about the Paula Abdul song I heard?"

"He did. My forensics collected samples from the clearing behind your property earlier this afternoon—beer cans, cigarette butts, and condom wrappers.

We sent them off to the lab. But my gut tells me we won't find anything that links to Hoover or Cassie. That clearing is a smoke pit. More than likely, kids have been smoking weed out there for decades."

Sensing his lack of conviction, I toss out Kingsley's aha moment. "Hoover had a neighbor, Emily Rose. She claimed she saw him in her basement after his New Jersey family shore home burned and he was deemed dead."

"I know all about Emily Rose. She has Alzheimer's disease. Like many Alzheimer's patients, Emily experiences hallucinations."

"Well, Kingsley and I, we—"

"You talked to Reverend Shasta. The reverend just called me. He's certain the man who stayed at his farm, Roger Stone, wasn't James Hoover."

I tear crust off my sandwich bread. "Seriously?"

"Yes, seriously."

"Well, the reverend must be backpedaling because he's worried about this camper, Maria. Actually, he's terrified of something else too, only he wouldn't tell Kingsley and me what it was. But whatever it is, it has to be major. I can't understand why anyone would let a serial killer go free like he did. It's irresponsible, reprehensible. You need to question him, get the truth out of him. You should—"

"Roger Stone isn't James Hoover," Leeds says, interrupting me.

"How'd you know that? What makes you so certain?"

Leeds wiggles his fingers. "Roger Stone's fingers are all intact."

"That doesn't make sense. We told Reverend Shasta about Hoover's missing finger. He said Stone and Hoover were the same person."

"The reverend only said that to get you to leave his farm. He didn't think you'd go unless he told you what you wanted to hear. He said you and Kingsley made him uncomfortable, that he felt threatened."

"That's ridiculous. It wasn't like that. We weren't harassing him. Kingsley and I just went there to tell Reverend Shasta about Cassie." I frown. "I'm confused. If you don't think James Hoover worked at the reverend's farm, why are you talking to me now?"

"We're looking into all possibilities, not just scenarios involving the Worm Man." His gaze traps mine. He nods.

"Oh, come on. You can't seriously think I took Cassie? That's silly."

"Is it? Why'd you touch Cassie's sneaker?"

"I wasn't thinking. I was upset. The search stirred up memories. I'm sorry."

Leeds' eyes shift to my breakfast nook walls. All are adorned with drawings of my students. Leeds points to the wall. "You draw your students a lot."

"I do. They inspire me."

"You especially like drawing Cassie Rossi. Evelyn Taylor said you showed her a sketchbook and that half the drawings were of Cassie."

"Cassie's a good subject. She's pretty yet unconventional. And her emotions are always just beneath the surface, ready to be captured."

"But you care about her more than your other students. You've spent a lot of time with her. You told me that at the station yesterday."

"Yes." I say, "We've already covered this, but I'll elaborate. Cassie is below grade level in math. When she was in my class, I tutored her privately twice a week, hoping to get her math skills up to speed. I continued tutoring her afterschool when she moved onto fourth grade. Also, she liked my architect husband, and he liked her too. Not many little girls are fascinated by arches, angles, and load bearing walls. Cassie is a unicorn in that respect." I shake my head. "Cassie's super creative, a naturally gifted 2d and 3d drawer. But the reality is, those talents are only going to get her so far. If she does pursue a career in architecture someday, she'll need to know algebra, trigonometry, and geometry. So, mastering basic elementary level math skills now is essential." I smile. "Cassie's got so much talent. But the other kids could care less. She's sweet, sensitive, driven. It's hard not to root for her, to care about her."

"Gotcha." Leeds sips his soda. "Joyce Hadley was in your ground search group," he says, eyeing me, "she said you insisted on searching the park. She said you made Randi Green switch maps with another group. Why'd you do that?"

I exhale. "Because we were originally assigned to search the area by the school. I knew Cassie wouldn't be there. Hoover grabbed Whitney from a park playground, not a school playground. Plus, Cassie doesn't like school." When Leeds frowns, I explain. "Cassie has ADHD. It's hard for her to sit for more than a few minutes when she's not medicated. Focusing enough to get passing grades is difficult for her. Also, Lauren's so active at school. I've always had the impression that Cassie felt overshadowed by her mother."

"Overshadowed? What are you saying?"

"Just that Cassie can't be herself when she's at school. It sometimes happens when moms are super involved."

"You don't like Lauren Rossi," Leeds says.

"No. I don't. But I wouldn't take Cassie to spite her, if that's what you're implying."

Leeds stares at me. "Why'd you lie to Liam Messer? Tell him you were going to the teacher's supply store when you were really going to talk to Reverend Shasta?"

My cheeks burn. "How did you ... Never mind." Leeds clearly talked to Liam. I take a bite of my sandwich and force down the bread. "I didn't tell Liam because he doesn't believe Hoover's alive. He would have said I was wasting my time and getting worked up over nothing." I shove my plate aside. "Anything else?"

I want Leeds to leave, but for some reason, he isn't budging. "Look," I say, "You may not like how I've handled myself, that I touched Cassie's sneaker, and that I lied to Liam about visiting Reverend Shasta. But I have no motive for taking Cassie. Why would I grab her and hide her? It makes no sense."

Leeds raises a finger. "See, I've got three theories. Number one, you like the attention your association with the Worm Man brings you."

"Not true. I could lose my teaching and drawing jobs if my connection to that Hoover goes public. I'd rather be known for anything but that."

"Really? In today's world of reality TV, infamy and fame have become synonymous. Studies show that more people want to be famous than rich. You ask kids what they want to be when they group; they don't say a doctor or a fireman. They just want to be known, internet famous."

"I'm a middle-aged woman. That's not me. If I wanted to be famous, I would have stayed in New Jersey. I had connections in New York. I was establishing an art career as a portraitist. Like I said, I'm super private about my past. Your theory has no merit."

He lifts a second finger. "The majority of female abductors grab children because they want a baby of their own. Prior to your husband's death, you miscarried."

"I did. But I've got a whole classroom full of children. Besides, if I wanted a child, I could adopt or become a foster parent. I could remarry, try in vitro, or get a surrogate. I've got options."

"What about revenge?"

"Revenge?" I laugh. "That's your theory number three? Who am I avenging?"

"Lauren Rossi. Word is, she had an affair with your late husband, Glen."

I spill what's left of my soda. "See, that's not even funny," I say, wiping up the syrupy liquid with my napkin. "That's just mean. Who told you that? 'Cause whoever did is lying. You really need to consider your sources before you … I'd like you to leave."

Leeds nods. He doesn't push or question me further. Perhaps he knows I'm done talking, or maybe he retreats because he's gotten what he wants from me, a reaction, a big one.

I escort him out of my kitchen and to my foyer. As I grip the doorknob and open the door, he grabs his jacket off the coatrack. It's no longer raining. Leeds hesitates on the welcome mat. The porch light flickers above him, illuminating the shadows beneath his eyes.

He says, "Oh, about that source."

"Yes?" I want to know who the lying gossip is.

He winks. "I'm not at liberty to reveal it."

He turns and descends my porch steps. Though it's pitch-black outside and my driveway is slippery from the rain, I don't wait for him to get safely into his sedan. I slam the door and lock it.

My breaths come kick. Screeching, hyena-like, I stomp back into the kitchen, jam my sandwich plate into my dishwasher, toss in a detergent pod, and push the start button hard.

To say I'm angry is an understatement. I'm angry at Leeds for coming to my home and spewing his BS. But, logical or not, I'm mostly pissed at Lauren for being curvy and beautiful, for making me doubt Glen's faithfulness. I feel like driving straight to her house and spitting on her. I could do it too. I know where she lives, in that little Cape Cod with the yellow shutters, about a mile from the elementary school.

But I'm not stupid. Confronting Lauren will only make things worse for me. I'm not prone to physical violence. But you see it all the time on the news, polite law-abiding citizen pushed to the brink, snaps. The *Oxygen Channel* has an entire docuseries dedicated to people who lose it and lash out at others. The interviewees are all in prison and sporting orange jumpsuits.

Don't put yourself in that situation, I tell myself. *Lauren's not worth it. Plus, her daughter's missing, for God's sakes, being held captive by a psychopath. You should feel bad for Lauren. She needs your empathy, not your jealous rage.*

But the bitch went after your husband, I counter.

You don't know that, I reason back. *Leeds knows nothing about your marriage. He barely knows you, and he's never even met Glen. He's baiting you.*

Some people run for miles when they're upset; others drink. Randi downs containers of Ben & Jerry's. I draw. I grab my sketchbook off the counter. I can barely hold my pencil. My hands are that shaky. As the dishwasher hums, I sit facing my breakfast table. I sketch the curve of Leeds' chin, the wrinkles fanning from his eyes, and his thick, almost triangular-shaped, brows. Drawing his features should give me a sense of control. I'm the one in charge. He's merely the subject. But as I shade his cheekbones, my pencil point breaks, and Leeds' words echo in my head, *Word is, she had an affair with your late husband, Glen.*

I shove my sketchbook aside, snatch a feather duster from the utility closet, and swat at the bookshelves lining the hallway. My mind races.

Okay. So maybe you guys weren't perfect. But hey, what couple is? So what if Glen offered to drive Cassie home after her tutoring sessions? Big deal. Glen was helpful like that. He drove Cassie to make things easier for you. He was happy with you.

But as I work my feather duster, waffling through the dining room and office, moving into the sunroom and the den, my words sound empty even to me. *Oh, who are you kidding, Kate? What man buys a five-bedroom house with a backyard the size of a soccer field in the best school district in the state, if he's content with just his wife?*

Glen had wanted children. This was no big secret. After my miscarriage, we tried to get pregnant again, but I didn't conceive. When I brought up in vitro and adoption and he brushed me off, I thought, *It's too soon. He's still grieving our loss.* When he passed fourteen months later, I figured he'd had a premonition, sensing he was ill. *He wasn't stepping out on you. He loved you. Don't even think that*, I tell myself.

But though I don't want to believe Leeds' statement, something about it rings true. Me tutoring Cassie was Lauren's idea. I was floored when she asked for my help. I'd been nominated for New Hampshire Teacher of the Year the previous year. At the time, I reasoned that Lauren had heard about the nomination, and that she'd put our personal differences aside for Cassie's sake. Still, because of the awkward tension between us, I hesitated to accept the tutoring job. I hadn't tutored a student privately before. Teaching a classroom of kids was draining enough. But it was Lauren's connection to the whole tutoring thing that rattled me.

"Oh, just tutor the kid," Glen said, the evening after Lauren propositioned me. "It's not like Lauren's gonna be there the whole time. Though if ask me, you being intimidated by her is just plain silly." When I told him that I wanted to create a website and spend more time drawing instead, he pushed harder. "What makes you think you can't build your art business and tutor Cassie? Why miss out on this opportunity? Yesterday, you told me Cassie was a blast."

My smile came fast. "She is. She's a firecracker. Smart as a whip. Cute too. She just needs someone to keep her focused."

I didn't tell him that Cassie made me think of Whitney, or that personality-wise Lauren reminded me of Whitney's mother, Lilly Bay, and not in a good way. But Glen seemed to get this. He got that my past haunted me and often held me back. Hell, it crippled me.

"Look," he said, "You and Cassie can come straight here from school in your SUV. When you're through tutoring her, how about I drive Cassie home? That way you won't have to deal with Lauren."

"You don't have to do that," I said. "I'm a grownup, a teaching professional. I should be able to handle this situation."

He kissed my forehead. "My point is, you don't have to handle anything. I'll be Cassie's taxi driver."

"But you're so busy. Why would you do that?"

"Because we're a team," he whispered, his breath warming my neck. "And because you're so damn sexy."

But was Lauren the sexy one, not me? Did drop-off flirting, lead to an affair?

Once, when Glen thought I wasn't looking, I caught him ogling Lauren at church. Dressed in a tight pink pencil skirt, her hips swaying, she strutted down the aisle before sliding into an empty pew. Beside me, and clutching a hymnal, Glen had lowered his gaze as if he were praying. But he wasn't praying. He was peering over the top of his hymnal, watching her, wanting her. Not that the wanting was anything unusual. A lot of men want Lauren. Most men want Lauren. What was unusual was that Lauren wanted him back. I could tell. The swaying of the hips and the pink skirt that hugged her curves, they were for him. How did I know this?

After the service, during coffee hour, she puckered her lips and blew him a kiss. Glen and I were standing across the fellowship hall. When I said something about it, he laughed.

"Christ, Kate," he said. "The coffee's damn hot. She's blowing to cool it off. You're being absurd."

As he turned to chat with Deacon Tucker, I got myself a cup of coffee from the ten-liter stainless steel coffeemaker where Lauren had obtained hers. The brew was tepid.

The church and the tutoring incidents were just two of many tiny exchanges, all easily explained away. Individually they meant nothing, but together they told a story, one I'd chosen to ignore.

I shut my eyes and picture the mysterious grey Volvo cruising up Old Main Street. A visual memory of the fresh daisies on Glen's headstone follows.

"It was you, Lauren!" I shout. "You ho! You left those flowers for my Glen!"

Chapter 6

I clutch my pillow, lean against the headboard of my bed, and moan. A week ago, before Cassie's abduction, Randi and I agreed to set up our classrooms together. The reality is, having concluded that Glen and Lauren likely had an affair, I don't want to leave my house or talk to anyone. But Randi isn't just anyone. She's my Oprah. She always has a fresh perspective. She keeps me sane. Plus, school is starting soon, and I need to start prepping. There's that, and there's my fear that if I stay home, I'll obsess over Cassie and what the Worm Man is doing to her, and I'll go nuts.

As images of Lauren's tight pink skirt flicker through my mind, I shower, dress, grab my supplies from the hall closet, and hightail it to the elementary school. As I'm pulling into the teachers' parking lot, Randi texts me.

Running late. Sorry!

I text back, **No problem**.

I teeter out of my SUV, lug my box of supplies through the deserted lot, and trudge into the building. Zombie-like, I enter the empty corridor. As I lower the large box in my grasp to the floor, a chill zips up my spine. My classroom door is ajar.

It's nothing, I tell myself. *Janitor Henry just forgot to lock it. It's an oversight. Relax.*

But I can't help but worry. Hoover was only at the blueberry farm a couple of weeks, but that's enough time to make a friend who might tell him if someone was snooping around.

Fingering the pepper spray in my purse, I take a cleansing breath. When I slip into my nine hundred-square-foot classroom space, I half-expect to hear the Paula Abdul song seeping out of the intercom. I don't. Even so, as my gaze drifts from the back of the room, forward, my heart thuds. I don't see Hoover or anyone else inside, just your basic unused summer classroom: bare walls, empty desks, and vacuumed carpet. I hone in on the supply closet, and my body goes cold. Last spring, Jake Davis hid in that closet for two periods, flattened himself like a ferret, to avoid taking his NH SAS tests.

Tiptoeing, as if I'm crossing lake ice, I move toward the closet. I fling the metal door open with one hand, and aim my pepper spray at the opening with the other. I let out a nervous laugh.

The closet's packed with stuff—paper, glue sticks, rulers, and markers—everything under the sun. But what matters is that no one's inside. *Jesus, Kate. Get a grip.* As I shut the metal door, a dull ache spreads to my temple. I'm a wreck. My limbs won't stop twitching. Even though I'm clearly alone, I can't shake the feeling that someone is watching me. I clutch my pepper spray and do a wide visual sweep of the room.

I've always considered the elementary school, and especially my classroom, a safe zone. But that doesn't mean I haven't thought about how I'd handle an attack from an intruder. I know which windows open the fastest, which drawer my pointy scissors are in, and how to unscrew the flagpole quickly so I could use it as a weapon. I'm careful too. During the school year, when I'm not in it, I keep my classroom door locked. I don't stay in the building late or arrive super early.

The administration is vigilant too. Though security at Kearsarge Elementary isn't Fort Knox tight, September through June, Janitor Henry patrols the grounds. Visitors check in and wear badges. Last spring every teacher took a self-defense class and active shooter training. Bottom line, Principal Jane runs a tight ship during the school year. The problem is, summer vacation is a different animal. Rules are looser. Teachers come and go. Doors, like mine, are left unlocked. Summer school students soar onto the school grounds like geese on a pond and then vacate.

I stare at the supply closet. *Check it again. You know you have to be certain.*

My pepper spray at the ready, I slowly reopen the closet door. Paper, glue sticks, and a box of hand sanitizers greet me, again. Sighing, I shut the door, push my cardboard box into the classroom, and remove the lid. Though my hands shake, my fingers work.

Enough, I tell myself. *You're being silly. Hoover's not here. No one's here, but you. Get something accomplished while you wait for Randi. Some physical work will do you good. Focus.* And I do, at least try.

My box contains life-sized cutouts of my incoming students. I drew them over the summer. I plan to use the cutouts instead of nametags. They're a tradition of sorts. My incoming students look forward to them, just like Randi's new students eagerly await the special cheer she does annually on the first day of school. Randi, who went to Plymouth State, is an ex-cheerleader.

Using my seating chart, I tape a dozen cutouts to their appropriate chairs. The more I move and work, the less jittery I am. But as soon as my fight-or-flight response switches off, I start envisioning Glen and Lauren together, bodies entwined. As I'm reaching back into my big cardboard box, Randi hurries into the room carrying a large plastic bin of chapter books.

"What a morning," she says. "Mikey spilled his OJ all over Bill's laptop. Justin, poor guy, couldn't find his toothbrush."

"Let me help you with those books," I say, hurrying toward her. Together, Randi and I tote her bin of books over to a shelf and lower it to the floor.

Randi rubs her bicep. "Thanks."

I glance at her engagement ring. Leeds' words drop from my brain. *Word is, your late husband had an affair with Lauren Rossi.*

Though I told myself I needed Randi's objective viewpoint, now that she's here, the thought of talking to her about Glen and Lauren makes my cheeks warm. It's like that time my period blood seeped through my Lilly Pulitzer dress, soiling the seat cushion at Lake Sunapee Country Club. I'm embarrassed, ashamed. Intellectually, I know that if Glen truly cheated on me, like I'm pretty sure he did, it wasn't my fault. But it feels as if I should have done something to prevent it—been more creative in the bedroom; gone on all those hiking trips Glen begged me to go on; been better, prettier, or more entertaining; not let my appearance slide; waxed my bikini area; worn perfume; baked his favorite ziti dish more often; or forced him to attend couples' therapy after my miscarriage even though we seemed fine.

What were you thinking? I ask myself. *Confiding in Randi? Randi's happily married. Bill worships her toenail clippings. It's not as if she can relate.*

As Randi retrieves a bottle of water from her bag and sips, I retape incoming student, Maxine Lemon's cutout to Cassie's old seat.

"We should probably reorganize the room," I say, motioning to Maxine's cutout. "Maybe move the desks into clusters. That way, Maxine won't feel so weird. Probably no one will realize that it's Cassie's old desk, but you never know." I point to the windows. "It's so strange. I keep thinking Cassie's gonna run across that playground any second."

Randi nods. "Me too."

We push the chairs and desks together and take stock.

"I should have taped the cutouts on after we did all this reorganizing," I say, securing Maxine's paper arm to her chair again.

Randi shrugs. "Doesn't matter. The cutouts survived. By the way, they look awesome."

"Thanks. Have you been working on your cheer?" I ask.

She makes wiggly spirit fingers. "You know I have." She looks at me. "So how have you been? I haven't seen you since the search, since ..."

"Since I lost it at the park? Wow. Was that two days ago?"

She nods. "Yup. How are you?"

"Okay. Hanging in there."

She touches my arm. "Hey, I should have called to check up on you. Don't know why I didn't. Got busy with the boys and Bill."

"No worries. I get it. You've got your own life."

Her gaze holds mine. "And you're a big part of that life. Don't forget that."

"I could have called you too," I say.

"Yeah. But I *should* have called you."

A lump clogs my throat. Not wanting to cry, I jump into work mode. Randi follows my lead. We tape the rest of the cutouts to the chairs. When all the cutouts are secured, I sharpen pencils and put erasers, markers, rulers, and scissors into baskets. Randi hangs multiplication and division posters. She hums

"How Far I'll Go" from the movie *Moana*. I start to put away the books from Randi's bin.

"Principal Jane wants you to be the lead teacher for the third grade again," she says, tacking a telling time poster beside a money chart depicting coin values. "You should do it."

I think about how I was lead teacher two years ago when Cassie was in my class. I picture Lauren's pouty lips kissing Glen, and the Judy Moody paperback in my grasp falls to the floor. I kneel and knock over a jar of pencils. Tears cloud my eyes.

Randi crouches beside me. "Oh, Kate? I know you're upset about Cassie. But they're gonna find her. I know it."

"It isn't just Cassie," I say, scooping up the number twos. "That FBI guy Leeds came to my house yesterday. He kept asking me questions, which I suppose is his job. But then out of the blue, he says someone told him Glen had an affair with Lauren Rossi."

Randi groans. "What a shit-stirrer. I never said Glen had an affair. I said there was this rumor."

I feel like I've been punched. "You told him?"

We stand and she wipes imaginary dust off her yoga pants. "I did. Sorry. Leeds kept badgering me about you, about the ground search. He wouldn't let up. He kept saying, 'Why did she want to go to the park? Why did she grab the sneaker off the slide?' And then he asked me about you and Lauren and why you didn't like each other."

Randi paces. She steps on a yellow crayon and it breaks. "I told him that some people just don't like each other. That it's like that with kids and dogs too. That sometimes Bill despises his clients for no good reason. He just hates them at the first handshake. But Leeds wouldn't let up. So, I told him about the rumor. I told him we'd never spoken about it and that I didn't think you knew, but that maybe you'd sensed something. Me telling him was like you grabbing Cassie's sneaker, an impulse. The second the rumor popped out of my mouth, I wanted to take it back, but I couldn't." She plays with the pocket zipper on her yoga pants. "You're mad."

I shake my head no. "Why didn't you ever tell me?"

"Because I didn't know if it was true or not. I heard it a couple of months ago. Glen had already passed. It seemed irrelevant. Telling you would only hurt you." She steps toward me, gestures at the tears in my eyes. "And I was right. You're devastated."

I cross my arms over my chest. "Who told you?"

Randi stares at the carpet, at the yellow pieces of crayon. "No one. I overheard it. Celine and Janet, you know those soccer moms, were talking. I had afterschool playground duty. They were sitting on the bench by the cafeteria. Their daughters, Jillian and Megan, were playing hopscotch. Anyhow, I was over by the water fountain, behind them. They didn't see me."

"What did they say exactly?"

"That they were surprised Lauren had kept Cassie in your class. Celine said it was ballsy, given the circumstances, given Lauren's affair with Glen, and wasn't there a statute of limitations for cheating. Then Janet said the affair was old news."

My heart drums. *Old news?* "Did Janet and Celine say when the affair, when they—"

Randi's eyes shoot to Cassie's old desk. "About ten years ago. I'm guessing it happened when you first came to New London."

My body goes numb. Up until this moment, I'd assumed that the cheating began when I'd started tutoring Cassie. That it was a fling, a short-lived meaningless romance, spurred on by Glen's approaching fortieth birthday, my miscarriage, and Glen and Lauren's interaction during Cassie's tutoring drop-offs. But what if Glen and Lauren actually had a relationship that spanned ten years, from our arrival in New London until his death? What if he loved Lauren? What if Cassie is Glen's daughter? My words squeak out. "Did Janet and Celine say if Cassie was Glen's—"

"No, and I don't know if …"

I make two tight fists. Anger surges through me—anger at Glen and Lauren, but also at Leeds too. Why couldn't Leeds have left my marriage alone? I admit, that the fairytale image of Glen I've clung to isn't spot-on. But it's that Prince Charming illusion that's kept me going, given me strength. The need to know if Cassie is Glen's daughter beats through me like a pulse. Organizing my classroom seems both trivial and overwhelming.

I say, "Can we finish up here some other time. I'm—"

"Of course."

As Randi nods, Karen, a fellow third-grade teacher, enters the room. Karen and Lauren live on the same street. Though they're not friends, just seeing Karen, knowing she interacts with Lauren daily—while putting out her trash bins, collecting her mail, and heading to her car in the driveway—makes me want to crawl underneath my desk.

"I'm out of staples, Kate," Karen says. "Do you have an extra box? The main office is closed."

I gesture at my supply closet. "If you can find one, it's yours."

Karen, a fifty-something bleached blonde, makes a beeline for my closet. As she rummages through the items on the shelves, I fight back tears. Beside me, Randi nudges me with her elbow. She pats my hand, I breathe, and everything feels doable again, like I'm going to get through this.

But then Karen screeches. She throws something pink across the room and wails. "OMG! Cassie's sneaker! It's Cassie's other shoe!"

I have to see the pink Converse for myself. Randi seems to understand this. She clutches my arm. Together, we walk toward the pink sneaker. I eye the pink low-top Converse like it's a python.

"Look!" Randi points to the shoelace eyelets.

Instead of laces, the holes contain strands of white-blonde hair.

* * *

I call Liam because I don't want to deal with Leeds. But, of course, Leeds comes too. Though he marches into my classroom wearing loafers, slacks, and a navy polo—what appears to be his usual attire—he looks different than he did last night in my kitchen. Under the stark classroom lights, he seems older and grittier. A faint scar I didn't notice during our two previous encounters zigzags below his left brow. He looks less like someone's laidback uncle, more like an actor playing the part.

"Fancy seeing you again, Ms. Boswell," he says.

Liam follows Leeds into the room. He stands beside Maxine Lemon's cutout. As Liam nods at me, gratitude and a spark of attraction shoot through me. That I can feel anything for him in this moment, surprises me. I'm reeling from the unearthing of Glen's affair and the implications of its timing. And seeing Cassie's sneaker has me beyond shook. I feel like I'm in a *Lifetime* movie. Nothing seems real.

"Thanks for coming," I mouth to Liam, needing him to ground me.

"No problem," he mouths back.

"So where is it?" Leeds asks.

Karen gestures at the pink sneaker on the carpet near the whiteboard.

Like a firing squad, Karen, Randi, and I line up in front of the backpack cubbies. As we press our spines against the coat hooks, the classroom door opens, and two agents dart past us. Both wear latex gloves. One carries a canvas bag.

Leeds points to Cassie's sneaker. "On the carpet." He motions to Karen, Randi, and me. "To the hall, ladies. FYI, until I say so, no one is authorized to reenter this room. I'm going to need to speak to each of you separately in the teachers' lounge."

Randi and I grab our bookbags and purses. We slip into the hallway. As Leeds and Liam talk in hushed voices, I lean against the cinderblock wall and attempt to steady my breathing. Beside me, Karen, who's been quiet since the shoe-tossing incident, trembles.

Randi pats Karen's arm. "Do you want to talk to Agent Leeds first? Get this over with?"

As Karen nods, Liam and Leeds join us in the hallway.

"Karen wants to go first," Randi says to them.

"I'll take Ms. Boswell and Ms. Green to the library," Liam says to Leeds.

Randi, Liam, and I watch Karen and Leeds march toward the teachers' lounge.

* * *

Ten minutes have passed. I'm in the school library. Randi is sitting at a small computer desk, staring at the wall. I'm not sure what she's thinking, but I'm guessing she's afraid for herself, for me, her boys, our students, the rest of the school staff, and especially for Cassie. Not only did Cassie's disappearance change our town, finding her sneaker in my closet has soiled our school. Like dung tracked on a carpet, the evil here is impossible to ignore.

"Hoover put that sneaker in there to scare me," I say to Liam. "He did it because Kingsley and I got too close to him in Waterboro."

Liam stands on the carpet beside me. He looks awkward, too tall beside the kid-sized chairs and tables. "Don't worry. We'll get to the bottom of this. I'm just glad you, Randi, and Karen are all safe."

"Me too."

I glance at the book-filled shelves. I can't see behind them.

Liam follows my gaze. "No one's here. I checked. And the door's locked, so you can relax. Leeds' men are combing the premises. If someone who doesn't belong is here, they'll find them."

I shudder. "Cassie's hair was in the laces."

Liam touches my shoulder. "Don't get ahead of yourself. We don't even know if it's Cassie's hair in that sneaker. It could be a doll's hair or from a wig. Or somebody else's hair entirely. Could be whoever put Cassie's sneaker in your closet, did it to get a rise out of you. Some sicko who's following the story on the news. Everyone in town knows you were her teacher. And don't forget, you were in the paper and on social media because of your art award. It's possible that one of the other artists from the show is angry that Evelyn gave you the award and not them. Art is a competitive industry."

I frown. A jealous artist...I hadn't considered this scenario. "You think that's what's going on here?"

"It's a possibility."

Leeds has a different theory.

* * *

After being interrogated, Karen and Randi are sent home. Now, I'm the one in the teachers' lounge hot seat. Leeds has got me making a timeline of events—everything I did from the moment I arrived at school up until the time Karen found the sneaker.

"Did you notice anything unusual, out of place, when you entered your classroom?" Leeds asks me.

"No. Just that the door was open."

"Were the lights on or off?"

I frown. "Off, I think. But it's hard to remember."

"And you didn't go into the closet prior to Karen opening it?"

"I did. But I didn't see the sneaker. I just checked to make sure no one was in there. I was on edge because my classroom door was open."

Leeds' brows furrow. "But if you were on edge, why didn't you wait in your car for Randi, find Janitor Henry and ask him to escort you in, or call Officer Messer? Those seem like the logical plays."

"One would think that. But …" I lower my voice. An image of the brick walls of the Carrier Clinic fills my mind. "I have an anxiety disorder. I suffer from panic attacks. I have for decades, actually since Whitney Bay's abduction. If I waited around or called for backup, every time I was anxious, I'd have no life. Truth is, I've learned to keep my fear in check. I use strategies to function. James Hoover's angry with me because I questioned Reverend Shasta. He's sending me a message. He put that pink Converse in my classroom," I say, determined to steer him back to what really matters. "There's no one else who would do it."

"Except …"

"Except what?"

"Except Hoover's dead."

"He's not. Like I said, no one else would put that shoe in that closet other than him."

Leeds looks at me. "I disagree."

"Oh, come on. Me? Why would I put Cassie's sneaker in my own supply closet? That would be stupid."

"Why? Because you're a person of interest. You had to figure my men would follow you to the school. You couldn't risk tossing the shoe out in a dumpster or the woods."

"And why am I throwing away the sneaker?"

Leeds taps his forehead. "Because the shoe implicates you." The randomness of his next statement throws me. "If I had to guess, I'd say you hid Cassie's sneaker in that big cardboard box you dragged in. Then you stashed it in the closet before Randi showed up."

"But I could have just grabbed the staples for Karen," I counter back. "Why would I have allowed her to rummage in my closet if I'd put the sneaker inside?"

"Because you were distracted by your conversation with Randi. The two of you were talking about Glen and Lauren's affair."

I swallow. I'm the third teacher to be questioned. Apparently, Randi told Leeds what we talked about. "Not an affair," I snap, not wanting to admit to Leeds that I believe Glen was unfaithful. "A rumor, one I didn't hear until yesterday, so that in itself refutes your theory."

"Don't give me that," Leeds says. "You've known about the rumor for a long time, since before your husband passed away."

"Not true."

"Then why did you yell at Glen in the hospital after your miscarriage?" He makes air quotes. "'This is your fault. This wouldn't have happened if you

hadn't f-ed her. I crashed because of you. We lost our baby girl because of you.'
You screamed that in the ER so loudly that the whole waiting room heard you.'"

* * *

I close my eyes. I lost my daughter when I was five months pregnant,
minutes after I careened into a telephone pole. At the time of my car crash my
baby's face, body, and organs were fully formed. If she'd been born, she would
be almost two now. Glen and I had picked out the name Georgia. In my mind, I
envision Georgia as the perfect mash-up of Glen and me. I can see the freckles
splattering her nose, her sun-bleached auburn hair, and the half-moons of her
fingernails. But though my mental image of who'd she likely be is vivid and clear,
those days surrounding the accident and my miscarriage are a blur.

I remember metal crunching and sirens, and Glen holding my hand
and then releasing it. Dr. Franklin, the ER doctor, prescribed pills, sedatives. An
image of Glen pleading with me, his eyes filled with tears and his fingers clasped
in prayer, surfaces. Why did Glen plead with me?

I lost blood. This I know. And I likely took more pills than I was supposed
to, blue ones. I downed them like candy. I needed them to block the pain, to stop
the bad thoughts from seeping from my brain. Days and nights morphed together.
Dreams, nightmares, and reality entwined.

Then Glen took the pills away from me. "No more," he said. "You've
had your fill."

As I lay staring up at the ceiling, Glen sat in the armchair beside my bed
reading *Dwell* and *Architectural Digest*. He studied my drawings of my students
too. One day, he handed me a sketchbook.

"I drew her," he said, "with your colored pencils."

"Who?" I asked.

"Our daughter, Georgia."

I stared at the page. The girl in his drawing was still and rigid, like a
stick figure. But he'd given her brown eyes to match mine. And she had my
auburn-colored hair. Her smile was crooked, like his, and her spindly arms were
outstretched as if she were ready for a hug. When Glen rose and opened his arms
like the Georgia in his drawing, I fell into his embrace.

"I'm sorry," I said.

"Me too," he murmured.

He didn't say what he was sorry for exactly. I assumed he was sorry for
our loss, maybe for something else too. Yes, there was something else, except I
was too tired and my thoughts were too fuzzy to care about that something else
anymore.

"What happened?" I said to Glen. I pulled my cotton nightgown away
from my sweaty abdomen, which was now flat, empty, and void of life.

"You were in a car accident and banged your head. We lost Georgia," he said. "You cried. Mostly you slept."

* * *

I'm back in the teachers' lounge. Leeds swivels in his chair. A salt shaker sits on the table between us. He shakes it and licks the salt that tumbles into his palm.

"What's wrong?" he says. "You think of something?"

"No." I spring to my feet. "James Hoover put that sneaker in my supply closet. He did it to spook me, to make me look guilty, and to punish me for talking to Reverend Shasta. And if he didn't, someone else did," I say, though I don't really believe this.

Leeds leans toward me. "Like?"

"Someone with access to my classroom."

He smiles. "You got a beef with Janitor Henry?"

"No. But don't forget it works both ways. I'm pretty sure, Lauren Rossi doesn't like me either. Talk to her?" I hesitate by the door. "Aren't parents the number-one suspects when kids go missing?"

Leeds squints at me. "If you had to guess, where would you say Cassie is now?"

"With James Hoover. He's definitely close by. How else would he have gotten into my supply closet? I need to go home. Either book me, or let me go."

He motions to the door. "You're free to leave."

I dart into the hall, and shut the teachers' lounge door. Liam is waiting beside the water fountain.

"You look rattled," he says, hurrying toward me. "I take it that it didn't go well."

"Don't know. I mean, I don't know how Leeds is when he interrogates other people. You saw Randi and Karen leave the lounge. Did they seem dazed?"

"Like deer in headlights." He tugs at my hair, playing with it like a kitten. *You can trust Liam,* I tell myself. *He's not like Leeds.* But as I press my forehead against Liam's chest, he says, "You should probably get an attorney."

I pull away from him. "An attorney?" I suddenly feel alone, vulnerable. The aloneness is deep. It jerks me back to those days following Glen's death. "You think I had something to do with Cassie's disappearance?"

"Of course not. But innocent people need lawyers too. I'm just saying, as a precaution." He whispers, "Don't panic, but Leeds is probably going to search your house."

My heart races. "I've got a family friend who's a lawyer. I'll call him."

"Anyone I know?" Liam asks.

"Someone you've likely heard of. Thurston Bay, Whitney's father."

Chapter 7

Wednesday, August 22nd, 4:02 p.m.

Thurston Bay arrives at my farmhouse three hours after I phone him. He parks his Land Rover in my gravel driveway, and we sit in Glen's home office. Though I offer him coffee, he declines. As Thurston reclines in Glen's leather chair, my spine taut, I sit in the wing-back chair facing him. The cotton fabric of my sundress brushes against my calves, itching me.

"I need some advice, Mr. Bay, I mean Thurston," I say, crossing and uncrossing my ankles.

Often parents of murdered children divorce, but after Whitney's death, it was her parents and my parents who couldn't look one another in the eye. Unable to deal with their memories, the Bays moved from Lawrenceville to Brooklyn a year after Whitney was murdered. Though my mother and father never rekindled their friendship with Thurston and Lilly, the Bays appeared at my father's funeral. Apparently, they'd heard about Dad's death through a mutual friend. After the service, we reconnected.

So, when holiday cruises for windows and widowers became Mom's thing, Glen and I started spending Easter, Thanksgiving, and Christmas at the Bay's Brooklyn home. Glen, who had clients in Vermont, often visited the Bay's vacation house in Stowe without me. I haven't seen Thurston and Lilly since Easter. I like Thurston, but Lilly makes me nervous. She's warm and welcoming. But I have this sense that she wishes Whitney had survived, not me. I'm a jittery mess around her, but because she's Whitney's mom, I haven't given up on the idea of us being close.

I glance across the office, at Whitney's father. Thurston is fair-haired and balding. Age has weakened his vision. He wears wire-rimmed glasses. Semi-retired, he dresses casually for our consult: slacks, a golf shirt, and oxford shoes.

"I'm in a bit of a bind," I tell him. "I earned a chunk of money recently, but I used it to pay my mortgage and property taxes. So, I can't give you a retainer."

Thurston raises his hand. "Don't worry about that. I've already discussed it with Lilly. You're like a daughter to us. I'm remodeling my Brooklyn office, the one on Court Street. I need art for the walls. You can sketch Coney Island, or Prospect Park for me. Pay for my services that way."

"You sure?"

"Absolutely." Thurston frowns at me. "Don't take this the wrong way, but you don't look good. Are you eating? Sleeping?"

"Not much." Determined to avoid a Dr. Phil counseling session, I get right to the purpose of our meeting. "This morning my cop friend Liam—well, he's not just a friend, the truth is, I'm thinking of dating him—anyhow, Liam told me that Leeds, the FBI agent assigned to Cassie's case, will likely search my house. Can he just do that?"

Thurston nods. "If he has a search warrant or an arrest warrant, he can. Is there anything incriminating on the property?"

I visualize the legal papers in my file cabinet, picture the pills in my bathroom, consider my Google search history, and make a mental note of the contents of my closets. Despite my Worm Man paranoia or perhaps because of it, I've never purchased a gun.

"Incriminating? I don't think so. But I didn't know Cassie's sneaker was in my classroom supply closet, and somehow that got in there." A wave of helplessness flows through me. It's as if someone nudged a boulder off a cliff and it's rolling toward me, about to crush me.

"This is all so unfair," I say, squeezing my chair arms. "All I can think about is Cassie, what might be happening to her. And Leeds keeps coming after me. It's such a waste of his time. He should be looking for James Hoover, not hounding me. Hoover grabbed Cassie. His MO's all over her abduction. All his victims were blonde girls. They all disappeared from parks," I add, though Leeds hasn't publicly stated where Cassie was grabbed. "And each girl was taken on a day when the weather was inclement, raining or snowing." I shake my head. "I'm sorry. Why are my telling you this? You already know Hoover's habits, his game." I exhale, attempting to regroup. "What were we talking about? Incriminating stuff on my property? I don't think any exists, but who knows?"

I point to the doorway. "I always lock my doors, and I have an alarm system. But if my car's not in my driveway, pretty much everyone knows I'm not at home. I'm not the only one with a key."

Thurston lifts his briefcase off the floor, opens it, and retrieves a yellow pad and pencil. "Who else has one?"

As I list them, Thurston prints the key owners' names on his pad.

"My mother, my best friend, Randi, and my closest neighbor, Gene McKinley. Gene owns the apple orchard and cornfield up the road. And Glen had two." I frown. "I don't know if he gave keys to anyone."

Thurston nods. "Well, should the feds decide to search your property and should they find something, that will be our defense, that other people have access to your home. But let's not borrow trouble." Thurston studies at me. "You don't honestly think Hoover has this little girl, Cassie? He's dead, Kate."

I tell him about the "Straight up" incident, about how Reverend Shasta admitted to employing Hoover and then backpedaled, and about how Hoover's New Jersey neighbor spotted him in her basement after his supposed death.

Thurston shakes his head. "I'm sorry, Kate, but that's all circumstantial and hearsay. But I get it. I understand your reluctance to write off Hoover. When the cops first told me Hoover was dead, I didn't want to believe it either. I didn't want it to be true, because if he was dead, that meant I couldn't punish him. And

I wanted to punish him. I wanted to smack him silly and set him on fire." He motions to the ceiling. "I guess God beat me to the punch."

He fingers his pen. "My point is, I wanted Hoover to feel pain. But mostly, I wanted to tell him what losing Whitney did to me and to Lilly. His death robbed me of that chance." Thurston's gaze holds mine. "But it's true, Kate. He's dead. If he were alive, believe me, I'd know it."

"But what about the timing? Cassie went missing right after the gallery show." I look down. "I'm sorry I didn't invite you and Lilly. I exhibited a drawing of Hoover's hand. I thought the drawing might offend you."

Thurston shrugs. "No worries. I heard about the show. You received a lot of recognition, which brings me to my next point. Can you think of anyone who might benefit from bringing Hoover back into the spotlight?"

"Just this reporter, Kingsley. He published a book about the Worm Man a decade ago. Leeds thinks he's writing another one, or promoting the old one. The truth is, before Kingsley and I met up, I thought Leeds was right, that Kingsley could be writing about me. Maybe not writing a book, but an article. But Kinsley swore to me that he wouldn't do that, and I believe him."

Thurston chuckles. "Come on, Kate. Writing articles, books. That's what reporters do."

"No. I don't think Kingsley's using me. I've spent time with him. He seems genuinely motivated to find Hoover and Cassie. Quite honestly, being around him is refreshing. He takes me seriously, listens to me." I look directly at Thurston. "Leeds and people who don't know Hoover think thirty years is a long time. They say I'm obsessed, that even if Hoover's alive, he doesn't care about me anymore. But they're wrong. Thirty years is nothing. I remember Whitney's abduction, the police interrogation, and her funeral like they were last Thursday."

"Me too."

"So, you'll help me if Leeds arrests me?" I ask.

"Of course. But let's not get ahead of ourselves. You're probably not the only suspect. Usually, the parents are at the top of the list. But just in case the FBI does decide to move forward and search your place, it's best if you're prepared."

"How do I get ready?"

"First off, don't let the agents in your house unless they show you a warrant. And once they're inside, don't leave." Thurston taps his yellow pad with his pen. "And you're gonna want to get yourself a notebook. Write down everything they look through and take while they're in your house. Don't talk to them either. They might try to extract information from you. And you should call someone so you're not alone while the search is occurring. That would be helpful. And don't leave. You don't want them to search unattended. Oh."

He points to the file cabinet. "Clean your house. Get rid of anything embarrassing, anything the cops might deem incriminating." The cell in Thurston's pocket pings. He glances at the screen. "That's Lilly. She's concerned about you."

"How's she doing?" Lilly was depressed when I saw her at Easter. Her niece was getting married. The wedding reminded her of the milestones she didn't get to celebrate with Whitney.

"Better," Thurston says. "She enjoys her water aerobics at the Y. And she's been teaching a Sunday school class. I thought being around children might upset her, but it appears to help. I guess you can relate to that since you're a teacher."

"Children are God's Prozac," I say, repeating Randi's mantra. I glance at my wedding band. The beating, the pulsing, and the need to know if Cassie is Glen's daughter pounds inside me.

I say, "I have to ask you something about Glen."

Beneath his bifocal lenses, Thurston's blue eyes narrow.

"Did Glen ever talk to you about a woman named Lauren Rossi?" I ask.

Thurston frowns. "Lauren Rossi? Isn't that the missing girl's mother?"

"Yeah. Lauren's the reason Leeds thinks I'm involved in Cassie's disappearance." My throat tightens. "There's this rumor that Glen and Lauren had an affair. Do you know anything about that? Did Glen ever talk to you about Lauren or Cassie?"

"Not that I recall." Thurston's cell pings again, another text. He looks at his wristwatch, slips his pad back into his briefcase, and stands. "But I'll ask Lilly. She and Glen were close, almost like mother and son. They often met for lunch when I was at the office."

I walk Thurston down the hall. We take a detour through the kitchen, and I show him a drawing of one of Randi's former students.

"Her name's Kendall," I tell him. "She was in my coworker's Randi's class three years ago. Her mom hired me to sketch her portrait. The mom wants to give the drawing to Kendall's grandmother for her eightieth birthday."

"Did you get the job from the gallery show?"

"The Internet. I've got a website."

Thurston smiles. "I'm glad you're staying busy. I credit my law practice for keeping me sane after Whitney's death."

I escort Thurston out the door and watch him climb into his SUV. As he drives away, I hear a third ding. This time it's my phone alerting me to a text. I retrieve my cell from my pocket and glance at the screen. It's Mom. She's in Paris. Though I need her desperately, I can't tell her I'm in trouble. I don't want to burden her. For years, she worried I'd never get over Whitney's murder. She was overwrought when I was admitted into the Carrier Clinic. We both dealt with Dad's heart attack and his passing. After that, she helped me cope with my miscarriage and most recently with Glen's illness and death. Mom deserves to be happy, at peace. Hoping to keep her out of the fray, I write her a simple cheerful text, **Love and miss you! Send me a postcard from the Louvre!**

As I push the send button on my cell, I hear knocking on my front door. I peer out the window and see Leeds' and unmarked sedan and two other official looking vehicles in my driveway. My stomach twists.

You should have cleaned up. Not that there's anything to throw away. You don't smoke weed, Glen didn't watch kiddy porn, and you don't have Cassie. Don't panic. You're fine.

Still, when I unlock the door and Leeds waves his badge, I flinch.

"We're here to search your property, Ms. Boswell. I've got a warrant," he says, handing me the document. "Do you have any firearms on the premises?"

"Of course not," I tell him.

I skim the warrant, return the paper to Leeds, and allow the crew of five men to enter my foyer. The agents all wear plastic gloves, two carry canvas bags, and one lugs a camera. Leeds' eyes bear into mine. As he glares at me, his men swarm around me like moths.

Don't let them intimidate you, I tell myself.

But I am intimidated, by the briskness of their movements, the intensity with which they swoop into my house, their lean muscular physics, and the jarring neon-yellow FBI decals on their jackets. I grab my purse off the end table. Leeds' hand flies to his pocket.

"Whoa," I say. "Chill. I'd like to make a phone call. Is that okay?"

He nods. I phone Thurston, but my call goes straight to voicemail. *What the heck? He was just here. Randi. Call Randi.* I do, but she doesn't answer either. I leave her a voicemail and text her too. *She's at Pilates*, I conclude, noting the time on my wristwatch. I consider calling Liam, but figure that because of our close relationship, that his presence on the scene might create an issue. *Thurston will call back*, I tell myself. *More than likely he's already turned around and is on his way back here.*

As I search for something to write on, the men move through my home in an organized fashion. They separate, making it impossible for me to record their individual actions. One goes to Glen's office, another to the second floor, and a third sprays chemicals in my laundry room. I assume he's looking for signs of blood. A fourth agent snaps a photo of a stain on my den carpet. A fifth, heads toward the barn.

I grab my sketchbook off the breakfast table. I don't know who to monitor, who's the most dangerous, because they all seem potentially lethal.

Suddenly parched and needing water, I head to the cabinet above the kitchen sink and grab a glass. As I'm filling the glass with tap water, Leeds enters the breakfast area. He plucks my drawing of Kendall off the table, and slips it into a clear plastic bag.

I point to the drawing. "You can't take that. A parent hired me to draw that. She's already paid me a deposit for my work. That drawing belongs to her."

Leeds closes the bag. "We'll return it when we're through."

"But she needs it by Friday," I say.

"Like I said, we'll return it when we're through."

I hear a thud and hurry toward the sound, toward Glen's office. As I stumble past Glen's desk, one of the agents lowers my laptop into a plastic bag and seals it.

I motion to the computer. "My lesson plans are on that. I need them to teach."

The agent nods. "I understand, ma'am. But we've got a job to do."

He turns toward the bookshelf above the desk and begins thumbing through Glen's photo albums. The albums contain photos of architecturally significant buildings Glen visited: the Chrysler Building, the Flatiron Building, the Woolworth Building, the Gable House, the Glass House, and St. Patrick's Cathedral. The agent flips through the first album. When he's through, he tosses it onto the floor, retrieves two more albums from the bookshelf, flips through one, and skims the other. I write in my sketchbook

1. Photos and drawing of Kendall
2. School laptop

As I lower my pen, the agent kneels and studies a fourth album, one I've never seen before. His lip twitches. Something has grabbed his focus. I glance over his shoulder, expecting to see a photo of the Eiffel Tower or the Sydney Opera House. Glen and I visited both on vacation. But instead, a baby's face gazes up at me: blue eyes, wisps of white-blonde hair, and a single dimple on her left cheek. The infant, who appears to be about three or four months old, is propped against a pillow. I study the curve of the infant's eyes and the shape of her tiny lips.

"No. It can't be," I murmur.

But I know it is. A portrait artist by nature, I was born with the ability to perceive and recognize facial features. Though time alters complexions and body shape, life doesn't change bone structure, mannerisms, and expressions. I know the baby in the photo.

"Cassie," I say, reaching for the album. "Let me see that. That's Cassie Rossi."

As the agent shuts the album and bags it, behind me, someone clears their throat. I whirl around. *Leeds.* He nods, seeming to take in my shock. Whether or not he believes it's genuine is another story.

My heart thuds. *Cassie truly is Glen's daughter. Why else would he have her baby album?* I want to sink to the floor and curl into a ball, but I can't lose it, not here and not yet. Leeds will see my pain and use it against me.

As I trail him, Leeds marches upstairs. He empties my dresser drawers, sifts through my wastepaper basket, and confiscates the pills in my medicine cabinet. I continue to follow him. He enters the second-floor nursery, still decorated for the arrival of my baby. Though he doesn't remove anything from the frilly pink room, he stands beside the changing table and makes a notation in his notebook. I shadow him as he exits the nursery, marches back down the stairs, and reenters my kitchen.

Leeds removes the drawings from the wall behind my breakfast table. He dumps the images of my students into bags and zips them. I eyeball the nails and empty wall space behind him, and sway. It's all too much. I bolt through the backdoor, collapse onto the steps, and cover my face with palms. Someone coughs, and I look up. An agent steps out of my garage. In his gloved hand, he carries a red plastic shovel. The agent drops the red shovel into a plastic bag.

As I stare through the bag at the toy, the memory from that rainy night at Bucklin Beach returns. I see Cassie and Glen building their sandcastle and Lauren watching them intently. It's the same scene I pictured when I was driving through the rain with Kingsley. But though the image contains the same wet sand and same grey clouds, and Lauren is still wearing the same ill-fitting tankini, I see everything differently now. I see Glen, Lauren, and Cassie as a family. It's like I've had Lasik.

* * *

Leeds and his men leave my home an hour after the discovery and bagging of the red plastic shovel. Though they found some blood splatters in the laundry room sink from when I cut my finger on the mesh of the dryer lint screen, they don't arrest me on the spot, and for this I'm grateful. As soon as the government cars exit my driveway, I call Thurston. He answers this time and apologizes for not picking up earlier. The mountains blocked his cell reception. Unable to keep still, I pace while I tell Thurston most of what went down.

I keep the discovery of Cassie's baby album to myself. It's a fresh wound. I need time to disinfect and dress it.

"Don't panic," Thurston says when I finish with my account. "Panicking never benefits anyone."

The call ends. As I clean up the mess created by Leeds and his crew, I call Randi and Liam. Though Liam plays down the seriousness of the search, the edge in his voice tells me he's worried. Randi seems shell-shocked, like when her obstetrician informed her that she needed a Cesarean. I don't tell either of them about Glen's photo album and what I'm almost sure it means. The knowing is too much. There's still a part of me that refuses to believe that Cassie is Glen's daughter. Because if I believe that, I also have to believe that Glen bonded with Lauren in a way he never did with me.

As I'm hanging the clothes Leeds' men dumped onto my bed back in my closet, Kingsley calls me. He knows Leeds' men searched my house. His mole filled him in. He starts ranting about my Fourth Amendment Rights and privacy laws. I interrupt him and tell him that Reverend Shasta did an about face and said Roger Stone wasn't the Worm Man, and that Shasta told Leeds we threatened him. Then I tell Kingsley about finding Cassie's sneaker in my classroom closet with the lock of hair in the laces. I don't tell him about Glen's affair with Lauren. Chances are, he already knows. "So did you learn anything at the Warner Pharmacy?" I ask Kingsley.

"Just that a man collected a prescription for a Roger Stone on Monday, July 30th. The time on the receipt was 9:02 a.m. Neither the clerk nor the pharmacist remembered the transaction." Kingsley chuckles. "I sweettalked the manager into showing me the video coverage of the pharmacy counter. But though the video was in color and clear, whoever picked up the oral steroid wore a raincoat. His hood covered his face."

"In other words, the video is useless."

"Not useless. The customer was definitely a man. His body type, stature, and stance were undeniably masculine. It could have been Hoover. But it also could have been some guy helping him. The pharmacy is on Main Street. It's a very public area. My gut tells me that James wouldn't risk going there. Anyhow, whoever picked up the prescription paid cash. They also bought a bag of chips and a Red Bull energy drink. The Red Bull and the phone conversation Reverend Shasta overheard make me think that James' brother, Samuel, made the purchase. Samuel drives a bus," Kingsley explains. "Seems like a bus driver might need a Red Bull pick-me-up. Also, the video customer's slacks and shoes looked to be standard uniform grade. So, I checked out Samuel's employer's website. The pics of the employee uniforms on the site matched the video guy's pants and shoes in color and style."

"Then it's a no brainer," I say. "We have to talk to Samuel!"

"Already tried." I hear the whoosh of traffic and car horns and figure Kingsley's in Boston. "I've been to his house in Bradford three times since Cassie disappeared," he says. "The guy won't open his door. He's scared, skittish. Not that I blame him. I'd hide too if my brother was a serial killer, and a local girl who matches my bro's victim profile was missing."

I start in on the rumpled clothes the feds dumped out of my dresser. "Maybe he'll talk to me. I mean, I'm not a journalist," I say, folding a sweater.

"True, but he doesn't know that. You want to talk about his psycho brother. That makes you the enemy. Doesn't matter your intent." Kingsley chews. Images of hot dogs and pizza slices pop into my head. "When the feds searched your place, what'd they grab?" he asks.

I picture Cassie's baby album and the red plastic shovel. "Pretty standard stuff: my school computer, pills from the medicine cabinet, trash, and my drawings. My attorney says it's nothing to be alarmed about."

"But you are alarmed," Kingsley says.

"Of course."

"Makes sense." I hear the creak of a door opening. "I'm entering my office building," Kingsley says, giving me a play-by-play. I imagine him lumbering grizzly-like and bearded into a crowded lobby.

"What bus company does Samuel Hoover work for?" I ask.

"Dartmouth Coach," Kingsley replies. "You know, the bus service that transports people to and from Logan Airport, with drop off and pickup points in New London, Lebanon, Hanover ..."

"I'm familiar with it," I say, balling up two socks.

Kingsley exhales. "I would attempt to corner him at the South Boston Station tomorrow, but my editor's got me covering a farm-to-table restaurant opening over on Tremont Street."

"I still think I should talk to him. He's seen you before. He'll run as soon as he spots you. Maybe I can engage him, get him to open up. He might feel guilty and not blow me off because of my connection to Whitney."

"Go for it," Kingsley says. "I've got a pic of him. I'll text it to you. Let me know how it plays out."

"I will. Enjoy the fresh veggies," I say, jamming my jeans into a drawer.

Kingsley grunts. "Just downed a pastrami on rye. That's how much I'm into this green farmer fad shit."

I end the call, drive to the Best Buy in West Lebanon, and purchase a new laptop. When I get home, I check the Dartmouth Coach Bus schedule and the airlines linked to the various airport terminals. After familiarizing myself with the info, I hibernate in my den and listen to the local news. I'm hoping to hear something about Cassie. I get nothing, just the basic facts replayed.

Unable to keep still, I call Thurston again. "Has Leeds contacted you yet?" I ask him.

"No," he says, "but if he's got forensics running tests, it might be a week before we hear from him, if we do at all."

"Seriously?" I grip my cell and pace. "James' brother, Samuel, drives the Dartmouth Coach. It's a bit of a long shot, given scheduling and all, but I'm going to take the bus tomorrow, see if Samuel's working, see if I can get him to admit that James is alive."

"Kate, we've been over this. Hoover's dead."

"Well, I'm not convinced. And I can't just sit around when Cassie's in danger while Leeds builds a case against me."

"I know you're frustrated, but confronting Samuel Hover isn't a good idea."

"I won't cause any problems. I promise."

Our conversation ends. I burrow into the couch. Clutching my cell, I stare at the doors and windows and shiver. While *American Housewife* and *Modern Family* play on the TV screen, I listen for sounds, for creaks, for footfalls. Trembling, I flip the TV station and watch replays of the 2018 Winter Olympic Super-G and downhill events.

As the television flickers, I fall asleep and dream that earthworms are slithering down the slopes at the Mount Sunapee Resort. Their slithering causes an avalanche. In my dream, I watch in horror as the fast-moving snow buries Cassie alive.

Chapter 8

Thursday, August 23rd, 9:32 a.m.

*W*hen morning arrives, my sinuses are blocked, probably from all that dust that Leeds' men unearthed. Not only do I feel stuffy, I'm amped up too. I'd hoped daylight would squelch my worries and fear, but the sun's rays only seem to heighten my anxiety.

Sniffling, I grab a carry-on from my closet, shower, and change. I put my sketchbook, a pencil, earphones, a sandwich, bottled water, and a sweater into my bag. Sneezing, I slip pepper spray into my purse and drive to the local Park and Ride, the commuter lot located off Highway 103A. I find a parking spot, head for the covered waiting area, glance at my watch, and sit. I have no idea which bus Samuel Hoover drives, if he's even working today.

Ten minutes pass. I hear the squeak of brakes. The 11:00 a.m. bus pulls into the lot manned by a twentysomething male driver with a scruffy beard. Definitely not Samuel Hoover. I remain seated and sketch the commuters milling around me, mostly tourists. Finally, the noon bus rumbles in. A brunette, a fortysomething woman with mauve gloss on her lips, clutches the steering wheel. The bus slows, and the loading door opens.

"Do you know if Samuel Hoover is working today? He's an old friend," I ad lib, plastering on a smile. "I haven't seen him in ages. I wanted to surprise him."

The female driver grins. "You're in luck. Samuel's manning the next bus. He'll be here in an hour."

As the female driver helps the noon riders with their luggage, I nibble nervously on the sandwich I packed. When the bus exits onto the main road, a brown sedan I recognize as one of the agent's cars, eases into the lot. The agent, who isn't Leeds, coasts and eyes the license plates of the parked cars. He stops in front of my Subaru, drives slowly toward the waiting area, and rolls down his window.

"Where are you off to, Ms. Boswell?" he asks me.

"To the airport," I say. "I'm catching up with an old friend. He's driving the next bus," I say, wanting to keep my story consistent. "I'm not going on the lam. Tell Leeds not to worry."

The agent nods, drives to the edge of the lot, and hovers.

The young woman, seated beside me, whom I recognize as a hairstylist from the local salon, rubs the tattoo on her wrist and frowns. "Ever since that little girl went missing, those suits have been hanging around the shopping center where I cut hair. I feel horrible for the kid. But those stiffs are scaring away my tourist walk-in business." She motions to the hovering sedan. "Like where we go and what we do is any of his business."

I nod. "I know, right?"

Having lost my appetite, I put my sandwich away. The stylist retrieves a cigarette from her fringe bag, lights the end, and exhales. I shut my eyes, grip the bench beneath me, and wait. Leeds says I'm free to do as I please, but his men are clearly watching me. In my mind, I hear the clink of handcuffs. I blink and picture Cassie, tied up and gagged.

By the time the one o'clock bus arrives, about a dozen passengers are lined up beside the covered waiting area. The bus stops. I spring off the bench and join them.

A deep male voice jolts me. "Ma'am, do you want me to put your bag in the lower storage compartment?"

I look up. Steely grey eyes leer at me. "I …"

It's not him. It's just his brother, Samuel.

My words squeak out. "Yes. No. My bag … it's small. I'll just keep it on my lap."

Samuel rubs his chin, seemingly oblivious to my elevated pulse rate. "What airline are you flying, Miss?'

I shove my hands into my pockets, fidget.

I need to question Samuel alone, not that I want to be alone with this man. He's an altered version of my nightmare, tweaked but terrifying. I know from having done my research that the Dartmouth Coach drops off all departing passengers before collecting new ones, and that British Airways is located in the last terminal, Terminal E.

"British Airways. London," I stammer.

Reeling, I purchase a bus ticket. As Samuel adjusts his cap and greets a woman from Wilmot Flats, I climb onto the bus. The seats are half-filled. As the passenger in the aisle in front of me jams a bag into the overhead compartment, Principal Jane's voice echoes in my head. *Keep potential problems and trouble close.*

I sit directly behind Samuel's seat, two rows back. I hear the lower storage compartment shut and then footsteps as Samuel boards the coach. Standing in the aisle, his back to the windshield, Samuel motions to a box of snack-sized pretzel bags and a cooler of mini water bottles on the seat behind him. "Folks, the water and pretzels are complimentary. Help yourselves. You've got free Wi-Fi. Today's movie is *Grease.*" He points to a screen. "Relax and enjoy the ride. We're about two and a half hours from Logan."

He takes his seat. The engine roars. We zoom out of the Park and Ride and onto the highway. I'm in a window seat and alone in my row. I put in my earbuds and place my bag onto the empty seat beside me. As the other passengers rest, watch the movie, and chat unaware of their driver's murderous family history, I study Samuel's reflection in the rearview mirror. Though his eyes are the same steel color as his brother's, Samuel's are wider-set. A cleft slices his square chin.

I sneeze, remove my earbuds, and crack the window.

Samuel points to the dashboard vent. "AC's on."

"Sorry."

As I shut the window, Samuel grips the steering wheel. In my mind, I see the Worm Man's fingers wrapped around Whitney's throat. Nausea rocks me, causing me to gag.

"You okay?" Samuel says.

"Motion sickness," I tell him.

He nods. "If you can help it, don't hurl in my bus. Last time someone puked, it took me three weeks to get the stench out."

I retrieve my plastic sandwich baggie from my purse and wave it. Keeping my baggie handy, I find my sketchpad and pencil and concentrate on sketching Samuel. Twice he catches my gaze.

The highway curves and arches. Buildings replace pines and oaks. The clouds drift, and we hit the city. Ahead of the bus, the airport looms. It's busy. Cars, transport vans, and buses zip about. Samuel seems immune to the intensity of it all. He stops at each terminal. He helps the passengers disembark and collect their bags. He smiles and wishes everyone a safe journey. His steely grey eyes twinkle and blink.

When we reach Terminal E, only an elderly couple and myself remain. As Samuel pulls the bus to a stop in front of the British Airways sign, I grab my bag. We all exit the bus. Samuel opens the storage compartment. He gives the elderly couple their luggage.

"Do you need assistance?" he asks the gentleman. "I can call someone if ..."

The elderly man shakes his head. "No, sir. Fought in two wars. I'll be damned if I can't haul my wife's bag up to the ticket counter." As the war vet pulls the rolling bag carry-on, he winks at me. "Christ, this one's heavier than a dead soldier. What the hell you got in here, Ester?"

Ester frowns at the carry-on and her husband. "What's the matter with you, Clyde? That's not our bag. We packed two big tan ones. We didn't bring our little blue bag. Remember?"

When Clyde releases the handle of the blue bag, I grab it and wheel it over to Samuel. The elderly couple enters the terminal.

Samuel looks at me. "This yours?"

"No. I was just ..."

He scowls. "You're not really flying to London Heathrow."

"I am."

"Yeah, right. Who takes one carry-on on a transatlantic flight?"

Before I can respond, Samuel lugs the small blue bag onto the bus. I trail him, close. He wants to ditch me. But I'm on the steps so he can't shut the door on me.

He turns as I board. "You're a reporter."

"No, I ..."

We're standing in the aisle, sandwiched between the vinyl seats. Samuel nods, like he's sizing me up.

As a horn honks, he jerks his chin toward the windshield, at an airport cop. "I'll tell him you threatened to blow this place up. That you left this bag and claimed it's filled with explosives. He'll pin you down on that pavement so fast it'll make your head spin. They'll interrogate you for hours, days."

"I'm not a reporter," I say, hoping my even tone will convince him.

He glares at me. "How dare you bother me while I'm working. I need this job. I've got a kid in college, tuition to pay." His eyes fly back to the windshield, to the airport cop beside the terminal. His lips pucker. He's going to whistle. I'm about to be body-slammed by the airport cop.

"You're fed up," I say quickly. "You're tired of this Worm Man business. We all are."

"We?" he snaps. "What could you possibly know about it?"

Outside, the cop circles us. I stare at his Taser. The bus is parked in an unloading zone. Samuel's allotted time is likely over.

I go with the truth. "Whitney Bay, your brother's first victim, was my best friend. I was at the park when he abducted her. Look," I say. "I know your brother's alive. I think he grabbed a former student of mine, a girl from my town, from New London, New Hampshire. You've probably heard about her abduction. It's all over the news. Did Leeds, the FBI agent, contact you?"

Samuel's jaw drops. The airport cop marches onto the bus.

The cop frowns at me and nods at Samuel. "Everything okay, Sam?"

I hold my breath, stare at Samuel. *Please don't be soulless like your brother.*

Samuel motions to me. "Poor lady missed her flight. Was just calming her down. She's supposed to meet her boyfriend in London."

The cop glances at my ring finger, at my gold wedding band.

Samuel winks. "A rather delicate situation."

"Gotcha." The cop waves, leaves the bus, and makes a beeline for a Hertz Rental Car van.

A mixture of relief and fear flows through me. I won't be patted down and interrogated by the airport cop, who in essence is a Massachusetts State Police Trooper. But I'll have to face Samuel on his home turf. He'll have the advantage. That's never a good thing.

"You're a good liar," I say, hoping a compliment will disarm him.

"A necessary skill given my family situation." He glances at his wristwatch. "I've got ten minutes. Got to collect passengers down at arrivals by 4:30 p.m. Airport's got a cell phone lot. We can talk there."

He doesn't ask me if I'm okay with this. He just eases the bus away from the curb and into traffic. Meanwhile, I sit, stare at the remaining pretzel packages in the cardboard box, and breathe. Cars, buses, and transport vans whiz by us. Horns honk. Jets roar. We don't speak until we reach the lot that's filled with people waiting for texts and phone calls. I glance at the waiting cars. I'm glad for their presence. Samuel Hoover is unpredictable, friendly, and then aggressive, carrying bags for seniors one minute and lying through his teeth to the airport cop the next. I can't read him. My guess is he's perfected his public persona, keeping the real Samuel under wraps. But if I pry, chances are, he'll emerge.

When the bus motor quiets, Samuel towers over me. "You're afraid of me," he says.

"I don't like flying. I'm always nervous at airports. It isn't you."

He grins, as if he doesn't believe me.

"Look," I say, "I'm in a jam. Like I said before, a former student of mine has gone missing. She's a sweet girl, special. She's dear to my heart. Anyhow, this FBI agent thinks I had something to do with her disappearance, which I don't. But someone's framing me, and the agent's all over me. So, I'm trying to find the missing girl. Like I said before, I believe your brother is alive, that he has her, and that you're in contact with him."

Samuel laughs. "What am I, the Long Island Medium?"

"Cute. When did you last see him?"

Samuel rubs his chin. "A decade ago. In Jersey, at the Jackson Funeral Home, in his coffin."

"You know what I mean."

"Actually, I don't."

"Look. I've done my research. A month ago, James obtained a prescription using the alias, Roger Stone. A week later, someone filled and picked up that prescription at the Warner Pharmacy... a man, wearing a Dartmouth Coach uniform." I point to Samuel's black rubber soled shoes and blue polyester slacks. "The pharmacy has video surveillance at the counter."

"Wasn't me. I'm nobody's errand boy."

My voice rises in pitch. "Please, Samuel. A ten-year-old girl is missing." I gesture at the Red Bull can in his cupholder. "The man who picked up the prescription also bought a Red Bull. You're clearly a Red Bull drinker."

"A third of the U.S. population drinks Red Bull."

"A third of millennials. Not baby bombers."

"Wasn't me at that pharmacy."

"Come on. We're both casualties here. Every time a news story about Whitney runs, I'm terrified that someone's going to uncover my connection to the Worm Man. I live my life waiting for the other shoe to drop. You and me, we're dealing with the same crap. Please help me out here, Samuel. I'm begging you. Give me something."

Samuel sighs. "Not much to tell."

"I'm listening."

Samuel sighs. "A month before he died in the fire, James surprised me at a Denny's up in Nashua. I was sitting in a booth. When he tapped me on the shoulder, I nearly shit in my pants. He'd been in hiding, laying low for years. We shared a burger. That was July 2008. That was the last time I saw him breathing."

"That's odd 'cause Reverend Shasta, the minister who hired..." I make air quotes. "'Roger Stone' to work at his blueberry farm, said he heard Roger talking to you on the phone two months ago."

"The reverend's mistaken."

I glance at the Honda parked beside us. The woman waiting inside nods repetitively as if she's listening to music. I face Samuel. "Don't give me that B.S. Your brother's not dead. You're helping him hide. Not that I'm faulting you for this. If someone I loved committed a crime, I'd probably protect them too. You're in an impossible situation."

"It might seem like that to you. But trust me. I've got my head on straight." Samuel retrieves an empty water bottle from beneath a seat and flattens it with his palm. "My son, Hollister, goes to Dartmouth. He's a sophomore. The Ivy Leagues, that's a big deal for a blue-collar guy like me. Kid's smart, hardworking. Was an Eagle Scout and president of the Math League. Perfect SAT scores. The whole nine yards. Even if James were alive, I'd never help my brother, like you're saying. I wouldn't jeopardize my son's future like that. The burned body in that shore house was James'. I don't know who was working at that blueberry farm and yacking on the phone. James never used the alias Roger Stone. You're barking up the wrong tree." He fingers his bus keys.

"One more question," I say. "When you saw James at that Denny's, would you say he was still physically capable of abducting a ten-year-old girl?"

"And dismembering her? Absolutely. What happened behind that diner was downright scary."

"What do you mean?"

"James chased a pit bull, caught it, and ripped off its ear with his teeth. That was after he'd eaten two burgers."

"You're lying," I say.

"Exaggerating some." He glances at the blue carry-on in the aisle. "Almost forgot about this thing." He fingers the handle. "No tag. Better take a peek inside and look for an ID." He unzips the bag. It's empty except for a backpack. As I watch, Samuel sifts through the pack's contents. "Girl's softball equipment. Someone must have an away tourney."

I take in the helmet, the gloves, the ball, the cleats, and the R on the pink uniform. The Channel Nine reporter's words seep from my brain. *Cassie was wearing a New London Rec backpack containing softball gear.*

"Rossi!" I say, motioning to the name on the backpack. "That's Cassie Rossi's stuff."

Samuel shoves the backpack back into the carry-on and zips the small blue bag. "That the girl from your town who went missing?"

I nod and motion to the bag. "Let me see that."

"No." He clutches the carryon. "You put this in here. You're setting me up."

"Me? Why would I?"

The radio crackles. A voice seeps out of the dashboard. "Sam? This is Jim from the South Station. Where are you, buddy?"

Samuel presses the radio control button. "On my way, about to pick up arrivals."

I peer out the bus window. The woman in the Honda listening to music drives away. Everyone else has left the lot. As Samuel glances at the empty parking spots, I sense a shift in him. I stand too quickly and bump my head on the overhead bin.

"I'm getting off."

Samuel blocks me. "You're not gonna tell anyone about the carry-on and the backpack with the gear in it."

"But that would be withholding evidence," I say. "If someone finds out we found the backpack and carryon and kept quiet, we could go to prison. Besides, there could be forensic evidence on the stuff in that pack: blood, hair follicles, and fingerprints. Evidence that might clear me from suspicion or lead us to Cassie: carpet fibers or dog hairs."

"But you said before that someone's framing you. How do you know that whoever left that carry-on didn't put one of your fingernails inside, maybe a strand of your hair? They obviously dumped it knowing you were going to be on this bus. They figured I'd find it, and turn it into the cops."

I nod. "I see why it makes sense for me to keep quiet. But what about you? What's your motivation? Why do you want to keep this between us?"

He smiles. "I've got a new woman in my life. Helena's amazing, a keeper. Not many women want to be involved with the brother of a serial killer. I lost Hollister's mother because of mistakes I made, but also because of my brother. I'll be damned if I'm gonna lose Helena over him too."

I nod. If I go to the feds about the backpack, it could backfire on me. Bottom line, telling Leeds about the backpack is a gamble, one I'm not willing to take. "So, what do we do with the backpack and carry-on?"

"We put the backpack inside the carry-on. I'll take the carry-on to the baggage claim area and leave it on one of the carousels. When no one comes to collect it, baggage will store it at the terminal for five days. Then the carrier will ship it to a central warehouse. After sixty days, it gets purchased by the unclaimed bag center in Scottsboro. No one will be the wiser. You won't be implicated, and I won't get dragged into this Cassie Rossi mess."

I chew on my lip, unsure if I should trust him. "How do I know you're not involved somehow? I mean, how did the thing get in the luggage compartment to begin with? Don't passengers hand you their luggage?"

"Most do. But the impatient ones and the regulars simply leave their bags on the pavement in front of the loading zone. They trust me to collect their belongings."

I picture the woman from Wilmot Flats and the hairstylist with the tattoo. "You don't remember who gave you the bag?"

"Nope."

As Samuel shakes his head, images of the red plastic shovel and Cassie's baby album fill my head. Another visual of Cassie's pink sneakers follows. "All right. Get rid of the carry-on and the backpack. Leave them on the carousel," I say. "But if the feds or the cops find out we dumped them, you're gonna tell them it was your idea and that you forced me to keep quiet. Let's exchange contact info," I say, handing him my business card. "Call me with any problems. I'll call you, if need be, too."

I give him my cell, he punches his number in, and returns it. I squeeze past him and bolt off the bus. Trembling, I request an Uber and instruct the driver to take me to the New London Park and Ride. The fee is nearly two hundred dollars. But I don't care. I'll do anything to get away from James Hoover's brother.

I'm in the backseat of the Uber, a Toyota Prius, when Kingsley calls me.

"So how did you make out with Samuel?" he asks. "Do I need to hound him tomorrow?"

"No. Samuel talked to me. But the guy's a piece of work," I say, picturing the backpack and the blue carry-on.

"What'd he do? Smack you and then threaten to charge you with assault?"

"No. He threatened to tell the airport police I was a terrorist."

Kingsley laughs. "That's a good one. So, did he tell you anything notable?"

"Just that a decade ago, that his brother was still physically strong and healthy enough to abduct and murder a ten-year-old girl. He refuses to admit James is alive, or that he picked up James' prescription, and is helping him."

"Why doesn't that surprise me?" Kingsley's phone beeps. "That'll be my editor. Catch up with you later." Our call ends.

As the Prius glides up Highway 93, my sinuses tighten. I find a Claritin sample at the bottom of my purse and swallow the tablet. Cocooning into my seat, I lean against the window. The glass pane feels too cold against my forehead. The sensation jars me.

* * *

When I return home from the Park and Ride, Lilly, Thurston's wife/ Whitney's mother, is waiting for me on my front porch, and her Lexus is in my driveway. Clearly, Lilly's here to tell me about Glen and Lauren.

After everything I've just been through with Samuel, talking to Lilly about Glen's infidelity isn't something I want to do right now. But Thurston is essentially helping me pro bono. I can't exactly blow Lilly off. I take the front path across the lawn and brace myself for a tense conversation. *Don't initiate anything,* I tell myself. *Let her take the lead.*

As I near her, Lilly springs off my Adirondack chair. Her wrap dress presses against her abdomen. Though age and Lilly's love of baking have added pounds to her once-thin frame, Lilly's addiction to water aerobics keeps her spry.

She slides her manicured nails through her pixie cut, rifling it. "I hope you don't mind me just showing up. We're staying at our Vermont house until October. I was at a dinner, up the road at the Historical Society. Figured I'd pop in. Oh, who am I kidding?" She grins and hugs me. "I came just to see you. I've been thinking about you, Kate. Given all that's happening with that missing girl."

My decongestant kicks in. *Lilac. Lilly still wears lilac.* An image of a thirteen-year-old Whitney dabbing perfume on her wrists, a woman-sized beaded cocktail dress dangling past her knobby teen knees, fills my mind.

"How are you doing?" I say, blinking away the memory. "Thurston said you were teaching Sunday school."

"I am. And I love it. It satisfies my grandkid fix. The new hymns they're singing at my church are pretty catchy too. They have a band and professional singers. Oh, and they're renovating the fellowship hall."

As she describes the new hall layout, I unlock the front door and escort her into my foyer. The hardwoods creak beneath me. Unease drowns me. It's like I'm thirteen again—shy, nervous, and guilty because I'm alive and Whitney isn't.

"How's your mother?" she asks.

"Great. She's touring Europe. I think she's in Rome today. Maybe Tuscany. It's hard to keep track. Would you like tea?" I lead her toward the back of my house. "I can boil water. But if you prefer something cold, I'm pretty sure I've got Snapple."

"Hot tea would be wonderful." She straightens a photo in my hallway.

We pass the powder room and enter the kitchen.

When we near the breakfast table, Lilly motions to the cookbooks heaped on the floor. "Thurston told me about the search." Her eyes drift to the nail holes in my breakfast nook walls. "So intrusive."

I nod. "I can't believe they took my drawings of my students." Lilly sits. I fill a teapot with tap water, put the kettle on the stove, and turn on the burner. "It's weird," I say, glancing at the naked walls, "but I miss them, my drawings. After Glen died, I used to talk to the children, their images. They made me feel better, less lonely. Silly, right?"

Lilly shakes her head. "It's not silly." She lowers her canvas bag onto the floor and looks at me. "Do you know why I came here today? Do you know what day it is?" she asks.

My stomach knots. *Shit. What if today is the anniversary of the day Glen and Lauren met, or the anniversary of Cassie's conception?*

I frown. "I don't know why today matters. Should I know?"

She shrugs. "Perhaps. But maybe it's good that you don't."

I expect her to reveal the day's importance straightaway, but Lilly merely smiles. It's like I'm on the edge of a diving board, about to jump, but time is frozen, and I'm teetering. The tea kettle whistles. I pour boiling water into mugs and grab spoons and sugar packets. I want her to tell me why she's here. I hate that she's holding back. But Lilly's like that. She takes her time with things. Perhaps all those decades of waiting for the feds to find the Worm Man taught her patience. More than likely, she grasps the weight of revelations, especially meaty ones. My hand shaking, I lower her mug onto the table, nudging it toward her.

"It's been two years since your miscarriage," she says, "two years exactly since you lost your baby girl, Georgia."

I exhale. I'm descending the diving board ladder. I'm not going to jump, not yet. And I'm okay with this for now. We're going to have a semi-normal conversation. She's not going to blurt out something about Glen and Lauren. Lilly sips her tea. Still shaking, I sit and sip mine too.

"Last year you gave me roses in remembrance of Georgia," I say.

"Yes. Yellow ones."

I nod. "I put them in a vase on the dining room table. The blooms lasted for weeks. They were lovely." I hand Lilly a napkin.

She folds it and leans toward me. "How are you holding up? How's everything? You've got a lot on your plate. That poor girl's abduction and this FBI business. And Glen's been gone what? About a year now?"

"It'll be a year next Thursday." I count the brown flecks in Lilly's eyes. I picture Leeds' hazel eyes and Samuel's steely ones and ask, "Did the police ever interrogate you when Whitney was taken?"

Lilly purses her lips. "They did. It's standard procedure when a child goes missing to look into the parents, even when there's a witness and a description of the abductor. More than likely, they theorized that one of us hired a third party to grab Whitney and something went wrong."

I frown. "I've never thought of that."

"Before they interrogated me, I hadn't either. But cops consider all sorts of possibilities."

We drink our tea. Shifting gears, I ask her about her water aerobics classes. She's thinking about getting certified as an instructor. I tell her about Reverend Shasta's blueberry farm and his Bible school for the children of his seasonal workers.

"You'd like him," I say, finding comfort in our small talk after my intense run-in with Samuel.

Lilly's eyes sparkle. "You're not going to believe this. But I know Reverend Shasta. Small world, isn't it? He's wonderful. He was at a Habitat for Humanity event I attended several years ago. We repaired a roof for a family up in Waterboro. He and I had a nice conversation about contradictions in scripture. He's a fascinating man. He sometimes visits our church in Brooklyn. After the Habitat for Humanity event, I toured his farm."

We talk about the upcoming school year and Randi's boys, Mikey and Justin. Lilly doesn't ask me about Evelyn's art show, and I'm glad about this. I don't want to talk about my drawing of the Worm Man's mutilated hand.

When we finish our tea, we head to the backyard. Instead of erecting a grave marker for the daughter we lost in the cemetery, Glen and I planted a birch tree in our yard. As black flies flit, Lilly and I stand beside that birch. She says two prayers, one for Whitney and one for Georgia. As Lilly prays, I touch the birch's white bark and finger a leaf.

Do it, the voice inside my head prods. *Ask her about Glen and Lauren. You imagining them together is far worse than whatever she might say to you.*

"Lilly," I say. My voice is so quiet. It's barely audible. "Did Thurston ask you about Glen and the missing girl's mother, Lauren Rossi?"

The fading sun illuminates the fine lines fanning Lilly's lips. "He did."

"Did Glen ever talk to you about her?"

She nods.

"And? What did Glen say? Tell me the truth, all of it. Don't sugarcoat anything."

Lilly's lashes flutter, causing mascara to darken the hollows beneath her eyes. "Oh, Kate. Why?"

I stare at the grass that needs cutting. "Because Lauren is the mother of the missing girl, my former student, Glen was my husband, and I need to understand."

"But Glen's dead," she says.

"Yes. But so is Whitney. And you still want to know everything about her." Lilly stiffens. "Not really. Not everything. Not the bad stuff."

I study the birch, taking in its slender white trunk and green oval leaves. "Look. I know Lauren and Glen had an affair. And I'm almost positive that Cassie is Glen's daughter. If you don't tell me the specifics, I'll find out from someone else. If I have to, I'll ask Lauren."

"Okay. Okay."

Taking my hand, she leads me to the cellar door, and we sit on the warm metal. I lift my bare legs and hug them. I don't like that metal door. Silver and shiny, it reminds me of the slide in the Lawrenceville park.

"From what Glen told me, he didn't love her," Lilly says, twisting a strand of her short hair. "It was just sex. The affair lasted a couple of months. It happened when you were living in New Jersey."

My stomach nosedives. "In Jersey? But Lauren lives here in New London."

"Apparently she came to New York City with girlfriends to celebrate her 30th birthday. She and Glen met at the Rainbow Room. Glen was there with a client. Evidently the client had gone to college with one Lauren's friends."

My heart pounds. I want to shove my fist down Lilly's throat to stop her words from coming out.

"According to Glen, it wasn't anything you did, or didn't do. It was more about him needing something different, a change. Which is why when Lauren got pregnant, he decided to move to New London."

"Ahhh?" Ever since Leeds brought up the affair, the idea that Glen could be Cassie's father was out there. And since the discovery of Cassie's baby album, the stark reality of Cassie's paternity has been crystalizing, hardening, and becoming solidly real. I thought having certainty about Cassie and Glen's biological connection, would help me. And it does ... sort of. But the timing inconsistencies throw me.

Initially, I thought Glen and Lauren's affair began two years ago, when I started tutoring Cassie. Then, after talking to Randi, I concluded that Glen and Lauren began hooking up soon after we moved to New Hampshire. But hearing this new truth about the affair's origins rocks me. I want to hightail it to the cemetery, dig up Glen's coffin, and shake his corpse until his dental fillings dislodge. Mostly, I want to beat Lauren to a pulp and tear out her white-blonde hair until she looks like a cancer patient. I know that white-blonde hair got him, that and the curve of her hips.

Like dead leaves, Lilly's words catch the breeze. "Glen convinced his partner to move to New London when he learned about the baby."

"Convinced Harris?" I say, choking on this detail. "No, that's not right. Glen's partner, Harris, was the one who insisted we move. Harris was the instigator," I say, though logic tells me that if Glen and Lauren met in NY, their affair likely set our move in motion. "Harris was tired of commuting to Manhattan from Hoboken," I squeal, not caring that I sound dolphin-like. "He wanted a quieter, less hectic life. He said they could work remotely, that they could shift their focus off commercial and onto residential vacation properties. Be more creative."

Lilly's words pierce me. "I'm sorry, Kate. But it was the other way around. Glen had to give Harris a lot to leave New York metro: a golf membership at Lake Sunapee Country Club, a month off in the summer, and a bigger percentage of the profits."

I leap off the cellar door. The ground is quicksand beneath my feet. How did I not notice that something was amiss when I reviewed the firm's financial statements after Glen's death? Of course, Glen blew me off, when spurred on my father's fatal heart attack, I suggested we make up our wills. He had Cassie and Lauren to consider too. I clutch my throat. "Glen did all of that for Lauren?"

"No. The affair was over by then. He did it for his daughter, for Cassie. And for you too. He moved for you too. He wanted to take you away from New Jersey and your memories of Whitney. He was worried about you, Kate. You'd just been treated at the clinic. He thought if you got away from where it happened, it would help. And it did," Lilly says, nodding. "Am I right? You got your credential at Colby Sawyer. You started a teaching career here, and your relationship with Glen deepened."

"But he lied to me for nine years."

"He was afraid you'd leave him if you knew about Lauren and Cassie."

Images of a pregnant me jamming my suitcase into my car trunk, flash in my mind. I see myself driving too fast, tears clouding my vision, skidding toward a telephone pole. The me in my memory screams, hugs her abdomen, and braces for impact.

"I've upset you," Lilly says, rising off the cellar door.

I point to Lilly's wedding ring. "You're a wife. Didn't you think I deserved to know that my husband had a child with another woman?"

"It was complicated. Listen. You need time to process this. I'm going to go now. We'll talk again later."

Lilly walks toward my driveway. Without turning around or glancing back to make sure I'm okay, she climbs into her Lexus, and leaves.

Chapter 9

*T*he rumble of Lilly's sedan motor fades, and I look west. The once yellow, orange, and red sky has darkened to an inky evening shade. I stare at Georgia's birch, and a cool breeze clips me. I'm cold. But instead of going inside and rinsing out the coffee mugs in my grasp, I sink to the ground. As Gene McKinley's Ford pickup zooms by me, its high beams shining, I drop the mugs and claw at the grass.

Why Glen? I scream in my mind, my fingers raking and tearing at the ground. *Why did you have to build our lives around that slut?*

I want to drive to Lauren Rossi's house, shake her, and shout, "How dare you lure my husband here! What kind of woman plays games with another woman's life?"

Lilly said Glen and Lauren's relationship ended before we moved to New London. But I don't buy this for a minute. Clearly Lauren kept Cassie in my class and hired me as Cassie's tutor hoping to remain close to Glen.

And Glen, the human I loved with all my being—who was this man I spent two decades with—cooking his meals, showering naked beside him, and following him to New London like a gypsy on crack? After he tasted Lauren's lips, did he ever truly love me, or was I simply a convenient substitute? What an idiot I was. That rainy evening Glen and I bumped into Lauren and Cassie at Bucklin Beach was definitely prearranged. Of course, Glen encouraged me to tutor Cassie. He needed to keep me occupied so he could be with Lauren. Christ, why didn't he just divorce me? Was it because he couldn't choose between the two of us?

I think about my parent-teacher conferences and how Lauren smiled at me from across the desk. Back then, had she feared I'd find out about her affair with Glen? Did she even care? And what about Glen's partner, Harris? Did he know about the affair from the beginning? An image of Harris peering up at me from the base of the Outing Club Park slide, his cheeks flushed and his eyes wide, fills my mind.

I have this urge to charge into Harris' firm and interrogate him. I want to do something crazy, something drastic, something the "Kate" Glen married would never do. My memories of my life with Glen are like marked playing cards. There's this sense that my years with him were counterfeit, that our marriage and Glen's persona were carefully crafted. My affection for Cassie feels like the only thing I can still trust.

As I blink back tears, through the window and illuminated by my chandelier, I see my dining room table. A visual memory of the yellow roses, the arrangement Lilly gave me last year to honor Georgia, fills my mind. As I envision the vibrant rose petals, a piece of remembered conversation tugs at me.

So, what makes you so sure James Hoover's alive?

Not what. Who. Emily Rose.

That day we lunched at Tucker's, Kingsley mentioned James Hoover's neighbor, Emily Rose. Kingsley's aha moment occurred while talking to her. I suddenly feel compelled to talk to Emily Rose too. Leeds says she's not credible because of her Alzheimer's, but I need to judge for myself. I took Glen's words as truth, trusted naïvely, and believed. I won't do that again. I'm going to find Miss Emily Rose and vet her.

I stumble across the semi-dark yard, hurry into my kitchen, and call Kingsley. He picks up, like he's expecting to hear from me.

"What nursing home is Emily Rose, Hoover's old neighbor, in?" I ask.

"Wedgewood Gardens Care Center. The place is in Freehold, New Jersey. Why? What are you thinking?"

"That I want to see her. You said Freehold? I'm gonna call the airlines."

"Whoa. You're gonna fly there now? Just like that? That's hard-core. I'm impressed."

"Well, once school starts up, leaving town is out of the question. I'll be too busy. So, it's now or never."

Kingsley clears his throat. "I don't have anything pressing going on right now. Want company?"

Thurston's comment about Kingsley possibly benefiting from Cassie's abduction gives me pause, but my gut tells me Kingsley's a good guy. Besides, I could use a bodyguard, Kingsley's a seasoned traveler, and he's met Emily Rose. Plus, proper Kate, Glen's wife, would never invite a male acquaintance on an overnight trip with her. So, there's that.

"Actually, yes. If you could join me, that would be great."

"Excellent. I'll pack my bag."

* * *

I buy the plane tickets for Kingsley and I. We take the 11:10 p.m. flight from Manchester to Newark, and obtain a rental car at Liberty International Airport. After grabbing two 7-Eleven Big Gulps, we drive south on Interstate 95. An hour and a half later, we reach Freehold, a town located off Highway 130. From what I can tell, the area's a mix of suburban and farmland. But darkness and exhaustion likely blur my perception. Having lived in New Jersey, like most garden state residents, I've been to the shore. But Freehold isn't the shore. It's thirty minutes west.

Kingsley and I check into the Radisson, each taking our own rooms. The sleepy motel clerk gives us our keys. She mentions a mall and some places to grab food. Yawning, I roll my suitcase out of the lobby, across the parking lot, and toward my room. A thin veil of trees separates the motel from the road. Cars whoosh behind it.

"I'll see you in the morning, at the breakfast buffet, say around eight," Kingsley says. "Knock or call if you need anything."

I yawn. "Will do."

Kingsley slips into his unit, two doors from mine. I enter my room and deadbolt the door behind me. I turn on the TV, with what is likely a germ-infested remote, and listen to the local news. But despite my efforts to keep it together, I can't. I keep thinking about my marriage to Glen.

How could Glen tell me I was his universe, his solar system, and his galaxy, buy me donuts on Sundays, draw me a bath nightly, hold my hand as we walked down Main Street, and pretzel his legs around mine in the darkness of our bedroom, but lie to me for nine years about Cassie and Lauren? Was I thinking about Lauren when he was kissing me? Those times I caught him staring into space, was he fantasizing about her curves? When he told me he was hiking alone, brainstorming his latest design project, was he actually meeting her? I envision the condom Liam and I found in the clearing. Did Glen and Lauren ever sneak into that clearing for a quickie? Me, being so close, within earshot, did it turn them on?

Glen's dead, I tell myself. *Nothing he and Lauren did or didn't do behind your back matters now.* But even though it's his infidelity, it's a part of me. Like a scar, it mars me. It makes me question everyone, everything, and especially myself and my judgement. I take a shower, scrubbing my flesh raw. Shivering, I step onto the bathmat and put on sweats and a T-shirt. I find a map of the tri-state area on the nightstand and skim it.

I think about Lawrenceville, my hometown and the site of Whitney's abduction, and how it's less than an hour away from where Kingsley and I are staying. One would think I'd want to go back to the place where I grew up. But I don't. Whitney's death overshadows my happy childhood memories. I sleep maybe two hours. Tossing and turning, I dream that Kingsley and I are back on the plane. In my dream, I peer out the window. Ice-encrusted worms cover the jet's wings. As the jet accelerates down the runway, terrified of crashing, I frantically push my call button. But the airline stewardess, who looks like Lauren, ignores the blinking light above my seat. The jet soars into the sky, wobbling. I dart to the front of the plane and burst into the cockpit. Glen's sitting in the pilot's seat, manning the jet.

* * *

I wake with a start and squint through my bedside window at the motel parking lot. Though it's barely 7:00 a.m., the sun's bright. It's more humid here than in New Hampshire. My motel room AC is already churning. As my stomach growls, I rub my forehead. I feel off, disoriented from the flight, the car ride, and my nightmare.

What are you doing here? What were you thinking? I ask myself. *Sure, Kingsley's easy company and a good investigative journalist, but you barely know him. Plus, if the Worm Man finds out that you're here talking to his old neighbor, he could come after you or hurt Cassie.* Perspiration slides down my back, slick, like slippery fingers.

I put on a maxi skirt, cotton top, and sandals and twist my hair into a topknot bun. Jittery, I grab my room key and purse and head to the motel café to meet Kingsley for breakfast. My unit is on the ground floor, so physically getting there is easy, mentally not so much. Just like with Samuel and the airport, this is James Hoover's old stomping ground. If James truly is here, if he's actually followed me, he's got the upper-hand.

I move past the other ground-floor units separating mine from the motel café. Ahead of me, a man drops quarters into a soda machine. I can't see his face, just his T-shirt and the broadness of his back. As a Dr Pepper falls from the dispenser and thuds, the man looks my way. *Brown eyes. Thin lips. Not Hoover.* Though I'm hunting Hoover, a wave of relief hits me. I welcome it, but a breath later it vanishes, and vulnerability swallows me.

I slip through the café door, make a beeline for the buffet, grab coffee and toast, and spot Kingsley. He's seated in a booth, downing French toast and drinking orange juice and coffee.

I plop into the upholstered seat across from his. Kingsley's grey hair is ruffled. He's got bedhead. Wrinkles crease his collared shirt.

He grins at me. "Top of the morning to you, Kate."

I nod. "You're up early? How'd you sleep?"

He rubs his neck. "Mattress was hard as a coffin." He wipes syrup off his bearded chin with his napkin. "Speaking of coffins, before we go to the nursing home, you should see where James Hoover supposedly died. It'll give you perspective."

As I bite into my toast, a family of four crams into the booth beside ours. The kids, a girl and a boy, look to be about Mikey and Justin's age.

Kingsley follows my gaze and cocks his chin at the family. "Great Adventure, the amusement park, is close by."

"Sounds like fun," I say, sipping my Maxwell House blend.

Kingsley rolls his eyes. "If you like lines, crowds, and whiplash, which I don't."

I nod. "I hear ya. I'm always lining up my students at school. I avoid lines in the summer like the plague."

As Kingsley heads to the buffet and refills his coffee, I watch the kids in the booth.

"I want to go on the roller coaster!" the boy shouts, waving his cereal spoon.

"No!" His sister shakes her head, braids flailing. "Too scary. The Ferris wheel! Let's ride the Ferris wheel."

I attempt to catch the girl's gaze. *Do what you want, little sister. Don't give in to any boy, not even to your brother.* I smile at the girl, hoping to give her confidence. There's a stubbornness about her that reminds me of Cassie.

* * *

Twenty minutes after Kingsley refills his coffee, he and I are on Highway 18 driving south to Neptune City. Though I rented the car, he's more familiar with area, so I let him drive.

The two-lane road is jammed with summer beach traffic, people getting an early start on the weekend. Lined with Ma-and-Pa businesses, hoagie delis, and Italian restaurants, the local highway weaves around three traffic circles and then narrows. We pass a KFC and veer east toward the Atlantic. Modest 1960s ranches, Capes, and split-levels appear. The neighborhood is decidedly middle class. Only train tracks and the beach town of Bradley Beach separate it from the ocean. But though the distance to the sand is bikeable, only one and a half miles, it's enough to matter.

Though the house fire that allegedly took Hoover's life occurred a decade ago, for me, the details surrounding Hoover's reputed demise are frozen in time. I almost expect to see a vacant lot, or a charred structure reminiscent of the photos I saw in newspaper articles. I don't. Kingsley pulls up in front of a new build. A "for sale" sign sits on a sodded lawn.

Because he does, I climb out of our rental car. Though Kingsley marches across the sod and peers in the curtain-less windows, I remain on the sidewalk. It's silly. I know this. But I won't step foot on this yard. It's not even *his* grass. It's new, grown from different seeds. But evil seeps off people and into places. I firmly believe this. Like an oil spill, evil pollutes. I don't want to get any dirtier than I already am.

"So, what do you think?" Kingsley says, motioning to the new build.

"It's pretty." And it is. The new build, which is slightly larger than its neighbors, is a cottage style ranch with flower boxes and a fenced-in backyard. I stare at the lawn and imagine worms wiggling in the sandy soil and ask, "Do you think the realtor tells the buyers about Hoover?"

Kingsley huffs. "No way." He points to the ranch beside the new build. "That's Emily Rose's old house. Her kids rent it out now."

I turn toward Emily's white single-story home. A crack zigzags across the driveway, a peeling Safe Neighbor House sticker mars the front window, two boxwood shrubs and a maple tree adorn the yard, and a rain gutter spout points toward a path of seashells. I motion to the cellar door. "So, he just climbed in there and hid when his house started burning?"

"Yup. Stayed over a week. According to Emily, he wasn't needing for much. The fridge and freezer down there were stocked. She kept extra stuff on shelves: books, blankets, a radio, and a microwave." Kingsley glances at his wristwatch. "Visiting hours at the nursing home don't start for a half hour. Wanna drive by the shopping center where the Hoover family pizzeria and their bait and tackle shop used to be?"

"Sure."

We hop back into our rental and head west, away from the ocean. We cruise by the KFC again and turn into a shopping area with a grocery store, a pharmacy, restaurant, and a liquor store.

Kingsley gestures at the Miller Lite sign in the liquor store window. "That's where the bait and tackle shop used to be. The Hoover boys' grandpa ran it." He points to an Asian restaurant across the parking lot called China One. "That used to be James and Samuel's dad's pizza place. Back in the day, it was a hangout for the local firefighters and cops."

"So, it's possible that some old-timers on the force overlooked some pertinent evidence about the fire."

"Very possible. But you're not going to get anyone in town to admit it."

He pulls into a spot in front of China One and punches Emily Rose's nursing home address into the GPS.

* * *

Though the nursing home is on a busy street, it's set back from the road and the front hedges form a fence-like barrier. But just like at our motel, there's this sense of constant movement. Dust, engine noise, and the whoosh of cars traveling at high speeds overwhelm me. We climb out of our rental car. Kingsley's usually silent. I wonder if his parents are housed in a place like this or if they're even alive. I don't know anything about him, other than he works for *The Globe* and he's obsessed with the Worm Man.

As questions about his personal life whirl in my mind, Kingsley and I enter the lobby. We approach a desk. A middle-aged woman sits behind it. She's wearing a nametag that says "Rachel" and a sticker that says "volunteer trainee." Her ears are double-pierced. She's sporting eighties eyeliner. Like my Whitney memories, she's time-warped.

"Hey, Rachel," Kingsley says as if they've met before.

"I'm Kate," I say when Rachel eyes me.

Rachel nods at both of us. "You're gonna need to sign in." She stares at Kingsley. "Do you live around here? You look familiar."

Kingsley knocks over a jar of pens. The ballpoints hit the tile floor and scatter. As he scoops them up, I put my name on the guest sheet.

"We're here to see Emily Rose," Kingsley says to Rachel. "I'm writing a book about Neptune City. Just finished a draft. Anyhow, I'm revising the chapter about the flea markets, the ones held at the Stein and Son's Pajama factory in the 60's."

When Rachel frowns, he adds, "Emily Rose was a Neptune City resident back in the day and had a booth at the market. We're fact-checking. Just want to clarify a few details for legal and authenticity reasons." Kingsley taps my arm. "Kate here is my assistant."

Rachel speaks to Kingsley. "So, you're a writer! How interesting." She looks at me. "Emily is very social. She loves reminiscing. It's her short-term memory that's shot. She can tell you what she ate for breakfast on her sister's wedding day, July 1st 1952. But she can't remember if she brushed her teeth. I've been a volunteer here for three months. She still doesn't know that I volunteer here. The thing is, I can't promise you anything. She has good and bad days."

"As we all do," I say.

"Too true." Rachel motions to the hall. "Emily is in the art therapy room now. Her session's just about over. She enjoys painting with watercolors. She's quite good." Rachel joins us in the lobby. "Follow me."

I step behind Kingsley and Rachel. In Rachel's mind, I've all but disappeared. I'm the lowly author's assistant, and I'm fine with that. It feels nice to slip back into the shadows. I was Whitney's sidekick and Glen's. But since Cassie's disappearance, I've been in the spotlight.

As Rachel and Kingsley chat, I trail them down the corridor. When we pass a room housing a piano, the tap of Rachel's low heels ceases and cheap commercial-grade carpet replaces the tile floor. It's the kind of carpet that cleans up easily and doesn't show spills or vomit. The type of carpet that soaks up urine, medicine, sweat, and the scents of aging and death, and keeps them.

I stifle a cough. We move by more rooms. These contain beds, both occupied and empty. As a nurse pushes a woman in a wheelchair, the odor of institutional food floats down an adjoining hallway. Something about it all, the uniformed orderlies, the stale air, and the blank stares of the residents, reminds me of my stint at the Carrier Clinic. My knees weaken. A wave of dizziness hits me. My heart pounds. Hoping to distract myself and squelch my panic attack, I stare at snag in the fabric of Rachel's blouse.

As Rachel and Kingsley enter a large rec space, I spot Emily Rose. I know it's her because she's the only one painting. The dozen other residents in the room are working with clay. Emily's small, child-sized. Her white hair is so thin I can see her scalp. It's pink, irritated. Her buttoned cardigan is eschew. Her long-sleeved cotton T-shirt is too big for her petite bird-like frame.

Emily's eyes widen in alarm as we near her. She waves her paint brush, swordlike. "Get out! What are you doing in my living room Who are you?"

"I'm Rachel," Rachel says speaking slowly. "I volunteer here, remember?" She motions to the beige walls. "Emily, you're at the senior home. You live here now." She gestures at the other residents in the room. "Along with all these wonderful folks."

Emily frowns at Kingsley. "What about him? Does he live here too?"

"No," Rachel says. "This gentleman, Tom, and his friend, Kate, have come to visit you. Tom's working on a book about the old flea markets. You spoke with him about a month ago?" Rachel crouches to Emily's level. "Do you remember Tom?"

Emily nods and smiles, but I recognize a good performance when I see one. She has no idea who Kingsley is. When Rachel steps away from Emily's easel, I take in Emily's work-in-progress. Rachel is correct. Emily is a good artist. She's painting a cat, a Russian Blue. She's captured the feline's superiority and its aloofness perfectly.

I point to the image. "Is this your cat, Emily?"

"No. Belongs to the world. That's Storm. Lives outside." Emily motions to the patio doors. "Meows a ton."

Rachel speaks to Kingsley and me. "The residents aren't supposed to feed Storm, but they do." She shrugs. "Actually, we all do. Consequently, he sticks around."

Kingsley laughs. "Cat's no dummy

A bell rings and Rachel glances at her watch. "The residents are scheduled to go to music therapy now. I'll take them and leave you three to chat. No one will disturb you. You'll have the room to yourselves."

Kingsley and I sit and wait while the other residents clear out, assisted by Rachel and orderlies. Emily rests her brush on the easel ledge.

"Emily, we came to talk to you about James Hoover," Kingsley says when the last resident vacates the room.

Emily jabs the air with her finger. Her lip quivers. "Don't know a James. Know a Fred. My sister married a man named Fred. Fred was a soldier in the army."

"James Hoover isn't a soldier," Kingsley says.

"Then I don't know him. I only know a soldier named Fred." She cocks her age-spotted chin at her painting. "Fred had a cat, a dog too, a collie." She eyes Kingsley. "What's your name?"

Kingsley pats his chest. "Tom. My name is Tom Kingsley."

Emily rocks in her chair. "Tom, are you the army? Do have a collie? Do you know my sister, Irene?"

"This isn't working," Kingsley mouths to me. "We should probably go."

"Not yet," I mouth back.

Emily points at me. "Who are you?"

"I'm Kate. Emily, may I draw something for you?"

As her head bobs, yes, I slide a pencil and notepad out of my purse. As she hums, I sketch Emily's house, the way it looked from the street this morning. I draw the pair of boxwood shrubs flanking the front porch, the zigzag crack in the cement drive, the peeling Neighborhood Safe House sticker in the front window, the towering maple tree with a branch arching toward the detached garage, and the rain gutter with a spout that's angled toward the path made of shells. When I'm through, I rip out the page and hand the finished sketch to Emily. "So, what was living on Sixth Avenue like?" I ask, hoping to ease onto the topic of James Hoover. She squints at my sketch, nods, but continues to hum. I shake my head at Kinsley. Across the art room, the wall clock ticks. Kingsley stands, and heads to the door.

"It's too quiet here," Emily says, motioning to the clock. "Never heard ticking at my house. Too loud. Lived across the street from a house full of boys. Those boys made a racquet, morning, noon, and night."

"You don't say," Kingsley says, sinking back down onto his chair.

Emily's hazel eyes brighten. "Those boys and their friends were always outside, playing basketball and riding their bikes. When they got older, they smoked something awful. Kicked their cigarette butts down into the sewer grate, clogged it up. One of them, the chubby one, was our paperboy."

She looks at Kingsley. "I remember you, now. You asked me all those questions about that horrible James Hoover. Savage should be shot. If I'd have known he was in my cellar, I would have padlocked my door, imprisoned him. He would have starved to death eventually, once those Stouffers dinners and that Carvel ice cream cake ran out."

My heart thuds. "Emily, how do you know it was James in that cellar?"

"Because he wasn't like the other," Emily snaps back.

"The other?" I frown. "You mean his brother, Samuel?"

"No, silly. Not Samuel, Charles. From a distance you could barely tell James and Charles apart. But when you got closer, you could see the difference."

"You mean there were three Hoover boys? James, Charles, and Samuel?" Kingsley says raising three fingers.

"Yes. Samuel and the twins," Emily says.

My heart races. I open my sketchbook, and sketch two boys, side-by-side, both identical in appearance. The boys I draw resemble the boyhood photos of James Hoover I've seen in old newspaper articles.

Emily motions to one of the penciled boys. "He didn't have a mind, that Charles. Well, of course he did," she adds when I gasp. "Just not like a normal person, is what I mean. Could barely dress himself. Spoke a little. Used simple words. When he wasn't hidden in his house, they stashed him in the back of his grandpa's tackle shop." She winks. "I suppose that's where the kids got that nickname."

"What nickname?" I ask.

Emily laughs. "Why, the Worm, of course."

Kingsley and I exchange looks. I quickly draw an earthworm on the page beside my sketch of the two identical twin boys.

"Which one was the Worm?" Kingsley asks.

"They both were," Emily says. "James was the head because he was smart. And Charles was the tail. You know, if you separate a worm, it becomes two worms, both identical in appearance, like those Hoover twins."

I sketch two identical worms beside the larger one.

Emily nods. Her thin white hair shuffles, rearranging itself. She motions to the large worm on the page. "The kids all thought that stupid name was genius. They teased Charles relentlessly. One day they got carried away. Someone shoved poor Charles, and he hit his head on the steel rail of the train tracks. He was never the same after that, even duller than before. Never came out of the house, not that he ventured out much before that." She sighs. "The incident changed James too. Made him mean, angry. The local boys were afraid of him. We all were."

I can't believe what I'm hearing. Identical twins share the same DNA. I now know how James Hoover faked his death and fooled the authorities. Still, given the tenacity of the feds, Emily's story is hard to believe.

"Emily,' I say. "When the feds found that body in the Hoover's burned-down house, did you tell them about Charles?" I frown. "The FBI is thorough. It seems as if they'd be able to find a record of Charles somewhere. Emily?"

She starts humming Frank Sinatra's "Strangers in the Night", and I'm sure I've lost her. Desperate, I flip to a blank page in my book and I begin sketching a charred structure, James' family shore home after the fire.

Kingsley speaks to me. "One would think they'd have found some sort of record, Kate. But don't forget, things were different forty years ago. People didn't have an internet presence. You didn't have cameras on every block. Institutions kept records, for sure. But they used paper, and the papers were sometimes lost or got destroyed. Using electronic health records to provide better care wasn't mandated until 2009. I should know. I wrote an article about the mandate once."

"You're right. The world has really changed," I say, sketching.

Kingsley nods. "It sure has. Big brother is definitely watching us now. Big sister, big mother and father too."

Just outside the door, an aide pushes a metal serving cart. I stare at the cart's metal top and picture the metal file cabinet in Glen's home office which houses my birth certificate.

I pat Emily's hand and point to the sketch of Hoover's charred home. "Emily, do you remember when the Hoover's house burned? Did someone save Charles birth certificate?"

Emily stares at my sketch. "There wasn't one to save," she says, blinking. "Betty, the boys' mother, had the twins at home. Charles was never baptized or immunized. I know because Betty told me as much. She didn't need records for him. Charles didn't attend school like Samuel and James."

"But why? Schools have programs for special needs children," I say picturing the autistic boy, Ross, who attended my class with his aide last year. "They did, even back in the 70's. and 80's"

"Maybe. But the Hoover family wasn't like other families." Emily cups her hand over her mouth. "Mr. Hoover was a cobra."

"Define cobra," Kingsley says, scooting his chair closer to hers'.

Emily stammers. "Someone who squeezes all the joy and life out of you." Her voice quiets. "The Cobra was embarrassed that he'd fathered Charles. He made Betty keep the boy hidden in their house, treated him like a leper."

"But surely someone would have seen Charles?" I say, "Neighbors? Delivery men? You said one of the neighborhood kids shoved him."

"He did," Emily says, nodding. "And yes...lots of people saw Charles. Folks aren't blind. They caught glimpses of Charles through the Hoover's windows, heard him crying when his brothers went off to school."

"And no one did anything?" I ask, appalled. "Called the cops? Social services?"

"Why? Betty was a kind decent woman. People felt bad for her. Mr. Hoover spent all of his time fishing, courting the local cops and firemen at his pizzeria, and betting at the racetrack. When he did come home, he beat Betty. Made those boys watch while he knocked her senseless." Emily's voice cracks. "He controlled that household, especially Betty. One frigid January morning, he shoved her out the front door and handed her a shovel. She shoveled eight inches of snow in her bathrobe and slippers while he while smoked a cigar and laughed. Betty got frostbite. Lost three toes. Came down with pneumonia, nearly died too."

As she describes the snowy setting, I flip to a clean page in my sketchbook. I draw the snowy driveway, a woman in a robe and slippers, a shovel in her grasp.

Emily looks at the image and winces as if remembering. "People saw that Betty was lonely and suffering. But they also saw that Charles gave her great joy. I can't tell you how many times I peered out my window and spotted Betty and Charles together in their fenced in backyard, or heard Charles humming loudly through the window screen while she played her piano. How could we call the social services and take Charles away from her? If the authorities institutionalized Charles, Betty would have crumbled. Charles was her Bambino. Right or wrong, we all kept quiet."

I consider her words, flip to another page, and I draw a street, neighbors peering out their windows, two women flanking Betty, supporting her, and holding her hands.

"What you're telling me all makes sense, Emily. Perfect sense," I say, pointing at my finished sketch. "People in small towns protect one another. I get that. And records weren't as organized in the seventies and eighties, and they definitely weren't computerized. But Emily, the feds questioned you in 2008, too."

Emily nods. "They did. They talked to me after the fire. But by that time, Betty, Mr. Hoover, and Grandpa Hoover were all deceased and most of the original neighbors had moved away. The few neighbors that remained refused to talk. They feared that James would come for their daughters and granddaughters if they gabbed." Emily laughs. "My daughter's a bitch. She put me in here. I could care less what happens to her, if James chops her up."

As Emily chuckles, volunteer Rachel, two orderlies, and an angry-looking woman appear in the doorway.

"It's him!" the angry woman shouts, pointing at Kingsley. "That's the guy who got Mom so upset. He's not supposed to have any contact with her. He's on the list."

"I'm so sorry, Donna. I didn't realize," Rachel stammers.

"I don't understand... What list?" I leap to my feet, and turn toward Kingsley, but he's already rushing past Rachel, Donna, and the orderlies and running bull-like toward the lobby.

Chapter 10

I shove my sketchbook and pencil into my purse. Donna grabs my wrist.
"What's wrong with you people?" she says to me. "My mother is ninety-five.
She's ill. She doesn't know up from down. Can't you leave her be?"

"I'm sorry," I say. "We weren't hurting her, just asking some questions.
The questions were important. A little girl is missing."

Donna taps her forehead. "Yeah, and my mother's missing half her memory.
No way am I going to let you interrogate her." She points to the sketch in Emily's
hand. "What's this? Why does Mom have a sketch of her house?" She eyeballs
me. "You're targeting us. You're planning on robbing our tenants. You're scam
artists. Crooks."

"No," I say, extricating myself from Donna's grasp. "It's nothing like
that. That sketch is just a memory aide."

"Memory aide my ass! You think I'm stupid? I'm calling the cops!"
Donna shouts. I bolt into the lobby, and she yells, "Sickos, both of you. Should
be arrested. What's your name? Kate something? I'm putting you on the list too."

As Donna rants, I career through the exit door and stumble into the
parking lot. A police siren sounds and I jump into our rental car. Kingsley's
already inside. He's got the motor running. He presses the accelerator, and the
engine revs. As the police siren wails again, we zoom out of the nursing home
lot, zip onto the busy street, and lose ourselves in traffic.

Kingsley yelps. "Can you believe it? The feds, the cops … they're all
wrong. Hoover's alive. That body in that fire was James' twin brother, Charles,
Worm Tail. James tricked everyone."

I grip the seat beneath me. I feel alive, more alive than I've felt since
Glen's death. But I don't like being screamed at, and I'm not comfortable with
Kingsley's investigative tactics. He had to have known he wasn't allowed at the
nursing home.

Kingsley slams on his brakes and almost rear-ends the sedan in front
of him.

"Why didn't you tell me you were banned from that place?" I ask, gripping
my seat belt.

"Because I didn't want you to screw things up. You tend to be jumpy.
Besides, I'm a journalist. I push people. There's always trouble when I interview
folks. It's expected. You should have expected it."

"Perhaps. But what if someone other than Rachel had been at that desk,
not a volunteer, someone who knew enough to check the list? What would you
have done?"

"I would have talked my way in. I always do. Hey, I didn't lie," he adds when I frown. "I told her I was a writer."

That part was true. But I sense that I was his cover, his means of getting into the facility. More than likely when he'd come before, he'd come alone. "I don't know if I should feel privileged or used," I mumble.

Kingsley turns into a tract neighborhood too fast. "You should feel jazzed. Hey. You know how Hoover faked his death now. You know your theory about him grabbing Cassie has merit. It's not just a belief, a hunch. It's a solid hypothesis. It's got meat on it now. Emily might be up there in years, and she might not know what she ate for breakfast or some volunteer's name, but when it comes to James Hoover, she knows her stuff. I believe her. Don't you?"

"Yes," I admit as he coasts, "but the truth sounds like some nutty soap opera plot and Leeds doesn't think Emily Rose is credible."

"Then we'll give him something more, something that will stand up in court. What matters is that you believe. You won't give up now."

Kingsley drums his steering wheel. He looks at the houses surrounding us. They appear ordinary to me, nothing stands out. But Kingsley grins as if he's triggered.

He pats his belly. "I'm hungry. Let's eat. Then we'll figure out how to get you that proof for Leeds. You up for lunch?"

* * *

We head to a barbeque spot off Highway 35 called Local Smoke Barbeque.

"I write articles on food," Kingsley says. "I know good eats. Don't question my taste." When I glance in the rearview mirror, he frowns. "Who are you looking for?"

"The cops. You heard those sirens. Emily Rose's daughter thinks we're criminals. I'm nervous, okay?" I add when he chuckles. "All of this is weird to me, upsetting. I've got a lot at stake—relationships, maybe prison time, and my teaching career. You're just writing about it."

"Just writing about it." Kingsley pulls into the lot beside the barbeque place. He does a three-point turn and backs into a spot partially hidden by a dumpster, but with a view of the takeout joint. "Just," he says.

And that's when I get it. Researching and hunting down James Hoover is his life. He's got nothing else—no wife, no friends, and no kids. *The Globe* job is something he does so he can do this.

"I'm sorry," I say. "This is important to you too. I really do appreciate your time and all the help you've given me."

"As you should," he says. "'Cause I'm the bomb, the master, when it comes to researching this shit." He points to the barbeque joint.

I pull out a twenty. "You go in. Get me whatever. I think we should eat in the car."

He nods. "Keep your Jackson. This is my treat." He waves his cell. "Call if you need me to skedaddle."

He climbs out of the rental and strolls across the lot. Despite having just bolted from the nursing home and knowing that the cops could be after us, he appears at home here. I'm guessing that's part of what makes Kingsley a good journalist. He's comfortable everywhere, in all situations.

Shoving the twenty back into my purse, I watch him chat with a man who's exiting the barbeque joint. As they linger on the restaurant steps, Kingsley nods and grins. When the man walks to his truck, Kingsley goes inside the restaurant and heads to the counter to order.

I figure Kingsley's in his fifties, about the same age as James Hoover. I've never asked him what made him want to write about Hoover, what made him decide that come hell or high water, Hoover's story needed to be told. The news media often contends that criminals shouldn't be given a voice, a platform. But I'm curious. Why does Kingsley think differently? Why did he write a book about James Hoover?

Through the windshield, I watch Kingsley slouch in a booth. He skims a newspaper and glances at his cell. When the cook hands him his order, Kingsley salutes the guy and exits with our lunches. He starts munching greasy fries halfway across the parking lot. I unlock his door, and he slides onto the driver's seat.

Kingsley licks salt off his fingers, hands me the bag containing a pulled pork sandwich, and mumbles, "Yum. Delicious."

And it is, smoky and spicy, culinary heaven.

* * *

We devour our sandwiches and head back to the new build in Neptune City. Kingsley says that seeing the house after speaking to Emily Rose will give us new insight, a direction. Me, I can't think about any of that. I'm still worried about the cops.

"Chill. Emily Rose's daughter is all bark and no bite," Kingsley says as I fidget and peer out the rental car window. "I doubt she even called the police. If she had, they would have pulled us over by now." He motions to the road. "That street by the nursing home is like a racetrack. The po-pos we heard were likely heading to an accident scene."

"But we were on that same street. I didn't see any pileups."

Kingsley gestures at his windshield. "Do you see a cop car now?"

"No."

"Trust me. We're good. And," he grins. "we're also here."

As the noon sun hovers, Kingsley pulls to the curb in front of the same cottage style new build we visited earlier. He parks behind the mailbox, and I glance through the windshield. Dressed in slacks, a polo shirt, and trendy sneakers, a realtor is tying balloons to an open house sign. The realtor, who appears to be about forty, is tan and looks fit. A blue bicycle is tucked behind a trash bin in a side yard. More than likely, it's Mr. Coldwell Banker's Schwinn.

"Wow, they're having an open house today. That's unusual. They normally only have those on Saturdays or Sundays, not Fridays," Kingsley says, motioning to the balloons. "We really lucked out. If the realtor's local, chances are he can tell us something about Hoover. And from inside the property, we'll get Hoover's vantage point. See how much of Emily Rose's place he was privy to. Who knows? Maybe we'll figure out how Hoover slipped into her basement undetected after the fire. You never know what a home tour might lead to."

I frown. In my opinion, Kingsley's grasping at straws. His plan of attack, his means of getting proof for Leeds, seems random, not well thought out. I think of the hundreds of the lesson plans I've written up over the past ten years and all the project proposals Glen prepared.

"You're not a planner, are you?" I say.

Kingsley laughs. "Nope. I'm a seat-of-your-pants kind of guy. But if you've got any solid well-thought-out ideas, I'm all ears."

I shake my head. "I don't think … Look. Maybe we should head back to the airport now, or at least lay low while we're in the area. We talked to Emily Rose and figured out how James Hoover faked his death. We accomplished our goals."

"No way. We're here. May as well learn as much as we can while we're in Jersey. Like I said before, the cops aren't coming. All we did was visit an old lady. We didn't hurt her. If you ask me, she probably enjoyed our company, the excitement. We likely made her week."

Before I can argue with him, he unlocks the door. As he unclasps his seat belt, I stare at the sod fronting the new build. I can't help it. I'm still imagining evil seeping out of the grass, Hoover's badness latching onto me.

I shake my head and look at Kingsley. "I can't do it. You go in there. You don't need me."

"Sure, I do. Come on," Kingsley says. "You have to move around and work off that pulled pork."

I huff. He means it has a joke, but his comment isn't funny. First off, I'm underweight. Second, there's nothing humorous about James Hoover's kind of evil. It's insidious, sticks to your bones. "I'm not stepping foot on that yard."

He smiles. "I'm not banned from open houses if that's what you're worried about." When I don't move, he steadies my knee with his fingers. "I don't get it. You bolted from those goons at that nursing home like you were Emmitt Smith running for a touchdown. You were awesome. And you fought off James Hoover when you were barely thirteen. You were a baller, even back then."

He motions to the yard. "It's just grass, fescue. Everything that was there when Hoover was alive, burned. It's all brand new. What is it they say? The body replaces its cells every seven years. It's been ten. Besides, James Hoover didn't even die here."

"But according to Emily Rose, his brother did."

"Yeah. But you heard Emily. Charles wasn't evil."

"True."

He climbs out of the car. "I'm going in. You should follow me. There's safety in numbers. We're a pack, you and me." He nods at the pavers leading to the front door. "You can hop across those. You don't even have to step on the sod."

I exit the rental and follow him. It's not because I believe his BS about packs and sticking together, or because I'm comfortable winging it. Neither is true. It's because Mr. Coldwell Banker is coming our way.

As I fidget on the sidewalk, Mr. Coldwell Banker grins. "Afternoon, ma'am. Sir. You folks in the market for a beach house?"

"We sure are," Kingsley says, plastering on a smile. He takes my arm. It's an act. He's pretending we're a couple. I'm no longer the author's assistant, like at the nursing home. This means I can be anyone I want to be. Given all that's going on, Cassie's disappearance, the Worm Man's resurrection, finding out about Glen's affair and becoming a suspect in Cassie's murder investigation, the idea of being someone other than Kate Boswell appeals to me.

"A beach house— Yes," I stammer. "We are looking for one. I'm Joan Cartwright." I extend my free hand.

"I'm George, George Lewis," Kingsley says as Mr. Coldwell Banker and I shake.

"My name's Ken Larson," Mr. Coldwell Banker says. "Welcome." Ken points to the house. "Flyers are on the table. Price is $450,000. Place is brand new, top to bottom. Take a look around. I'm here to answer any questions."

I step onto the first paver. Kingsley squeezes my arm.

"This is a big step for us," he says to Ken, diving straight into character. "Joan and I are moving in together. She's been freaking out all morning. And I don't blame her. I mean, we're not kids anymore. We've lived. Am I right, Joan?" he says, winking at me. "We know what can happen, how one bad decision can screw you up."

Ken nods. "Well, let me assure you. Buying this house wouldn't be a mistake. Everything's permitted. The builder who constructed the property is a personal friend of mine. You're not in a flood zone. Neighbors are super friendly. And the location is great. You're beach close. But you don't have the traffic and prices associated with Bradley Beach, Ocean Grove, or Belmar."

"Belmar," Kinsley says. "I hear that's quite the party scene."

"It is," Ken says. "But you're a couple of miles away. You can participate if you want to or not. Neptune City is the best of both worlds."

As Kingsley and Ken talk, I disentangle myself from Kingsley's grasp and

manage to hop my way onto the front porch. I feel ridiculous. I picture Kingsley
strolling into the barbeque joint. *Act like you belong. You're Joan Cartwright. Joan
wouldn't worry about James Hoover or his evil oozing off some lawn.*

I nudge the front door open and step into the foyer. I think about how
James' twin, Charles, burned, perhaps alive, in this very spot. I can't help it. I
imagine his ghost seeping up from the foundation and through the floorboards.
As panic overwhelms me, I breathe in and out, counting to ten. Trembling, I move
gingerly through the open-concept living area. Kingsley and Ken catch up to me.
Ken starts talking about the appliances, about how they're GE and the range is
gas. As he flips the lights on and off, Kingsley thuds across the hardwoods. They're
the fake kind, engineered.

As Kingsley inspects the wide planks, Ken stands beneath a doorframe.
Ken says, "The floors are perfect for the beach. Easy to take care of. No warping."

I nod. Kingsley heads to the bathroom. Ken says something about a
rain showerhead faucet. A sign-in sheet rests on the kitchen table. I finger the
pen beside it.

"Ken, I've got a question." I decide to be direct. I hear water running.
Apparently, Kingsley's testing the shower. "We know the home's history, who
lived here. I get that this is a different structure, a completely new one."

Ken, who's now standing beside the dining room window, stiffens. "Yes,
it is. It's totally new. The seller cleared the lot."

I bite my lip. "But …"

Ken drags his fingers through his hair. "I'm not gonna lie. On occasion,
curiosity seekers swing by. Probably the same weirdoes who take selfies at places
like the JonBenet Ramsey house, Nicole Brown Simpson's condo, and Michael
Peterson's Durham Mansion. But the true crime tourists just snap and go. It's not
a problem, not even an inconvenience. That's how infrequent it is."

"But what about …" I touch my cross necklace.

He smiles. "The karma. The bad juju. I don't believe in that stuff, but if
it makes you feel any better, a reverend blessed this house yesterday."

"You called in a reverend?" Kingsley says, emerging from the bathroom.

"No. Fella made an appointment to see the place. Had no intention of
buying the property. I figured that out pretty quickly. Just did his blessing and
left. If he wasn't a reverend and so darn nice, I would have been annoyed at him
for wasting my time." Ken scratches his chin. "Fella said he was in the area for a
religious conference. We've got a lot of those locally. Guy came all the way from
Maine."

My pulse quickens. "Maine? You're kidding?"

Ken heads to the kitchen. "I know. Quite a trek. The reverend gave me
this." He opens a cabinet, retrieves a jar of blueberry jam, and points to the
label. "Shasta's Farm."

My heart beats. *Holy shit. Reverend Shasta was here. A religious conference...I don't buy it for a second. We have to talk to Shasta!* I frown. *We drove to Shasta's farm unannounced. What if Kinsley doesn't have his cell number?*

"Listen," I say. "About the house. We might feel better about the bad juju if we spoke to that reverend. Do you know how we can get in contact with him? Is he still in town? If I knew all the dark karma was gone, we might consider making an offer. I love the layout and the location."

"And the price is reasonable," Kingsley adds, joining us in the living area. Ken remains silent.

"Please," I say. "The home really is perfect for us."

Ken exhales. "I usually don't do this. Respecting privacy is paramount in my industry. But you seem like nice people. The reverend's name is Shasta, hence the label on the jam. I'll give you his number." I hand him my cell. Ken punches in Reverend Shasta's number and returns it. He says, "Shasta mentioned that he was staying at the Majestic Hotel in Ocean Grove. I don't think he'd mind if you asked him about the blessing in person."

"The Majestic," Kingsley mutters. "We'll track him down. Thanks."

As we exit, Ken slips me his card. "This is a good house, solidly built. What it needs is good salt of the earth owners like yourselves to fill it with love and memories."

"Thanks for the information on the home. We'll be in touch," I say, darting down the front path. I climb into our rental car, Kingsley starts the engine, and we zoom toward Ocean Grove.

"What do you think Reverend Shasta was doing here?" I ask, as Kingsley takes a curve at warped speed.

"I dunno. But he didn't come to pass out jam."

I bite my fingernail. Kingsley's mole has him on speed dial, and Liam keeps me in the loop. We'd know if the feds found Cassie. No communication from New London means she's still in danger.

As Kingsley drives, I call the number Ken punched into my cell. My phone rings repetitively.

* * *

Ocean Grove, which is located seven miles from Neptune City and less than a mile south of Asbury Park, is a picturesque resort town. It has a boardwalk and boasts historical Victorian houses, replete with gingerbread trim. The Majestic Hotel sits on Main Avenue, a block from the Atlantic, within walking distance to shops and restaurants.

As we pass the famed hotel, Kingsley turns up the rental car AC and adjusts his driver's-side visor. It's a prime beach day, sunny, humid, and eighty-five degrees. We park on a side street, climb out into the heat, and scurry around beachgoers toward the hotel's wide front porch. After entering the moss-green lobby through double doors, we approach a twentysomething clerk seated behind the check-in desk.

"We're looking for a friend of ours. Tried calling him, but his cell seems to be turned off. Not sure if he's checked out or not," Kingsley says to the clerk. "Guy's a minister. Name's Reverend Shasta."

The young staffer, a guy, nods. "I know the guest you're speaking about well. Just checked out, not five minutes ago. Said something about going for one last walk on the beach before heading up north." The staffer motions to the doors. "If you're lucky, maybe you can catch him."

"Thanks. We'll try," I say.

We leave the hotel and walk east to the beach, passing bathing suit-clad tourists along our route.

"Shit," Kingsley says, motioning to the attendant positioned at the edge of the boardwalk. "Gotta pay to get on the sand. I forgot they do that here. It's a rip-off if you ask me. Access to the ocean should be free."

"You're right. But we've got a bigger problem." I motion to the sand. "There's a zillion people out there."

"What a zoo." Kingsley wipes sweat off his brow. "I'll head north to Asbury Park. You go south toward Bradley." He takes off his loafers and socks and groans.

I smile. "You're not a beach person, are you?"

"No," he says. "I'm not."

As I slip off my sandals, he says, "You?"

I fumble in my purse for my wallet. "I'm a lake girl myself."

Kingsley grins at me. "I could see that." He taps his cell. "Text if you find the rev. I'll do the same."

We pay the attendant for two daily passes and separate. It's late afternoon. The sun burns my shoulders. The sand is hot beneath my feet. Thinking I'll be able to cover more ground and possibly catch Reverend Shasta on the hard packed-down sand, I hop toward the water's edge. As the cool surf splashes my ankles and toes, I gather up my maxi skirt to keep it from getting wet. Another day, another time, I would enjoy this, the crowd, the sun, and the surf. But I'm on a mission. We could try to reconnect with Reverend Shasta in Maine, but time is of the essence. Who knows when Leeds will decide to arrest me, or if Emily Rose's daughter, Donna, will sic the cops on Kinsley and me? I don't even want to think about what James Hoover could be doing to Cassie.

I move and study the beachgoers. Some are lying on towels. Others are reading in beach chairs. Groups of teens play Frisbee and football. Dozens of people are walking like me. There are slews of swimmers in the ocean too. If Reverend Shasta's in the water, it's unlikely that I'll spot him. He could be under the waves. And if he's not wearing his clerical collar, I might not recognize him.

I pass a girl building a sandcastle, think about Cassie, and pick up my pace. The crowd of beachgoers thickens. A boogie boarder zips past me. Distracted, I trip over a plastic bucket. Three girls in matching bikinis trot by, coconut suntan lotion wafting off their bronze skin. A dozen people wearing the same pale-blue T-shirts march toward me. A family reunion? A church group? The T-shirt people swarm.

"This is ridiculous!" I kick sand and slip my cell out of my purse. I'm about to call Kingsley, to tell him it's futile, a lost cause, when I see Reverend Shasta a free-throw shot away from me.

He's carrying his shoes and dressed in slacks, a short-sleeved shirt, and his clerical collar. Our eyes lock. When he glances toward the boardwalk, I'm sure he's going to run from me.

"Kate?" he says, stopping in his tracks. "What in the devil are you doing in Jersey?"

I hurry toward him. I go with the truth. "I came to talk to James Hoover's neighbor, a woman by the name of Emily Rose." The surf surges, the ocean covers my feet, and I feel myself sinking, becoming rooted into the beach. "What about you? Why are you here?"

"Religious conference. Annual event."

Instead of a question, I go with an accusation. "You lied to Leeds. You told him Kingsley and I were harassing you. You told him James Hoover wasn't at your farm."

"I didn't lie," Reverend Shasta snaps. "I did feel badgered. And when we spoke before, I was confused. I thought Hoover was this fella, Roger Stone, but I realized later I was mistaken."

"Really? Then why were you blessing that house on Sixth Avenue, the one built on the lot where James Hoover lived?"

Reverend Shasta backs away and stares at me.

I lift my skirt and turn slowly. "I'm not wearing a wire if that's what you're worried about. I'm not recording you. I swear it."

The reverend points north. We start walking in the direction he was heading, back toward Ocean Grove. He bends, scoops up a shell, and flings it into the surf.

"Why are you here, really?" I prod. "Don't tell me you're attending a religious conference."

"Kate, please. Leave it be."

"Can't. I'm not going to let up."

He glances about.

"Talk to me," I plead. "Cassie Rossi is still missing."

"That doesn't surprise me."

My chest tightens. "Why would you say something like that?"

He lowers his voice. "Two days ago, I found another chalk drawing on my blackboard. It was a cartoon drawing of a girl. Whoever drew her, X'ed her out and scribbled 'August 30th' and 'Cassie' below the image."

Suddenly, despite the sun and the eighty-plus-degree temp, I'm cold, very cold. Goosebumps form on my forearms. "So, you came here and blessed Hoover's house because Hoover threatened to kill Cassie? I don't understand."

"I didn't come just to bless Hoover's house." He gestures to the boardwalk, to the crowds. "Ocean Grove is a special place to me. My family vacationed here when I was a boy. This beach is where I first truly felt the Lord's presence. I was twelve. I came back here because I needed to feel God in that way again."

We continue to walk. People dart past us, catch footballs, and leap into the surf.

The reverend's voice cracks. "Maria isn't just a camper. She's my daughter. Her mother and I had a relationship. I was in Mexico doing missionary work when we met and fell in love. I'd just graduated from the seminary. Valeria, Maria's mother, was married at the time. The circumstances aren't something I'm proud of, but I don't regret having Maria. When James Hoover was working for me, he overheard me talking to Valeria. Hoover didn't just threaten Maria, he threatened me too. He told me that if I turned him in, he'd tell the elders at my church that I seduced Valeria and fathered Maria. I couldn't ruin Valeria's marriage and hurt Maria. Maria doesn't even know I'm her father." His lip quivers. "Kate, you have to understand. I feel terrible about Cassie. I'm a wreck."

"Then come forward now."

"I can't. Nothing's changed."

"I see why you're torn. I get it. But it feels like you're sacrificing Cassie for Maria, your farm, and your reputation."

Reverend Shasta touches my wrist and halts. I stop too. "Kate, it's been five days since Hoover grabbed Cassie. Given Hoover's history of impulsive violence, you have to believe she's already dead. Besides, Hoover left my farm two months ago. What good would coming forward about his employment do now?" His words sputter out. "My charity, Blueberries for Betterment, is supported by conservative donors. If people find out about my indiscretion, I could lose my church, my farm, and my camp. Valeria's marriage might not survive. And if Hoover finds out I'm corroborating your theory, he'll go after Maria. The feds won't protect her, not really. They can't. You know how the Worm Man is. If he wants a girl, he takes her. We both know that."

"Look, I get that you're scared. But I can't convince Leeds to take me seriously, not without someone credible like you backing me up."

Reverend Shasta shakes his head. "I'm sorry. But Cassie's dead. I'm certain of it."

"See, I don't buy that. If you truly believed she was dead, you wouldn't be here seeking God's comfort?"

The reverend starts speed-walking. I have to hurry to keep up with him. "I'm not a bad man," he murmurs.

"I didn't say you were."

We hurry back to the Ocean Grove beach access entrance. Though I hound him about Hoover, hoping to uncover clues to the monster's whereabouts, Shasta remains tightlipped. I spot Kingsley sitting on a boardwalk bench, dripping with sweat and licking a snow cone, and shove on my sandals.

Kingsley nods at Reverend Shasta. "A little birdie told me you blessed a beach house yesterday, Reverend. What's on the agenda for today?"

Reverend Shasta points to the street. "I'm heading home. I suggest you two do the same. Instead of digging up dirt here, you should be supporting Cassie's family. Godspeed," he says, moving toward Main Avenue.

"Reverend!" I shout. "You're making the wrong choice!"

"It's my choice to make, Kate," he hollers back. "I'm the one who has to live with it."

"At least you get to live," I yell. "Cassie ... she ..." I run after him.

Kingsley tackles me, holding me back. "You're making a scene, Kate."

"Like you give a care about impressions," I say swatting Kingsley with my purse, as a crowd forms around us.

"I don't. You're right. But you can't make Shasta talk. Plus, for Christ sakes, the guy's a reverend. If you assault him, the cops you've been so worried about, will really come after you. You'll be all over the internet. Probably on the news. Relax. We'll find that proof to give to Leeds."

"But you don't understand," I say, "Hoover did another chalk drawing of Cassie. He said she's only got until August 30th to ..."

I look up. The reverend's no longer in my sight. My muscles slacken. Kingsley releases me, and we sink onto the bench. I glance around the boardwalk, at the street. Both are filled with staring people. Kingsley touches my hand. His fingers are sticky from his snow cone, but I don't care. I cling to them.

"Maria's his daughter, like his actual daughter," I mutter. "The reverend had an affair with Maria's mother, who was married."

"Well, that explains your outburst. Seems like the reverend and your ex have things in common."

I make a fist, motion to the lifeguard stand. "Is that why I want to bury Shasta alive in that sand over there?"

Kingsley chuckles. "Fathering a child out of wedlock and infidelity are definitely triggers for you. But I'm guessing the reverend's refusal to come forward about hiring James Hoover has got you seething too."

"I want to pound that ..."

"Take a chill pill. People flake. They get scared. It happens. Whatcha gonna do?" He gestures at the street. "Guy's gone."

"Yeah. Well, if he knows what's good for him, he'll run fast."

"Like you're gonna catch him in those Payless sandals."

I glance down. Kingsley's snow cone is lying beside my big toe, melted, the V-shaped paper sleeve housing it, soggy and flattened. I likely knocked it out of his grasp.

I point to the gooey liquid on the boards by my feet. "Sorry about your snow cone."

Kingsley shrugs. "No worries."

After leaving Ocean Grove, we zip to the Freehold Mall, where we rehash the day's events in the airconditioned food court. When Kingsley leaves the table to buy a fountain drink and a hot pretzel, I call Leeds, intending to tell him about James' twin Charles and the cartoon drawing on Reverend Shasta's chalkboard. Leeds doesn't answer, and I don't leave a voicemail message. What I need to tell him requires a conversation. All talked out, Kingsley and I wander through Macy's and eat dinner at the Cheesecake Factory. I spend a sleepless night in my motel room. The mattress is rock hard. As I toss and turn, images of Cassie, limp and covered in blackboard chalk dust, crowd my mind.

Chapter 11

B right and early the next morning, Kingsley and I check out of the Radisson. We hightail it back up Interstate 95, drop off the rental car, and head to the Newark Airport. I don't talk much on our afternoon flight. My conversation with Reverend Shasta has me conflicted. Kingsley is quiet too. Our visit to the Jersey shore seems to have impacted him. Seemingly lost in thought, he orders a scotch and soda and puts in earbuds.

Our plane lands in Manchester an hour and a half later. We locate my Subaru in the long-term parking lot, and drive back to New London. As the sun dims and becomes a gold dot in the early evening sky, I drop Kingsley off at the Fairway Motel.

As he climbs out of the SUV passenger seat, Kingsley squeezes my shoulder. "You did good," he says. "We now know how Hoover faked his death. We just have to get Leeds proof so he'll believe your theory. Be patient. The proof will come. We'll find it."

He salutes me, lumbers into his unit, and I take Seamans Road toward town and home. When I arrive at my farmhouse, I leave my bag in the foyer. After checking the downstairs rooms and finding them to be Worm Man-free, I stumble up to my bedroom. I collapse onto my bed, stare at the ceiling, and imagine Hoover doing unspeakable things to Cassie, making X patterns on her flesh with a razor blade. I spring off the bed and pace.

Be patient, Kinsley said. Is he for real? How can I possibly be patient when Cassie's life is clearly in jeopardy? August 30th is five days away.

Feeling as if I'm going to explode, I grab my cell off the bedside table and call Liam.

"Just came back from the Jersey shore," I say when he picks up.

"What? You came back from where?"

"From New Jersey. I went with Kingsley. Listen. We talked to Emily Rose, James Hoover's neighbor. She told us about seeing James in her basement. You're never gonna believe this. But James had a secret identical twin brother, same DNA. Parents hid him in the house because he was mentally challenged. James' twin died in that fire, not James. I know it sounds crazy, farfetched, and ridiculous. But it explains everything. James is here in the Lakes Region! We have to tell Leeds! We have to make him listen! We're running out of time!"

"Kate, hold on. Slow down. We've been over this before," Liam says. "That woman, Emily Rose, is senile. She was diagnosed with Alzheimer's over a decade ago. When the feds questioned her after the house fire, the details she gave pertaining to her James Hoover sighting didn't add up. Leeds isn't going to—"

"I know all of that. But when we spoke with her, yeah, Emily Rose was definitely confused. She didn't remember Kingsley, though they'd met before, or the volunteer working the reception desk. But when it came to James Hoover, she was clear as a bell. She remembers her distant past. It's the present that's—"

"Kate—"

"Listen, I didn't just call about Emily Rose. I called to tell you that Reverend Shasta was there too."

"The reverend was in New Jersey?" I've got his attention now. Liam seems genuinely surprised.

"It's weird, right? He claimed he was at a religious conference, but he wasn't. He was in Neptune City blessing this new house someone built on the lot where James Hoover's old house used to be. And get a load of this." I take a deep breath. "Maria, the girl I told you about before, the girl who's staying at the reverend's farm, is the reverend's daughter. And Shasta said that someone … no, not someone … the Worm Man used his chalkboard again. Only this time he drew a cartoon girl, wrote 'Cassie,' and put an X through it and the date 'August 30th.' The reverend will likely deny it. But I'm not making it up."

Liam exhales. "Did Shasta report the threat? Take a pic? Did anyone else see it?"

"No. None of that. But I know he wasn't lying."

"Kingsley was with you when the reverend spoke about all of this? He can corroborate this conversation?"

"No. Kingsley was on another part of the beach. It was just me and the reverend. But this is big, huge. I'm going to talk to Leeds. I'll call you back." I'm about to push the end call button on my cell, but the urgency in Liam's voice stops me.

"Wait! I think we should take a pause, to strategize," he says.

"But don't you see? August 30th is Thursday!"

"August 30th is also the anniversary of Glen's death. Doesn't that seem—"

My skin goes clammy. *Glen's death. I'd forgotten, or rather I'd tried to forget.*

Look," Liam says, "You have to be thinking about Glen. You were married almost twenty years."

I shake my head. "No. That's not what this is about."

Liam's voice softens. "Kate, I'm speaking to you as someone who cares about you."

"You think I'm losing it because of the anniversary?"

"No. I just know that you're under a hell of a lot of stress. I'm on your side here, Kate. I'm only saying that given the circumstances, I wouldn't run to Leeds with my theory, not unless I had my head clear and wasn't emotional. He's too good. You need to have all your ducks in a row, have all your thoughts squared up, before you talk to him. Otherwise, he'll trick you up."

"But Cassie ..."

"You're not going to be any good to Cassie if you're locked up."

I bite my lip. "So, what do I do?"

"My shift ends in two hours. Come over then. We'll talk things through. We'll figure out what makes sense. If you still feel the same way after we talk, then we'll go to Leeds with the information. Let's meet at my townhouse. I'll grab that pizza we didn't get before. How does that sound?"

"Your townhouse works fine. In two hours is fine too," I say, wishing it were sooner. "But I'll get the pizza," I tell him. "I need some air."

* * *

The Pizza Chef is packed with Colby Sawyer students celebrating the end of the summer term. Dressed in jeans and t-shirts, they devour slices and down soda and beer. I brush past them and hurry to the counter. George, the Pizza Chef owner, wipes his hands on his apron and slides a pencil behind his ear.

I retrieve a twenty from my purse. "Hey, George. How goes it?"

He rolls his eyes. "Crazy. Nuts. But I'm not complaining. Last week was deader than my Aunt Jenny's ghost."

I force a smile. "Glad things picked up. I'd like a large pepperoni pie with extra cheese."

George scribbles my order on a ticket. "Got it. Wait's twenty minutes."

I glance at the order tickets clipped to the holder wheel and scold myself for failing to call in or order online. Twenty minutes is reasonable. But the restaurant noise is already getting to me—the laughter, the giggles, and the young voices so eager, so optimistic. Desperate for quiet, I hurry past the crowded tables and booths, exit by the register, and wait outside beneath the roof overhang.

It's a warm evening. A choking humidity hangs in the air. It weighs on my flesh, making my limbs feel thick and swollen. I want to sit somewhere, but I'm antsy. I can't stop thinking about Cassie and the big X on Reverend Shasta's chalkboard.

You should have gone straight to Leeds, I tell myself. *Why did you let Liam stop you? Okay, so it's the anniversary of Glen's death. Of course, that's a big deal. But ...*

Have I been thinking about the date, dwelling on losing Glen? No, I decide, *definitely not. I've been so concerned with finding Cassie and coming to terms with Glen's infidelity, I haven't allowed myself to acknowledge the day's significance. Glen hurt and lied to me. He doesn't deserve my attention or tears.*

Though no one's occupying the bench outside the pizzeria, I stand by the entrance. There's an outdoor seating area behind the restaurant. But I don't go there either. Why? It's a gut thing. Trees surround the area. The patio tables aren't visible from the interior of the Pizza Chef or the parking lot.

Decades of thinking about the Worm Man have made me hyper-aware. I try to remain in plain sight, especially at night, and always when I'm feeling vulnerable, which I am right now. Normally when I'm feeling jittery, I'm drawn to lights—streetlights, interior lights, headlights, and flashlights. Lights mean safety, other people, and help.

A car horn honks. I turn toward the beep. That's when I notice Oscar Rossi's office light. It shines like a lighthouse beacon. Of course, I knew his dental office was there, tucked between that expensive gift shop that keeps changing owners and that clothing store that sells attire for mature women. I've been inside the revolving gift shop and the grandma store. But Oscar's not my dentist; nor was he Glen's. So, there was never a reason to enter his office. But I've got one tonight.

Oscar's blinds are up. He's facing a desktop computer. He's focused on whatever's on the screen. He doesn't see me or choose to see me, even though I'm lit by the neon glow of the Pizza Chef sign.

I step away from that sign. Darkness cloaks me. Though we chatted often when Oscar picked Cassie up from tutoring, I've avoided talking to him lately because of the investigation. But as I stare at his silhouette, I feel the urgency of time. Reverend Shasta refused to back me up. But if I can get Oscar to listen to me, maybe together he and I can get the feds to focus on Hoover. Liam told me not to talk to Leeds yet, but he didn't say anything about steering clear of Oscar.

I inch closer to the curb. *Not smart, Kate. You don't know what Leeds has told Oscar about you. If you confront him, it could blow up in your face. Most fathers would obliterate anyone they believe hurt their daughter.*

Maybe it's leftover headiness from my adventure with Kingsley at the shore. It could be my way of giving the finger to Glen, of saying "Cassie matters. You don't." Either way, I can't stop myself. I step off the curb and walk boldly toward Oscar's office. As I march, the thin soles of my sandals smack the hard pavement. Though my legs feel stiff from the flight, there's something freeing in what I'm about to do, necessary too. I picture the X over the chalkboard drawing Reverend Shasta described, and move toward the cluster of businesses.

In the semi-darkness of the parking lot, the exterior of Oscar's office looks like a movie set, quaint and old-fashioned. Awnings shield the front window from the moonlight. I inch toward those awnings. Even before I knock, before my toes hit the welcome mat, Oscar opens the door.

"Kate?" he says.

He steps back and ushers me in. His air-conditioning is on, and I feel it immediately. It's as if I've entered a freezer. Cool air blasts from a vent near the ceiling. Goosebumps form on my arms.

"Got a stack of paperwork to weed through. The cold air keeps me awake," he says, following my upward gaze. He shrugs. "Truth is. I can't concentrate. All I can think about is Cassie, and where she might be. If she's scared, if she's hurting."

Oscar's wearing a white medical coat and clutching a computer mouse.

When he looks at me, I see tension in his dark eyes. He blinks, and suddenly I'm so nervous I want to bolt. But I'm here, and he's here. And if I'm going to get the feds to listen to me about James Hoover, I can't wimp out. I enter the reception area. The door shuts behind me. Oscar stares at me like he's looking in a mirror. His face pales, and I know that he knows that Cassie is Glen's daughter. He didn't know when he picked up Cassie at my house after tutoring. I'm certain of this. I'm also certain that olive-skinned Ian, is Oscar's biological son. In my mind, Ian's paternity has never been in question.

"I take it, Leeds told you about Lauren and Glen?" I say.

Oscar's dark eyes narrow. "Yes."

"He told me too," I say, swallowing. Oscar fingers his computer mouse. Silence follows. I exhale. "I don't know what Leeds is saying to you exactly, but I didn't take Cassie. I don't have her."

Oscar nods. "Lauren thinks you do. But I never thought you took her, even now that you ..."

"That I might actually have a motive."

"Yes."

He walks over to a shelf above the reception desk. He places his mouse on a legal pad on the desk, and grabs a plastic mold of a set of teeth off the shelf. As he separates the upper teeth from the lowers, tears pool in his eyes. He doesn't hide them, doesn't even try.

"It's absurd," he says, staring through the window and into the night. "Now that I know Cassie's not my daughter, I'm even more desperate to find her. I have to tell her that I love her, that she'll always be my little girl." He gently places the mold of teeth onto his desk chair. "Don't get me wrong. I'm pissed as hell at Lauren for keeping her secret from me, for pretending, for stepping out on me. But finding Cassie is what matters now. Cassie's my princess. She and Ian are my world."

"Of course, they are." I motion to the stack of paperwork on his desk. "Look. I know you're busy, and that talking to me has to be uncomfortable. So, I'll get to the point. I just got back from New Jersey. I visited the town where this serial killer, James Hoover, was raised. Has Leeds told you about the Worm Man, about my connection to him, about the housefire?"

Oscar nods.

"Well, this elderly woman, this neighbor, she spotted Hoover after he allegedly burned to death. I spoke to her. I'm convinced James Hoover's still alive. I believe he took Cassie to get back at me. I think we should—"

Oscar raises his hand. "Kate, I'm gonna stop you right there." His next words startle me. "You were hospitalized in a mental health facility in New Jersey for paranoia and delusions before you moved to New London. Don't deny it. Lauren hired a P.I. to check you out. He told her all about it."

He frowns at me. "Paranoia and delusions are a big deal, Kate. You took students on field trips and supervised them in the playground. You tutored Cassie in the park after school. Who knows? You were probably there when the monster who grabbed Cassie was eyeing her. If you were medicated, or unwell, you could have missed things, things that should have been reported to the police, things that could have prevented Cassie from being abducted."

I blink rapidly. "No. It's not like that. Yes, I take medicine, but it doesn't make me fuzzy. I always watch for strangers. I never leave students unattended. If I'd noticed anything unusual, which I didn't, I would have reported it to the cops, to my principal."

"That all sounds good, but—"

"Listen. Please. Just listen to me. August 30th—"As my lips part, Oscar opens a drawer. He pulls out a gun. "Whoa," I say, waving my hands in surrender.

He strokes the gun nozzle. "You know, I actually taught Cassie how to shoot this thing. I took her to the range. Lauren thought I was nuts. She said Cassie was too young, too impulsive to handle anything more deadly than a butter knife, that New London is safe, not Roxbury or Mattapan, and that she'd end up shooting herself. But I took Cassie there anyway. I even hired a retired army sharpshooter to work with her, to teach her proper form, to school her on gun safety."

I stare at his gun. "But she's ten? I'm with Lauren on this. Oscar, what were you thinking?"

"Teaching Cassie about guns wasn't about gang violence or those school shootings you see all over the news," he says. "It was personal." His words jab me. "When I was a kid in Phili, my house was broken into. I was home alone. My dad had a gun in his bedside drawer. I knew it was there but didn't know how to use it. I hid under the bed and peed on myself while some meth loser robbed my parents blind. I thought, no way was I going to allow Cassie to feel that sense of powerlessness." He huffs. "Lots of good those shooting lessons did her. Guns aren't the problem." He looks at me with scorn. "People are. People like you, Kate." He stares at me. "You should have told the school administration about your issues, your psych hospitalization."

My words sound uncertain, even to me. "It was a long time ago. I'm better now. Yes, I still have panic attacks. But the paranoia and delusions are gone. They're under control."

"Don't give me that. You just flew to New Jersey to search for a ghost."

He shakes his head at me, as if the anxiety medication I'm on, Lexapro, is the same as heroine, like I'm careless, thoughtless, and irresponsible. And for a millisecond I decide I am. Then I look at the photo of Cassie on Dr. Rossi's wall, and I know I'm not. Since the moment I started teaching, I've put my students first, before myself, before Glen, and not just Cassie, all my students. No way did I ever put any of them at risk. I'm highly functional, rational. But it's clear Oscar doesn't believe this.

"I'm sorry," I say, backing away from him. "I'm sorry about everything."

Oscar puts his gun back in his drawer. I don't wait for him to pull it out again. Without saying goodbye, I dart out of his dental office. When I'm halfway across the parking lot, I hear the crash of glass shattering. I turn. Dr. Rossi's window is in a million pieces. His desktop computer is on the curb. Looking like a spirit in his white dentist coat, Oscar stands beneath his doorway, wailing. Some Colby Sawyer students getting out of a Honda rush to check on him.

My heart pounding, I quickly collect my pizza and hightail it to Liam's townhouse.

* * *

Liam's townhouse sits on the Lake Sunapee Country Club Golf Course. His back patio faces the tenth-hole green. The three-bedroom, three-bath, 1980s-style unit is a rental. Though Liam isn't a golfer, he claims the views of Mount Kearsarge lower his blood pressure and help him think.

The thinking part I can certainly relate to. My brain is going a mile a minute. As for my blood pressure, mine is likely through the roof.

I park crooked in Liam's driveway and switch off my headlights. My encounter with Oscar Rossi has me beyond rattled. My legs refuse to stop shaking. Every sound, each image I hone in on, is magnified. Instead of bringing clarity to Glen's affair and my current situation, seeing Oscar has muddied my perspective. No one's ever pointed a gun at me before. Even James Hoover, the demon from my nightmares, didn't do that. But despite everything, finding Cassie's backpack, confirming Glen's affair, meeting Emily Rose, uncovering Reverend Shasta's secret, and experiencing my run-in with Oscar—or rather because of it all—I want to see Liam. I need his comfort, his strength, and his calm, logical perspective.

I grab the warm pizza box off the passenger seat, and hurry through the semi-darkness to Liam's front door. I stand amidst the glow of his security light and ring his bell repeatedly. I've been here before, but not a lot, and only in the daytime.

Shifting my weight, I wait on the front landing until Liam's muffled voice seeps through the window screens. "Door's unlocked. Come in, Kate."

Balancing the pizza box on my hip, I rush into his foyer and look up. Liam is standing on the staircase in jeans and a polo shirt. His hair is damp, like he's just stepped out of the shower. Tall, dark, and buff he looks nothing like Glen, who was a ginger and artsy thin. Tonight, of all nights, the difference between the two men seems significant. I use it to support my belief that Liam isn't like Glen, not a liar or a cheat, that he'll have my back if Oscar comes for me.

As Liam descends the stairs, he frowns at me. "What's going on? You seem frazzled."

"I... he..."

"Let me guess. The Pizza Chef was a zoo."

"It was, but..."

Liam motions to the seating area in the living room. "Relax, Kate. Make yourself comfortable. George needs to hire another waitress. That's a given. I've been telling him to install another pizza oven since forever. Red wine?"

He pours and gives me wine. My heart thuds. "Oscar Rossi has a gun!" I gush. "He was waving it around his dental office. He smashed his office window too. Threw a computer through it."

Liam's eyes widen. "Jesus. Just now?"

"Yes. I went to talk to him. I saw him through the window when I was at the Pizza Chef."

"He threatened you?"

"No. Not really. But just seeing the gun, him having it, it scared the shit out of me." I chug some wine and tell him what went down. "Everyone is so on edge, so tense," I say, when I'm through catching him up to speed. "Even normal, rational people, like Oscar are acting crazy. And no one will listen to me."

"A missing child does that to people," Liam says. "And Oscar's been dealt a double whammy. Still, he has no business waving a gun around." He swivels toward the door. "I'm going over to his dental office."

"Don't. He wasn't going to hurt me," I say, though I'm not sure if this is true. "Please. Send someone else to check on him. I want you with me. You're not on duty," I add when he hesitates. "Please, don't leave me. I need you."

"I'll call the chief," Liam says, hugging me. He grabs his cell off the end table and speaks into it. "Kate Boswell just had a run-in with Oscar Rossi at his dental office. She's fine. But he's got a gun in his drawer. She said he wasn't threatening her, but that he was agitated, smashed his front window. Yeah. A welfare check. Proceed with caution. Let me know how things play out. Call me if you need backup."

Liam ends the call. We sit on his couch. He takes my hand in his. "Leeds told me he told you about Glen and Lauren. I'm sorry," he says.

I avert my eyes from his. "Thanks. But their affair wasn't why I spoke to Oscar. I was hoping I could convince him to talk to Leeds about James Hoover. I was worried because I thought Oscar would blame me once he knew Hoover grabbed Cassie. But the thing is, Oscar didn't even care about my connection to James Hoover. He found out I was hospitalized at a mental health facility in New Jersey. That's what set him off."

Liam looks at me and I explain. "It happened a decade ago, right before Glen and I moved here. I wasn't coping well because of Whitney's abduction. Though it had been years since it happened, the memories kept surfacing. I was having a ton of anxiety. I thought I could just keep powering through. But things came to a head. Anyhow, because of my issues, Oscar thought I might have missed something when I was with Cassie. Someone watching her in the park perhaps. He also thought I should have been upfront and told the school administration about my mental health history." I sigh. "Do you think he's right?"

"Don't do that to yourself, Kate," Liam says, stroking my hair. "Getting treatment when you need it is nothing to be ashamed of. It's a sign of strength. And your healthcare, mental or otherwise, is a private matter. It's your own business." He pats my hand. "Look, Oscar Rossi's upset in general. I mean, his daughter is missing. Then he finds out that his wife had an affair and that the missing girl he thought was his daughter, isn't even his. It's a lot. Too much. Of course, he lost it. He needs Lauren right now. He can't turn on her. So, naturally, he's gonna blame you and say you contributed to Cassie's situation."

Liam exhales. "Truth is, you caught Dr. Rossi at a bad time. I probably shouldn't tell you this, but you're gonna hear it from Leeds anyway. The hair in the sneaker, the one from your classroom closet, was Cassie's."

"Christ."

Liam speaks softly. "When I worked on the force in Boston, I was involved with a few child-abduction cases. When kids go missing, everyone looks for a scapegoat. The people who are hurting the most, the ones closest to the missing child, blame each other. It's human nature. It's our mind's way of coping and dealing with the guilt and pain."

I think of the Bays and my parents and how things between them changed after Whitney's murder. I suddenly want to call my mother. I'm regretting keeping her in the dark.

"We're going to find Cassie," Liam says. "You just have to hang tough. And remember, Oscar's rage and his nasty words are not really about you. Leeds is likely hounding him, like he's been hounding you."

I frown. "You just said *likely*. You don't know if he's hounding Oscar?"

"Nope. I'm not on the case anymore."

"What? Because of me?"

"It was my decision. Leeds and the chief need someone who can be objective, and that's not me."

"I'm sorry," I say.

"Don't be. It's for the best. And I'm fine with it."

I gulp down the rest of my wine. I don't believe him. Liam loves being in the thick of things. And from a career perspective, the Cassie Rossi case is high profile, career-changing.

I shake my head. "Wow. I'm sorry. You've given up a lot for me, too much. You becoming a detective...how does this affect that?"

"I'm still on track to take the exam. The chief reassigning me won't affect my career."

"You're lying. Don't do that. I'm not a big Leeds admirer, but I know you were learning a lot from him."

"I was. But it's no big deal. Besides, me being off Cassie's case means I get to focus on the important stuff—parking tickets, stray dogs, drunk college students, and you."

"Hey, you just lumped me in with all that crap."

I inch closer to Liam. I don't want to eat pizza right now. I don't want to argue about going or not going to Leeds about my conversations with Reverend Shasta and Emily Rose. One shaky trigger finger and Oscar could have ... I could have ... I don't like being the cause of Liam's career setback, but there's something sexy about Liam giving up his role in the case for me. Glen had to have everything: me, Lauren, Cassie, his career, and his reputation. He refused to choose. Liam's willingness to sacrifice for me makes him incredibly attractive.

I remove my wedding ring and slip it into my pocket. Kissing Liam on the mouth, I motion to the stairs.

"I don't think this is a good idea. You're upset," he whispers.

"I am," I murmur. "But, so what?"

He touches my lip. "This isn't ..."

"I want to be with you. I've wanted it for a while. It's not about Oscar, the gun, or punishing Glen. It's about us. I want ..."

I kiss his hand, his wrist, and his neck. Before I can rethink my actions, he scoops me up. As I cling to him, he carries me up the staircase and into his bedroom.

Chapter 12

I wake the next morning in Liam's bed. He's at the police station. A dozen white asters and a note rest on my pillow. The note reads, *"We'll talk tonight. Hang tough. We'll figure this thing out. Promise."* As images from our sultry night flicker through my mind, I dress and drive back to my farmhouse.

With everything that's going on with Cassie's disappearance, and my feelings about my marriage to Glen being so conflicted, building a relationship with Liam is hard to fathom. I don't know where things with us are headed, but I know I've got his support and more. Liam told me last night that of course there have been other women in his past, but no one special, no one like me. It could be a line. It could be all BS. But I want to believe him. But regardless of what develops between us, I feel good about last night. The sex was amazing, different and gentler than with Glen. I can see myself getting addicted to his touch. He makes me feel safe, as if it's okay for me to be myself.

Being with Liam makes me hopeful about my future, confident too. I decide to visit Leeds at the station. I'm going to convince him that James Hoover is alive. But first, I need to take a quick shower.

As the morning sun warms my windshield, I park in my driveway. But instead of going straight inside and up to my master bathroom, I head to the backyard, to Georgia's birch tree. I'm feeling sentimental. I want to place Liam's asters beneath its branches. As I move across the grass, the coos of a mourning dove comfort me. The raised beds of my tomato garden, brimming with life, give me hope. But when I duck beneath the clothesline, my blood goes cold.

The birch tree, which stands six feet tall and has a trunk as wide as a mini watermelon, is now severed at the base. Not only did someone chop down Georgia's tree, they cut it into pieces and tore off its branches. The tears are uneven, like a madman ripped it apart. I look down and shudder. Deep blade marks mar the ground around my sneakered feet. Like drops of blood, leaves splatter the grass.

I stare at the destruction. "You're not going to win this time, Hoover! I'm going to beat you!"

I place Liam's asters in my birdbath bowl and march to my garage. When I lift the manual door, it screeches like a howler monkey. Squinting into the shadows, I slink into the musty space. Hammers, cutters, a can of gasoline, and screwdrivers line the shelves.

I go for a saw hanging on the wall rack, and grab a wheelbarrow with my free hand. Moving quickly, I place the saw into the wheelbarrow's steel tray where I can reach it. Then I push the wheelbarrow through the wide garage door opening. Back outside, I start to collect the mangled birch branches, keeping my eyes peeled. Ten minutes later, sweating and trembling, I push my load to the cellar door, stack the branches beside the hose spigot, and enter my house through the kitchen, wielding my saw. As I'm turning off my alarm, the cell in my pocket chimes. I answer the call. It's Randi.

"So, Kate. Why didn't you tell me about that girl, Whitney?" she snaps. "I mean, I get that it was awful, traumatic, not something you want to share. But I'm your best friend. I've known you for ten years. What the hell! You've never once mentioned her or your hospitalization. Don't you trust me? I feel like you're a stranger."

"How did you? Never mind— Of course, I trust you. And you're right. I should have told you about Whitney, about my illness. The thing is, I didn't tell anyone about any of it, just the people who had to know—Glen, Liam, the feds, and this reporter who's helping me. Listen, Randi. I'm super sorry. You're a great friend, the best. And we can talk about all of it. I'll answer every single one of your questions." I peer around the breakfast table and into the shadowy hallway. "But the thing is, I'm dealing with a situation here. James Hoover could be...What I'm saying is, he chopped down my birch tree."

"It wasn't James Hoover," Randi says quickly.

I picture Oscar's shattered office windowpane, his computer on the asphalt. "Then it was probably Oscar Rossi. He and I had words. Things got a little crazy. Liam sent another cop over to check on him last night, but—"

"Could have been Oscar, but it could have been anyone."

I stumble backward. My dishwasher handle rams my buttock. "I don't ..."

"There's been a ton of social media posts about you," she says. "Ever since Leeds searched your house on Thursday, the parents from school have been posting— Lauren's PTA friends, Janet and Celine, the soccer moms. Some teachers commented too. I'm not sure if Lauren's prodding them. My point is everyone's riled up. Someone who read the posts likely chopped down your tree."

She exhales. "If I'd known about your past, about Whitney, about the clinic, I could have done damage control, at least tried to contain the backlash. But you left me in the dark. My God, we searched the park together. You climbed that slide. Your friend Whitney was snatched on a park slide, and you didn't mention a thing. No wonder you were so adamant about searching the park. I feel like an idiot." Her voice shakes. "Is there anything you want to tell me, Kate? 'Cause like I said before, you can trust me. I don't care if it's bad. I'd rather hear it from you."

"No. It's like you said. I saw my friend get abducted. Actually, I was grabbed too, but I escaped. I lost it two decades later, and was hospitalized. End of story."

"You sure? 'Cause no matter what, I'm your girl. I'm your ride or die. I'm not going to abandon you."

My eyes mist. "I know that. Your loyalty, your friendship, they mean everything to me. I'm sorry," I say. "I should have told you about my past. It's just that your life is so normal, so perfect. My life is messy. I didn't want you to think badly of me."

"I don't. I could never." Her voice quiets. "Newsflash, my life's not perfect either. Have you forgotten that Bill almost got that DUI after the Sunapee Realtor's Convention last April? If the cop hadn't been a previous client...And my sister, Sara, remember her? She had that affair with her kid's travel soccer coach. Oh, and last night, Justin wet his bed. I changed his sheets. I still smell like pee."

"But none of that's you, and compared to my baggage..."

"Stop it. I love you. End of story."

"I love you too."

"No more secrets?"

"No more secrets."

I glance around the kitchen. Except for the dripping of the faucet, it's quiet. As I inhale, attempt to regain my composure, the faint sent of Pine-Sol wafts off the floor. "So, out with it," I say. "What's everyone saying about me? Tell me. All of it."

"The basic gist is this: some people actually believe you've got Cassie stashed somewhere, which is ridiculous. But the majority are just mad because they think you put their children at risk."

"Are they blaming me because the Worm Man is here, in New London?"

"No. They don't think he's here. They think he's dead. They're convinced you're unstable. Not just because you were hospitalized a decade ago, but because you've been looking for the Worm Man now. You went to Maine to search for him and you flew to New Jersey to check out his hometown. Don't deny it. You told Oscar you went to see the Worm Man's neighbor." Randi's voice quiets. "Kate, you do know James Hoover's dead, right?"

"I ..." My knees buckle. I slide to the floor. The saw that's still in my grasp clanks on the tile. Now's not the time to tell her about my secret identical twin theory. She'll think I'm bonkers. Convincing Leeds that Hoover is alive suddenly feels impossible.

"Of course, it's all stupid," Randi says, rambling. "But stupid or not, it's out there. And people are taking it seriously. Like I said, it's likely that one of the parents chopped down your tree. Social media stuff makes everyone crazy. The social media hype is probably what set off Oscar. You should call Leeds and tell him about the tree."

"No," I say. "Someone will see his car heading to my house. They'll post something about it and twist everything up."

Silence follows. Randi seems to think. "Bill's home. He's in between clients. I'll send him over. He can look around for you and make sure your place is safe."

"No need to bother him. Those soccer and PTA moms won't do anything scary. They're all show, flash and drama." My throat tightens. I squelch a sob.

"I'm sorry this is all happening to you, Kate," Randi says. "It sucks.

Social media and smear campaigns suck. But they're gonna find Cassie, and it'll all blow over. People will forget. They should apologize to you. But more than likely, they won't."

I nod. "I don't need an apology. I just want everything to be normal again." I think about how nothing has been normal for me since Cassie's abduction. "What if they don't find Cassie?"

"They will."

"Promise?"

She sighs into the phone. When the call ends, I'm unsettled, but no longer terrified. I'm pretty sure it was just a PTA mom who went all Paul Bunyan on my tree. Even so, despite this belief, and the sunlight shining through the window above my sink, I shiver. I place my saw on the breakfast table, grab my cell, call the online nursery, and order a new birch tree.

I spend the rest of the day rereading Kingsley's Worm Man book. Five hours later, having finished his true crime novel, I stream a *Dateline* episode about James Hoover's second victim, the girl from the Poconos. Like the evidence in Kingsley's book, I'm familiar with the clues documented on the TV show. One thought sticks with me. Hoover held his three victims captive in different places—a hunting cabin, an abandoned warehouse, and a storage unit. My takeaway is this—James isn't afraid to mix things up. Frustrated, I make a list of potential holding places.

1. *A vacation cottage*
2. *Campsite*
3. *Basement with external access*
4. *Vacant RV*
5. *Barn*

Bottomline, Cassie could be almost anywhere. What she needs most now is the will to survive.

I spend the evening and night that follow at my breakfast table, drawing Cassie and attempting to breathe life and strength into her penciled image.

Cassie's a tough cookie, I tell myself, staring at the Cassie I create on the page. And even though she's not my daughter, and loving her seems inappropriate, as if I've crossed a line, traversed a professional boundary, I know I do...And not just because she's Glen's daughter, but because being with her brings me joy.

Thinking about my affection for Cassie, makes me think about Liam. My memories of our night together are so vivid and intense, I can almost taste the wine on his lips, the salt of his sweat.

Trembling, I rest my head on a sketchbook and pray for Cassie's safe return. I shut my eyes as the sun begins to rise. I wake three hours later. As I'm jamming bread in the toaster, I get a call from Principal Jane.

"Can you come to my office today?" she asks.

When Randi called yesterday, she didn't mention Jane wanting to see us. "When?" I ask.

Jane's words are clipped. "Now would be ideal. It's important."

I swallow. "I've got to shower and change. Give me thirty minutes."

* * *

Jane's office is neat, obsessively so. I sit in a chair facing her desk and stare at the erasers stacked on her blotter. As I fidget, Jane fingers a pen. Her long face and square forehead, combined with her short white hair, make her look like actress Jamie Lee Curtis.

"You're one of my best teachers," she says, holding my gaze. "You're dedicated. Your classroom test scores are awesome, but more importantly, your students love school. Trust me. I understand how hard it is to instill a passion for learning. That's no small feat. That's why this is so difficult for me."

I wave my hand. I don't care if she sees my fingers trembling. "Please, Jane. My students mean the world to me. I know there's a lot of buzz, a lot of craziness surrounding me with Cassie still being missing, but I didn't take her. You know that."

She nods. "Of course, I do. Anyone who knows you knows that."

"Then I don't see the issue. I can still teach even if my life is nuts. Trust me. I'm used to chaos." I motion to the door. "The second I walk into my classroom I block everything else out. I did it when Glen died. I can do it now. I won't drop the ball. I won't let you down. I promise."

Jane frowns. Desperation surges through me. I need my paycheck. But more importantly, my sanity is at stake here. Without my students, my purpose, I'll crumble. My voice rises. "Look. My life has been hectic, and I've always performed. I got all 'A's in high school while working a part-time job and playing varsity field hockey. When IBM laid off my father, I paid my college tuition waitressing and still graduated at the top of my class. And three years ago, I was nominated for New Hampshire Teacher of the Year. That was the same year I underwent IVF treatment. You ask anyone. They'll tell you Kate Boswell can juggle. I won't make excuses for myself."

"You're a survivor and an achiever," Jane says, nodding. "There's no doubt. But you should have told me about your connection to the Worm Man, and his lasting impact on your daily life. You should have been transparent."

"When? When you interviewed me that first time? You wouldn't have hired me."

She shakes her head. "That's not true."

"It is."

"Kate, if I'd known about the trauma you experienced, I could have supported you better, especially after Glen passed. But the way things stand now, by teaching at this school, you're putting my students at risk. It's my job as principal to be sure my students are in capable hands."

"But you just said—"

"I'm not talking about your students' test scores. I'm referring to your breakdown."

"I'm fine now. That was ten years ago."

Jane sighs. "I'm not talking about your New Jersey hospitalization, Kate. I'm talking about your current break down. You're not okay. You're struggling now. Look, I'm not faulting you. You've been through a lot, too much. This is about optics. I'm not judging you."

"It's because of the internet stuff, isn't it? Those trolls are pressuring you to fire me."

"Not trolls, parents. And no one said anything about firing you." Jane retrieves a sheet of paper from her desk drawer. It's a petition with one hundred and eight signatures. "Ninety percent of the incoming parents in the third grade signed it," she tells me. "The school board wants me to put you on a temporary leave of absence, just until things get straightened out. Don't look at me like that," she says, as my eyes pool with tears. "I'm not punishing you."

But it feels as if she is. And the truth is, I can't blame her. I probably should have been up front about my stay at the Carrier Clinic and my history with the Worm Man. But if you tell a potential employer that you witnessed your childhood friend's abduction and that you were hospitalized at a mental health facility because you couldn't deal with the lingering trauma of her murder, they look at you differently. They think you're tainted. It doesn't matter the circumstances, or the strides you've made.

I count my heartbeats in an effort to keep from losing it.

"I'll keep in touch. You stay in contact too." Jane pats my hand. "I'm rooting for you, Kate. But my hands are tied. Marsha Hanson from human resources will call you regarding the leave paperwork." Her gaze settles on the wall behind me. "I need your building and classroom keys. You're no longer allowed on school grounds. I'm sorry."

I fish in my bag for my keys and drop them on her desk. As I face the principal I've known and worked with for ten years, more tears bubble in my eyes. When Jane stands, I step away so she doesn't hug me. As I march out of her office with my head held high, there's this sense that my teaching career is over.

The office door slams shut behind me. I take in the New Hampshire flag in the hall, the awards case, the "Welcome Back Incoming Students" banner, and the mural of New London my students and I painted on the wall opposite the entryway. My throat catches. I'm torn between memorizing it all, every last detail, and bolting. I opt for a middle course. I look straight ahead and walk briskly out of the building and to my Subaru. Trembling, I jam my key into my ignition and zoom out of the lot.

* * *

Normally when I'm upset, I go to Glen's grave. But the cemetery, home to the bones of my unfaithful husband, is the last place I want to be. I drive toward the police station, determined to talk to Leeds about James' twin Charles and Hoover's chalkboard threat. But when I reach the parking lot entrance, I press hard on my accelerator and zoom by. If the school parents and Jane think I'm delusional, Leeds likely does too. Talking to him seems futile. Driving aimlessly, I take Main Street past the shopping area and drive toward Highway 89. I zip up the ramp and head south toward Warner. It's a brisk, sunny day. The lanes are uncrowded. The trees surrounding the highway make it difficult to see life happening around me, and maybe that's for the best.

I grip my steering wheel and scream. I'm angry. I feel helpless, like there's nothing I can do to fix the awful situation. Lauren, the Worm Man, Reverend Shasta, and Leeds, their faces shuffle in my mind. I speed up and cut off a minivan. I hate that Jane and the parents think I'm unwell. I want to set them straight. But getting them to see me as a healthy woman capable of guiding their children seems beyond my reach.

I drive for fifteen minutes. When I see exit 9, Highway 103, I turn. The Market Basket, a regional grocery chain, is located down the road. I head toward it. When I spot the store through the trees, it occurs to me that my fridge and cupboards are bare. I don't want to go to my local store any time soon, too many familiar faces. I picture the chopped-up birch tree and the signatures on the petition. *Best to get your groceries now.* I pull into the half-filled lot and park. My mind is running a mile a minute. I think about how James Hoover filled his prescription at the pharmacy near here. I'm so distracted that I trip over a cement parking bumper.

As moms with kids push carts toward and away from the store entrance, I grab my own cart and hurry inside. The store is old and cold. As a grocer sorts through a bin of peaches, tossing out bruised and overripe ones, I think about Cassie. Is she bruised? Is she expired? I shut my eyes and see her white-blonde hair matted and bloodied.

The produce grocer eyes me. "Do you need help, ma'am?"

I shake my head, place a bunch of bananas in my cart, and move toward the refrigerated section. As I drop milk and butter in the flip-up child seat, a woman in a cotton sundress frowns at me. I peer at my reflection in a glass pastry case. My waterproof mascara's intact, and my boobs aren't popping out of my V-neck. I shake my head and tell myself I imagined her negative reaction. But as I put a loaf of bread into my cart, one of the clerks points at me.

What the …? I hurry to the self-check area, bag, and pay for my groceries. As I wait for my change to spit from the machine, my gaze drifts to the newsstand. I gasp. My face is on the *Concord Monitor* and beneath it the headline, "Local Teacher, Award-Winning Artist, and X-Mental Patient Is a Suspect in the Cassie Rossi Abduction Case." *The Boston Herald* reads, "Prime Suspect, Kate Boswell, Wronged in Love Triangle."

Without waiting for my coins, I grab my bags and bolt from the store. I tear across the parking lot, jump into my SUV, and auto-lock the doors. I punch my steering wheel and look up. The sky, which only minutes ago had been bright and sunny, is now grey. I fumble in my purse for my cell. I want to call Liam, but what's happening is a lot, even for an understanding decent man like him.

He's going to dump you, I tell myself. *A cop can't be romantically involved with a kidnapping suspect. Plus, how can you trust him? You trusted Glen and look where that got you?*

But you love Liam? I argue, realizing for the first time that I do. *But if you truly love him, you'll let him go.* I counter, *You're a disaster. If you don't push him away, you'll drag him down with you and ruin his life. He's already been taken off Cassie's case because of you.*

Lightning flashes and raindrops pound my windshield. I flip on my headlights, start my engine, and switch on my wipers. As rainwater churns beneath my wheels, I drive back up Highway 89. When my windshield fogs up, I switch on my defrost and roll down my window. Raindrops splatter my arms.

Either Jane spoke to Randi or Randi saw the newspapers. Randi calls me eleven times. Instead of answering, I put my cell on vibrate and consider phoning Thurston, but don't. I can't deal with legal stuff now. Though at some point Thurston will have to look over my leave of absence papers.

Feeling the need to hide, to be camouflaged, I drive in the middle lane between two large trucks until I spot my exit. My farmhouse looks lonely and timid when I reach it ten minutes later. The shades are shut; the front lawn is slightly overgrown. Three circulars lay in my drive. I climb my porch steps and get as far as the front foyer before I drop to the floor, and my cell buzzes. This time it's my mother. Randi likely told her I'm in trouble. Either that or Mom's been checking the local news on the internet. I pick up this time. I have to. I've pushed Mom off long enough.

"Mom." Before I even hear her voice, tears cloud my eyes.

"Katie, my angel," she coos. She sounds far away. The travel itinerary she emailed me before her departure puts her in Venice. "I spoke to Randi. She told me what's going on. I'm taking the next flight to Logan."

"Don't. Nothing's really happened. I'm on leave. That's all."

"Come on, Kate. This is me you're talking to. That poor girl …"

"Cassie."

"Yes, Cassie. Have they found her?"

"No. It's been almost a week. Mom, it's been awful."

"I can't even imagine."

Yes, you can, I think.

"The feds keep questioning me," I say. "I hired Thurston Bay to help me with the legal part. I didn't know who else to ask. Mom, I'm scared. I don't know how everything got so messed up. Everyone's so angry, so mean. Instead of looking for Cassie, they're—Mom, I feel like they're all against me, attacking me." I press my palm against my chest and breathe.

"It happens," Mom says as I shut my eyes. "When Whitney was killed, the Bays were furious with your dad and me."

"What do you mean, furious? The Bays were mad at you? I knew things were awkward between you. But you never told me they were angry with you."

"We couldn't. You were punishing yourself enough."

"But why were they mad at you? I'm confused."

"It doesn't matter. It's water under the bridge."

"Mom, it does matter. Please tell me." I hiccup tears.

"Take a deep breath."

I swallow. "I'm good. Mom, just tell me."

Her words fill my ears. "The Bays were upset because the cops brought in a group of suspects for questioning, and your father and I wouldn't allow you to look at the lineup. You'd already given a description, helped their sketch artist with a drawing, and looked at two other lineups. We thought that was enough, that anything more would send you over the edge. You'd pretty much shut down at that point."

Mom exhales. "Well, it turns out James Hoover was one of the men the police dragged in that fifth day. The cops didn't have enough evidence to hold him, so they released him. He left and murdered Whitney a few hours later."

My heart thuds. "So, if I'd gone, she'd still be alive?"

"Maybe. Maybe not. Who knows if you would have even ID'd Hoover? But you not going to that lineup was our decision, your father's and mine, not yours. If anyone was to blame, it was us, not you. My point is, as time passed, the Bay's anger toward us subsided. They see things differently now. But people in the thick of things, like Cassie's parents, scared hurting people, they blame. You can't take it personally. But you do have to protect yourself."

"I am. At least, I'm trying too. Mom, why didn't you tell me about the lineup? At least ask me if I wanted to go?"

"You were fragile, hanging by a thread. As your parents, we had to make a choice: the investigation or you. Your father and I chose you."

"But Whitney—"

"I don't regret shielding you. I'd do it again in a heartbeat. You're my daughter. How could I not protect you?" Mom's voice quiets. "How are you feeling? Are you taking your pills?"

"Of course. Always. Mom, listen. I don't know how much Randi told you. I know it sounds crazy, but James Hoover's alive."

"Oh, honey. He's not alive. He's dead, been dead for ten years."

"No. No. He's not. I swear it."

Mom sighs. "Oh, sweetie. I think this thing with your student has done a number on you."

"Mom, I know what I know."

"Perhaps, but I'm coming home. You need me. I'll call you the second I arrive in Boston."

"Mom, don't come. It's not safe here. Hoover could come after you."

The phone line crackles. "I'll be fine," Mom assures me. "I'll text you my flight details. Love you."

The call ends. Mom's words echo in my mind, not just the loving ones, but her words about Hoover too. *They released James Hoover and he murdered Whitney a few hours later.*

Essentially, Whitney died because my parents saw me as weak. Guilt courses through me. And along with it, comes the shame of being perceived as helpless and unstable. Still sitting on the foyer floor, I hug my knees against my chest and rock.

If my own mother thinks I'm losing it, then maybe I am. I think about how I came to believe that Hoover was alive and holding Cassie. It was the worms in the jar, combined with the timing of Cassie's abduction and the art show, Kingsley's theories that coincided with mine, hearing the Paula Abdul song, Emily Rose's words, and Reverend Shasta's comments. It all seems flimsy when I think about it now, ridiculous and farfetched. Still, I stand by my theory.

But one thing is certain: Mom loves me regardless. *Family,* I think, *you can always count on family when you're in a jam.*

That's when it hits me, a possible path to finding Hoover. What if James Hoover didn't just contact his brother, Samuel? What if he reached out to his nephew too? A young man whose mother passed when he was an impressionable teen might be willing to give a manipulative psychopath a chance.

It's just a theory, and it isn't much. But it's enough to get me off the foyer floor, to keep me from withering. I have to do something. Me doing nothing, led to Whitney's death.

I find, and turn on my laptop. When we spoke on the bus, Samuel said his son was a sophomore at Dartmouth. He mentioned his son's name too, Hollister. I Google Hollister Hoover Dartmouth sophomore. An image of a nerdy teen pops on my computer screen. Below the image is the caption, "Local Bradford Boy Admitted to Dartmouth." I skim the brief article that highlights Hollister's high school accomplishments, print out the pic, and vow to track down Hollister in the morning.

Just get through tonight, I tell myself.

As the wall clock ticks and it starts to rain, I lock the doors, check the windows and my alarm system, and grab a steak knife from the kitchen utility drawer. Clutching my knife, I sit on the den couch and stare at the dark television. My phone keeps vibrating, but I don't respond. What's there to say? Hoover's alive. No one's willing to admit to this, except a journalist/true crime writer whom everyone says is desperate for new material and publicity, and an Alzheimer's patient the authorities deem delusional.

I place my knife on the coffee table, grab a bottle of white wine from the dining room cabinet, and down two glasses and a third. The alcohol makes me dizzy, reckless. I locate my computer in the kitchen, type in Reddit, and read the comments.

Anyone who saw that drawing from the gallery show knows she's off. Paranoid delusional people shouldn't be teaching our children.

No wonder her husband got so sick. The stress of living with her must have been monumental. Bitch is batty. A nightmare.

She lives in that farmhouse in the middle of nowhere. The cops should be checking those fields behind her barn for a body.

As my vision blurs, the doorbell rings. Liam's muffled shouts seep through the door. "Kate. It's me, Liam. It's pouring out here. Let me in."

I stumble to the foyer, and open the door. Too tall to fit, Liam is slouched beneath the doorframe. As rain pounds the lawn behind him, I usher him inside. He lowers his jacket hood.

"Listen," he says, stomping on my floor mat, "I know you're upset. Randi told me Jane put you on leave, but you can't go MIA. You have to answer your calls, your texts. Everyone's worried about you. I'm worried about you." He touches my cheek. Though his fingers are cold and wet, I don't pull away. "Last night was special to me," he murmurs. "I've been thinking about you, about us, all day."

"Me too, about you."

I shut the door behind him and we embrace.

"I'm sorry for turning off my phone," I say. "I'm sorry you were worried. But as you can see, I'm fine. Well, as fine as I can be under the circumstances. Come in," I say, attempting to smooth my wrinkled dress. "We don't have stand here in the foyer. Let's sit in my den."

As I stagger down the hall, he trails me. He motions to the overnight bag by the entryway table.

"I'm not running away," I say, gesturing at the bag. "I went to the Jersey shore with Kingsley, remember? I just haven't carried my bag upstairs yet."

We enter the den. Liam glances back toward the foyer. "Look, I didn't want to say anything last night," he says. "You had enough to deal with after your encounter with Oscar. And the truth is, I didn't want to ruin what was happening between us. Being with you was awesome, beyond what I ever imagined it could be like."

"I feel the same way."

He points to the nearly empty wine bottle and glass on the coffee table. "You've been drinking. Now's probably not the best time for a serious conversation. But you need to hear this, Kate. That reporter's got ulterior motives."

"Kingsley? No. He doesn't. He's helping me. He's as determined to find Hoover and Cassie as I am."

"No, your instincts were right that night at the gallery. Kingsley's writing another book. I'd bet my season Celtic tickets on it. Don't you get it?" he says, when I purse my lips. "You're his long-awaited sequel, Kate. His first book was about Whitney and the Worm Man's two other victims. This second book is about you: the only surviving witness. Kingsley's leading you on a wild goose chase, studying your reactions, and taking notes."

"You're wrong," I say, sinking onto the couch, my cheeks fiery. "Kingsley's helping me find Cassie. And the truth is, I need him. No one else is listening to me. Not Leeds. Not you. Not Randi. Kingsley's the only one. He connected me with Emily Rose. She..."

"That old woman with Alzheimer's? Did Kingsley tell you she mistook her son-in-law for Jeffery Dahmer and her nurse for Andrea Yates? Did he tell you that?"

When I don't speak, Liam says. "I don't want you to see him anymore."

I flinch. "Whoa."

"I'm sorry. That came out wrong. You're your own person. Obviously, you can see whoever you like. We're not married. We're not even an official couple. But I want us to be. I love you, Kate. There, I've said it. If I'm being honest, I've been in love with you for a long time, since before Glen passed, since that first day I saw you on that playground."

"You never...I..."

Liam's voice quiets. "You were kneeling on the blacktop. You'd just finished drawing this amazing chalk merry-go-round over by the jungle gym. The kids were all pretending to ride on it. They kept running in circles. You had chalk dust on your cheek, chalk in your hands, and you were grinning... not just with you lips, but with your eyes. I thought, this woman is incredible. You started humming that organ music they play on merry-go-rounds. When you hopped onto one of those imaginary horses you'd sketched and whinnied, and I knew I was a goner." He smiles. "My sister's work schedule at the bank changed after that. She didn't need me to pick up my niece, Emma, anymore. But I kept coming to the school anyway. I had to see you."

"I..."

"You probably don't remember any of that," Liam says. "You were with Glen. You probably didn't even notice me."

"Oh, I definitely noticed you," I say, peering into his eyes. "A uniformed cop carrying a pink unicorn backpack, tall, handsome. You stood out. When you lifted Emma onto that high jungle gym bar with one arm, I thought this guy can't be real. I actually pinched myself. I was sure I was dreaming."

Liam motions to the den window. "Come with me. Ride with me in my patrol car. Not much is going on tonight. Just some downed trees, a bit of flooding over by Murray Pond. We can talk. Figure things out."

He looks at me. I see the love in his eyes. I want to go with him. I want to let him protect me. But I allowed Glen to take care of me, and I didn't fare well. And looking back, I understand why. After I was hospitalized at the Carrier Clinic, Glen stopped listening to me. He started making decisions for me, as if I were no longer his equal. First, he stopped valuing my judgment. Then he stopped valuing me.

"I'll go. But we need to settle something first. James Hoover is alive. I'm not crazy," I say, my voice even keeled. "I'm not having issues like in New Jersey. This is different. It's not in my head. Do you believe me? Be honest."

Liam exhales. "I believe evil people live on, even after they're dead, in our minds. Because of the impact of the horrific deeds, they linger. Does he still affect people? Yes. Is he living and breathing? No. What I'm saying is that I believe Hoover's still here, but perhaps not in the same way that you do."

I frown. "See ... that's ..."

He shakes his head. "I'm sorry, Kate. But you asked me to be truthful. The evidence doesn't support your theory. Like I said before, I've gone over Hoover's file a hundred times. There is no secret twin brother. Don't you think the feds would have found some record of Charles if he truly existed? Emily Rose is an identical twin herself. That's probably where she got the idea from." He touches my shoulder. "Kate, James Hoover is dead. His death should bring you comfort. It shouldn't be the other way around. I don't want to argue about this. If you and I have different thoughts on this issue, so what? It shouldn't matter."

But it does, and we both know it. It's like being on the opposite sides in a war. It's like being a born-again Christian and loving an atheist. It matters.

Liam's voice softens. "We don't have to settle our differences now. Just come with me. I just need to know you're safe." His eyes swing to the knife on my coffee table.

That's when I know I can't go with him. He wants me to ride with him because he thinks I'm a danger to myself. He's not worried about Hoover, the storm, Oscar, or the internet trolls coming after me. Just like my parents, thirty years ago, he thinks I can't handle the stress of the investigation. He thinks I've lost it. In his mind, I'm a fragile monster.

I stand. "I'll call you if I need anything. Tell Randi I'm okay."

"Kate, please."

I point to the foyer. "Just go."

"Listen. I love—"

"If you love me, you'll leave me be. I need to be alone."

"But..."

"I'm begging you."

"Kate, don't..."

"Please leave."

"Call me."

He marches back into the foyer, exits out the front door, and darts through the pouring rain to his car. Though he turns off his headlights, I see his cruiser parked beside my mailbox. It's just a shadow, but I know he's there, watching over me. For a few breaths, his presence comforts me. But then I blink, and the memory of Glen keeping a bedside vigil after my miscarriage surfaces. I grab another bottle of wine from the cupboard, down a glass, and chug another.

Chapter 13

*T*he morning sun jolts me. I roll off the den couch and squint out the window. Liam's cruiser is gone, but three news vans are parked in front of my farmhouse. When I spotted my name in the Market Basket newspapers, I knew the reporters were coming. Even so, their presence shocks me.

I close my curtains, trip upstairs, and take a hot shower.

I'm dizzy, my legs feel hangover weak, I'm nauseous, and my head aches. And these are just my physical concerns. For the first time, things are shaky between Liam and me. I love him and he loves me, but maybe that's not enough. Wrapped in a towel, I turn on and check my cell. Though I have a zillion texts and my voicemail mailbox is full, I don't listen to or read any of my messages. Knowing Liam's, Randi's, and Mom's concerned thoughts will only make me feel worse.

I think about my plan to talk to Samuel Hoover's son, Hollister. In the light of day, tracking Hollister down on his campus and getting him to tell Leeds that his uncle is alive and where he's hiding feels like a long shot. But it's the only plan I've got. The complications don't end there. I'm trapped. If I leave my farmhouse, the reporters will follow me.

Get dressed, I tell myself. *You won't be going anywhere if you don't put on some clothes.* I open my closet and kneel on the carpet. As I drag my nails through the thick nylon weave, my eyes drift to the storage bin, the one beside my snow boots.

The clothes in that bin are mine, but from another time, a different life. I wore them when I lived in New Jersey and commuted to NY City, back when I was actively building my career as a professional drawing artist. I looked different then, dramatically so. I felt different too, hopeful and young, not exactly innocent, but definitely not jaded. I lug out and open the bin of chic designer garments, shoes, and accessories, so different from the conservative practical teacher clothing I sport in New London. I select a grey silk romper and black sandals with heels. I slip on a turquoise bangle bracelet and blow my hair out so it isn't wavy. The makeup comes next: eyeliner, matte lipstick, and blush. But what really seals the deal is the black Hermès bag. I peer at my image in the full-length wall mirror and don't recognize myself. I hope no one else sees Kate Boswell, the third-grade teacher, hiding beneath the designer garb.

Satisfied with my look, I transfer my wallet and keys into my Hermes Birkin, head to kitchen and force down a banana, some crackers, an Advil, and a bottle of Gatorade.

My next step is finding a vehicle. I can't use mine. The cops and press will spot it. I glance out the back window. Glen's pickup is still in the barn at the far edge of our property. I drive it biweekly to keep it running. There's an access road behind the barn. The road starts at the base of the cornfield and swerves to the main road fronting the orchard. Once I get to the orchard, I can simply drive out of town. The key is getting to the barn unseen. What I need is a distraction.

I find my Subaru key and consider setting off my car alarm. But the savvy reporters have likely seen that trick before. I could call Randi and ask her to divert them. But like everyone else, she doesn't believe James Hoover is alive. She'll tell me I'm going on a fool's quest. I don't need pushback. As my thoughts churn, I hear a rumble outside. I pull the curtain aside and peek at the street. A UPS truck, likely the one delivering my new sapling birch, is pulling into my driveway. The reporters are watching it. They're focused on the truck.

"Go!" I tell myself. "It's now or never."

I grab my bag off the table, scamper out the back door, and squint. The morning sun is bright, and the lawn shines with dew. Unstable in my heels, I stumble across the grass and to the barn. I haven't been beneath those rafters in ages. The barn was Glen's place, not mine. He tinkered on his truck in there in the fall and winter. In the warmer months, he opened the wide double doors and let the air in, and he and Cassie built miniature models of houses. Though he loved the space, I hated it. Even when the sun shone, to me, the workshop area seemed dank and musty.

As the reporters' voices sound from the front of the house, I press my body flat against the wide barn doors, which are padlocked. The lock is a combination lock, and I know the sequence of numbers, but as the reporters' voices grow louder, more urgent, my mind goes blank. My hands shake.

60 30 12
30 21 60
12 30 60

Finally, I get it right, and the lock springs open. I push the massive doors apart. Sunlight streams in and hits the truck's windshield. The reflection blinds me. Blinking, I dart toward the pickup and unlock it. I can see into the cab, but the hayloft behind it is dark. As I glance up at the loft, something moves. I scream. Wings flutter and flap. Something screeches.

"An owl. It's just a barn owl," I murmur.

I hop into the truck and jam the key into the ignition. As the engine roars, shouts come from the front of my property. *Step on it!* I tell myself.

And I do. I zoom through the open doors. Using the access road, I speed behind the cornfields until I hit my neighbor Gene's orchard. I move, camouflaged behind his apple trees, until I spill out onto the main road. My head thudding, I drive through town, glancing in my rearview mirror. I don't see anyone trailing me, no reporters or cops. Still, when I hit the highway, I keep my eyes peeled. Semis and family vans cruise by me.

With shaky fingers, I flip the radio on and adjust my mirror. As traffic reports and a replay of a Red Sox game seeps from the radio speaker, the pickup sputters and backfires. I clutch the steering wheel and drive. Forty-five minutes later, I arrive in Hanover, home to Dartmouth, the college Samuel's son, Hollister, attends.

I park on Lebanon Street and cross East Wheelock. I pass the Hanover Inn and make my way to the Dartmouth College Green. As students in T-shirts, shorts, and backpacks scurry down windy paths, I collapse onto a bench. No one's pointing. No one's whispering. No reporters are following me. My disguise must be convincing.

Four girls in J. Crew dresses, tennis shoes, and flat-ironed hair prance by me. I pull out my phone and look at my calendar. Colby Sawyer College and Dartmouth appear to be synched up. An internet search tells me that it's the last day of the summer term here at Dartmouth. As the J. Crew girls disappear into a building, I call Kingsley. We last spoke when I dropped him off at his motel early yesterday evening. So much has happened since: my run-in with Oscar, me sleeping with Liam, the destruction of my birch tree, Randi finding out about Whitney, and my meeting with Jane. It's overwhelming.

"I heard your boss put you on leave," Kingsley says after we exchange greetings. "Tough break. If it's any consolation, I got fired from two rags. You'll reinvent yourself. You're a transformer."

I grip the bench arm. "Well, I don't feel very transformative at the moment."

"That feeling like you wanna barf up a sandwich, it'll pass. Then you'll get pissed and have the urge to smack everyone within arm's length."

"So, I should keep my distance from people?"

"Quite the opposite." Kingsley laughs. "Lean in, and take up boxing."

I smile. Kingsley feels like a friend. He swore he wouldn't write about me, but I need to be sure. I say, "Tell me the truth. The night we reconnected, why were you at the gallery show?"

"Honestly?"

"Yes. Of course, honestly."

He chuckles. "My editor forced me to go. No offence. But I'm not much into art. But hey, your show was a zillion times better than squeezing into Cinderella's pumpkin coach at the Storyland Amusement Park. Far better than that Lake Winnipesaukee assignment. Let's just say pontoon boats aren't my thing. I'll take art over pumpkin coaches and pontoon boats any day." The bells in the library bell tower toll. "Where are you?" he asks.

"Dartmouth," I tell him, satisfied by his answer. "I'm visiting Samuel's son, Hollister. Listen, I probably should have asked you last night, given you more time to—"

"Out with it. I'm a bottomless pit of information. I'll bet you a drink at the Flying Goose Pub I've got the answer."

As a lacrosse player darts by waving a stick, I think of Glen, how we met at NYU and how Glen played lacrosse as a defender.

"I got Hollister's photo off social media. Do you know what dorm he's in?" I ask.

"Hitchcock Hall," Kingsley shoots back. "He's an engineering major in the Thayer School."

"Thanks. I'll head to his dorm. Ask around."

"Hmmm. That could be dicey. Kids might mistake you for a cougar."

I smile. "I'm thinking Hollister's aunt or mother, maybe his much older sister."

Kingsley's computer keys click. A professor type walks by carrying a briefcase, and glances at me. I look away. "Any new news about Cassie?" I ask.

"Yeah. Word is the Rossis are speaking to the media at four. Should have done that immediately after Cassie's abduction. Not sure why they're talking now."

"Given that Leeds is following the affair angle, I'm guessing they want to keep the focus on finding Cassie and off their marriage. What are you writing about now?" I ask.

"Miniature horses," he says. "There's a championship breeder located in Hancock. By the way, I drink Ragged Mountain Red Ale. You owe me a pint."

When he ends the call, using my GPS cell app, I cut across the green and head to Hitchcock Hall, a modern brick dormitory, carrying my pic of Hollister. As a breeze plays with the leaves of a nearby oak tree, an Asian girl in jeans exits the dormitory.

"Miss," I say, "I'm trying to find someone, a student …"

She waves her textbook, rushing by me.

Several minutes pass. A squirrel scampers across the pavement. I toss the critter an acorn. Three students, all boys—two with glasses and the third wearing a New England Patriots cap—ascend the steps leading to Hollister's dorm. All carry notebooks.

I say, "Do any of you know Hollister Hoover?"

The Patriots fan nods. "He's in applied mathematics with me. Final just ended. He should be heading this direction any minute." The boy frowns at me. "Wait. Are you?" He shakes his head. "Never mind."

As the boys enter their dormitory, I dip my hand into my bag, retrieve the pic of Hollister I printed out, and glance at my wristwatch. More students climb and descend the steps. Not wanting to miss Hollister, I study the faces of the boys meandering by. Some have pimples. Others sport beards. All look young.

I squint at a skinny kid walking quickly with his head down. The graduation photo I obtained from social media was spot-on. Hollister, lanky and awkward, ambles toward me. Dressed in jeans and a T-shirt, he looks fifteen. He seems skittish too, like if I came at him too quick, he'd bolt. But then I see his steely grey eyes. I'm thrown back to that snowy Lawrenceville park, to the slide, to Whitney. I drop my printout pic. It lands face-up on the pavement in front of Hollister.

He points to the image. "Hey, that's me. Where'd you get that? That's creepy. That's ..." he squints. Nods. "Wait. I know who you are ... you're that lady who cornered my dad on the bus. He said you might come here to try to talk to me."

"Then you know what this is about," I say, wondering what kind of spin Samuel put on our encounter. I scoop up the printout and extend my hand. "I'm Kate Boswell."

Hollister doesn't reach for my fingers. "My uncle killed your friend, right?"

"Yes, Whitney, when she was a thirteen."

"I'm sorry. That's wack. But I don't know what you want me to do about it." He starts to back away.

"Wait!" I say. "You've probably heard. It's all over the news. Another girl has gone missing, one of my former students. I'm pretty sure your uncle has her. Have you talked to him recently?"

"He's dead!" Hollister says. "How could I have talked to him?"

"Hollister, you don't have to pretend with me. I know he's alive. I'm not saying that you reached out to your uncle. But I'm certain he communicates with you."

Seemingly nervous, Hollister begins scrolling through pics. Kids' faces flash across his cell screen: nerdy boys, girls in glasses. One pretty face stands out.

I point to the image on his phone. "That's Maria. Maria from Reverend Shasta's farm. Your uncle stayed with Reverend Shasta. You visited him there. How else would you know Maria?"

"From Instagram," he says, jamming his cell into his pocket.

"Did you know your uncle threatened to kill Maria?"

Hollister's face pales. "You're lying."

"Don't believe me? Ask Reverend Shasta. Call him. Go ahead. His number's in my cell." I shove my phone at him.

Hollister pushes it away. "Let's get out of here." He walks fast and away from his dorm.

"Where are we going?" I say, struggling to keep up with him.

"To the cemetery. No one will bother us there. Lately everyone's been staying away because President Hanlon reprimanded the student body. Someone knocked over a row of tombstones. The mayor of Hanover is pissed."

"Understandably so," I say.

Hollister looks at me. "You don't think Uncle James would really hurt Maria?"

"I wouldn't put anything past him," I say, catching up to him.

We veer south, onto a quiet road. The sign on the post reads Cemetery Lane. As Hollister picks up his pace, leaves fall onto the pavement. He charges through them. He doesn't say anything until we reach the tombstones. There are several hundred of them, scattered over what must be three or four acres. Some markers look new and durable. Others, the ancient ones, are low-quality slabs, worn by the weather. The names and dates on the stones are now illegible.

Hollister's voice slices the air. "They used to bury only the college presidents and professors here. But the town owns it now, so they put other people here now too—babies, grandmas, and old dudes that own businesses on Main Street. Some junior drowned himself in the river after finals last spring. He could have been buried here, but his family didn't want him to be." He points to a bench and we sit. "Before the mayor got mad, kids used to have parties here. They weren't supposed to, but they did." He laughs. "Other kids, not me."

He retrieves a pinecone off the ground and tosses it. "I'm not like him. I'm not like my Uncle James. I would never kill someone. I hate that he did the things he did."

"But you still talk to him."

He nods. "I do. Not a lot. And like you said, he's the one who's always bugging me. He writes me letters."

"Any return addresses?"

"Nope. He calls me from random places too. Sometimes I hear cars, and I know he's next to a highway. He's been calling and writing me since I was in junior high, since he faked his death. Just snail mail. No face-to-face contact. Then one day he shows up here at my school, not at my dorm like you, but outside of the engineering building. It was January, cold as shit, snowing. He must have been waiting for a while 'cause he looked like a freakin' snowman. His hat and wool coat were white. He asked me if I wanted to get lunch. I was scared to go anywhere alone with him. So, we went to Lou's on Main Street and had burgers. He seemed normal. And he didn't hound me like my dad does about grades. He said he didn't do any of the things the cops said he'd done, that they framed him."

"And you believed him?"

"I wanted to. One time, I think it was June, he came for lunch and asked me to go to Reverend Shasta's blueberry farm, to see where he worked and lived up in Maine," he says. "It's like he wanted to prove to me that he was on the up and up."

"And you went up there?" I say, incredulous.

"I'm not stupid. I didn't get in his car with him. I borrowed my roommate's car and drove up myself. But I went. Yes."

His gaze drops to the ground. "I don't fit in here. I didn't fit in in high school either. I'm always on the outside. And it isn't because of what Uncle James did either." He taps his chest. "It's me. Kids just don't like me." He looks at me. "I felt bad for Uncle James. I know what it's like to not have friends, to always be alone. So, I went up to the blueberry farm to see him. I guess I was lonely too. Dad tries. But I can't talk to him, not about real stuff."

"Anyhow, I visited Uncle James up in Maine, like you said. And you're right. I met Maria there." He smiles. "Maria's different. She's not like the girls here. They're rich, super-smart, competitive, way too into themselves." He grins wider. "She's just good. You know, inside."

"You care about her," I say.

He nods. "She's coming here next year. She got in, early admissions. Reverend Shasta arranged a scholarship."

"That's great." My thoughts swing back to Hollister's visit to the farm, to the Worm Man. "What about your Uncle James? Did something happen at the farm, something that changed your opinion of him? You don't seem to be a fan now."

Hollister rises and stands in front of a grave. "I caught him with a little girl behind a blueberry bush, one of those Bible camp kids. He wasn't doing anything with her, just talking to her. But they were alone. She was maybe eight. He had this look in his eyes. It was messed up. So, I left. I told Maria to stay away from him. After that, whenever he called me, I told him I was busy."

"He's not at the farm anymore," I say.

"I know. He's ..."

"You know where he is?"

"Sort of, not really. I just know it's a house, a big house. Old and vacant. He said I could visit him. He said he had the run of the place." Hollister plays with a thread on his shirt. "I asked him if it was someone's vacation home, and he said no. That it was for sale, that he didn't think it would sell anytime soon. Something about the location, too isolated. He said the house needed a ton of work too. That it was a big-time fixer-upper, an obvious money pit."

"Did he say what town it was in?"

"Yeah. And he mentioned that a creek ran through the property. And it had a lake view, but only in the winter. 'New' something he called it."

My chest tightens. "Newport? Newbury? New London?"

"Not Newport. Newbury or New London." He nods.

We start walking again. We head back to the road. Hollister kicks a rock. "What will happen to my uncle if the cops find him?"

"He'll go to prison for the rest of his life. He might even get the death penalty."

"Even if he doesn't have that missing girl?"

"Yup. He's been linked to three murders. My friend, Whitney, and two other girls in the New York Metro area." I grab Hollister's arm. "You've got to come down to the police station with me. You need to tell the authorities that your Uncle James is alive and that you've seen him."

"No way. Can't," Hollister says, jerking free of my grasp. "I talked to you. That should be enough. If people find out my uncle's a serial killer, I'll be ostracized. My life will be hell." He motions to the brick campus buildings. "Here. Everywhere I go."

"But a little girl's life is at stake."

"Don't you get it? If I talk to the cops, I'm dead too." He points back to the graves. "Not dead like them, but I may as well be. Talking would be social suicide. My future will be ruined too. Every grad school or potential employer who Googles me will find out that the Worm Man's my uncle. I'll be screwed."

"Please." I say her name. "Cassie could die."

"He's in that house. I told you where he is. You just have to find him."

"If you change your mind …"

"I won't." We walk. He eyes me. "Are you gonna tell my dad I visited my uncle?"

"No."

He nods. "Just so you know, if you send the cops here to question me, I'll lie. I'll tell them you're crazy."

"But I'm not crazy."

He laughs. "Yes, you are. But it's cool. I am too. Everyone my uncle messes with is nuts."

* * *

Randi's husband's real estate office is on Main Street. I park in the small lot, adjust my sunglasses, and duck when a Fiat zooms by. Me being here is risky. Though Bill's office is on a part of the street that's not pedestrian-friendly, residents cruise by on their way to the shopping center. I could easily be spotted. I don't want the media, the cops, the feds, or some pissed-off parent to corner me.

I've come straight from Dartmouth and my conversation with Hollister. I'm all talked out, mentally and physically drained. I want to sleep. But time is of the essence. I've got to rally so I can get what I need from Bill. And I will be dealing directly with Bill. Randi's minivan isn't in the lot, a rarity.

During the busy summer months, when tourists enamored with the lake purchase cabins and cottages, Randi helps Bill with paperwork. She used to handle rental showings too. But Airbnb killed the majority of Bill's vacation rental business. I imagine Cassie's abduction has destroyed the rest.

I check my look in the rearview mirror and dart into Bill's office. He's alone. *Thank God. No clients and no receptionist.*

Bill glances up from the stack of papers on his desk. "Kate? Is that you?"

"In the flesh," I say, closing the door behind me.

He grins at me. "And all spiffed up. So where have you been? Randi's been going nuts, you know, blowing up my phone. She said you haven't been answering your calls. She's worried about you."

He frowns. "I'm sorry Jane put you on leave. A raw deal, if you ask me." He eyes me. "But seriously are you okay? Did anything else happen at the farmhouse? Don't tell me someone butchered another tree."

"Nope. All my trees are fine."

"Good. Your neighbor, Gene, is renting out one of his cabins. He was in here about an hour ago. He said the news vans have taken up residence on your road."

"That's why I blew Randi off. I didn't want to drag her into all my chaos. Plus, I needed to handle something. I had to sneak away quietly. I didn't want the reporters interfering."

Bill motions to my silk romper and my designer bag. "Hence the Manhattan getup, the disguise."

"Exactly."

He gestures at the empty office. "Randi's at the Outing Club Park with the boys. She mentioned something about soccer practice, or was it T-ball? She's been trying to keep things normal. Hasn't wanted to upset Mikey and Justin."

"Makes sense." Outside, a car whizzes by, and I jump. "I didn't come here to see Randi."

Bill grabs a pen. "You need somewhere to hide out for a while, a short-term rental? A modern cottage with a security system and easy access to the highway?"

"Now that you mention it, that does sound appealing. Truth is, I'm trying to find someone who's squatting in a vacant home, a property that's currently on the market."

Bill closes the shades and locks the door. "Let me take a wild guess. This squatter is none other than the infamous Worm Man." He shakes his head. "You really think James Hoover's alive, that he's got Cassie?"

"I wasn't sure initially, when Cassie first disappeared. But now, yes, I do think he has her. If you want me to explain, I can. But I'm not sure how much time I have." I glance at the door. "The feds. The reporters …"

Bill squints at me. "Kate, I think you should let that FBI and the cops, handle things. Hunting down a criminal is dangerous."

"I'm not going to actually hunt Hoover down. My goal is to simply locate him and give the authorities his address. That's it. Leeds has got blinders on," I add when Bill groans. "He's focused on me. I need to give him something solid, something real to work with, not just theories. And the reality is, I'm running out of time. That's why I came to you. Come on," I say when he folds his arms across his chest. "Help me out here. I could do an internet search, but the agency websites aren't specific enough."

"But if this monster is alive, like you say, the feds will find him."

I shrug. "Maybe. Maybe not. I can't risk the authorities pinning Cassie's disappearance on me. I've already lost my teaching job." My voice quivers. "I don't know what I'd do if anything happened to Cassie. Please, Bill. I'm desperate. I won't tell Randi you helped me. I promise. I'd pay you for your services, but I'm broke. But you can list my farmhouse when I sell it."

"You're never gonna sell that place, but that's not the point."

"What if I sketch your listings? You know, for your brochures." My eyes mist.

"Stop with the crocodile tears. Give me the specs. But not a word to Randi."

"Thank you. You're a lifesaver."

As Bill heads for his computer, the doorknob rattles, and someone knocks. I duck behind a file cabinet and hold my breath. The doorknob rattles again and then nothing.

"A big old house with a winter lake view and a creek running through the property," I whisper.

Bill types into his computer. "Location?"

"Isolated. Newbury or New London."

He smiles. "Sounds like your place, if you don't factor in the seasonal lake view."

"Ahh. Ahh. So, do any properties come to mind?"

"Three." He types on his computer keyboard. "The first two are in New London, one on Camp Sunapee Road and the other on Lakeshore Drive. The third is on Proctor Road in Newbury."

The printer hums. Bill retrieves the MLS sheets. "My money's on Proctor Road. They haven't had a showing for months. It's a trust sale, in probate. The owner's deceased. The heirs live in Colorado and have yet to visit. A tribe of Indians could move into that house and paint themselves blue, and no one would notice. The road leading to the property is a mixture of dirt and gravel. It's over a mile long. No way a plow's going down there in the winter." He points to the calendar on the wall above his printer. "It's almost September. If someone's in there, they only have a month to worry about interruptions. They could use that time to prepare. If they buy enough supplies, they'd be good until spring."

He hands me the printouts. "The driveway on the Proctor Road property needs reworking. Don't drive down there. You won't be able to turn around. There's no room. The trees and shrubs are overgrown. You'll have to back out. It's not a place you can exit quickly. That's what I'm saying."

I nod. "Thanks for the heads-up."

"No problem. Maybe park on the street and hike down to the house," he adds. "But I suggest you don't hike it alone."

"Black bears?"

"Definitely."

Fingering the MLS sheets, I hesitate in front of the door, as Bill unlocks the deadbolt.

"Do you want me to distract who's ever out there?" he asks.

I push the blinds aside and spot Agent Leeds. Feeling cornered, I start to shake.

Bill touches my arm. "Kate, are you okay?"

I slide Bill's MLS sheets into my purse and reach for the door knob. "Yeah. It's just Leeds. I may as well see what he wants. Tell Randi I'm fine and that I'll call her."

I exit Bill's office, impressed but not surprised that Leeds found me.

"Ms. Boswell," Leeds says, calling out to me, "We need an official statement. I'd like you to come down to the station.."

"Now?"

"It's standard procedure," he says approaching me. "You've got nothing to hide, right? You do still want to find Cassie?"

My heart thuds. I've been desperate to talk to Leeds since my NJ trip, but this is a damned-if-you-do-damned-if-you-don't situation. If I refuse to talk, I'll appear guilty. But if I cooperate and Leeds twists my words, I could incriminate myself.

Not wanting anyone to see me riding in his car, I say, "I'll meet you at the station."

Chapter 14

*A*fter climbing into my SUV, I call Thurston from my car phone. When he doesn't answer, I leave him a voicemail. *What kind of lawyer is he? I'm totally on my own here.*

Frustrated, I drive down Main Street, park, and enter the police building with Leeds. Leeds guides me into the same interrogation room we used during our initial encounter. As I sit facing the familiar rectangular table, my knees knock. I want to tell Leeds about Hoover's chalkboard threat, Hoover's twin Charles, and seeing Reverend Shasta in Jersey. But my belief that Leeds likely thinks I'm delusional, keeps me silent.

Leeds points to the video camera mounted to the wall. "You okay if we videotape you? It's for your own protection."

I glance at my cell. Thurston hasn't responded to my voicemail. "I suppose."

Leeds turns on the camera and pulls a small notepad out of his pocket. He asks me to state my name, the time, and the date, which I do. I figure he's going to ask me about the blue carry-on and the backpack. Since I harassed Hollister, I wouldn't put it past Samuel to throw me under the bus, no pun intended.

But instead of asking me about the carry-on, Leeds sinks into a chair and says, "You look different, dressed up. Is there a reason?"

"No. Just wanted to put my best self out into the world."

Leeds grins. "Don't want the news photographers to take any unflattering pics of you?"

"Something like that."

Leeds clears his throat and glances at his notepad. "When we conducted our search of your property, my men found a red plastic shovel in your garage."

"I remember."

"This morning Lauren Rossi identified the shovel as belonging to Cassie. Lauren stated that Cassie often used it to dig in the soil when she was collecting worms. According to Lauren, the shovel disappeared the afternoon Cassie went missing."

I frown. "How does she know it's the same shovel?"

"Because she wrote Cassie's initials on the handle with an indelible Sharpe after she purchased it from the Walmart in Claremont." He gestures at my hands "Your fingerprints are all over that plastic shovel handle. The question is, how did it end up in your garage?"

"Because I put it there. But that's irrelevant."

Leeds' brows arch. "I'm not following you. Why is it irrelevant?"

"Because that shovel didn't go missing the day Cassie disappeared. The day Cassie was grabbed, she must have been carrying a different one. Cassie and my husband built a sandcastle with the shovel your man found in my garage. Cassie left it on Bucklin Beach and I found it. I intended to return it to Lauren, but forgot."

Leeds appears skeptical. "Cassie built a sandcastle with your husband? When was this?"

"The beginning of last summer. Two months before my husband's death. A little over a year ago."

Leeds drums his fingers on the table. "Let's for argument's sake say that you're right and Lauren's mistaken. Are you usually that forgetful? You tutored Cassie many times during the school year. You never thought to return the shovel when Cassie came to your house?"

"My husband was hospitalized soon after the outing. I wasn't thinking about sand toys."

Leeds chews his lip, seeming to consider my words

"I'm sure if you remind Lauren, she'll remember. She probably doesn't want Oscar to know that she and Cassie were with Glen at the lake. Either that or she's confused."

Leeds waves a flyer. On the page is a picture of Cassie, a description of her clothing, and the items Lauren and Oscar told the cops Cassie had with her the day of the abduction. The red plastic shovel is listed, along with an umbrella, a bucket, and her backpack. "Where were you on the afternoon of Sunday, August 19th?" Leeds asks.

"I told you before. I was at home, gardening in my backyard. When it started to rain, I went inside. I worked on my lesson plans and did yoga and some laundry. I needed time to myself."

Leeds frowns. "Why?"

"The gallery show was a big deal to me, good but draining. I haven't been out much since Glen's death. I needed time to regroup, to decompress."

"Did anyone see you the afternoon of August 19th?"

"Not sure. Maybe Gene McKinley, the orchard owner. He lives up the road from me and drives by on occasion. But I was indoors and weeding in the backyard, so maybe not. And I turned off my cell. I wanted quiet. I kept my phone off until Monday. Check with Gene. Ask him if he saw me."

"Already did. He said he saw you digging in your yard." He looks at me. "Not on the afternoon of August 19th, but five days ago, last Thursday, August 23rd. Gene said you appeared frantic, distraught, that you were digging, not with a shovel, but with your fingers."

I grip the chair beneath me. "Last Thursday, someone chopped down my birch tree. The tree was important to me. I planted it when I miscarried my daughter. The 23rd was the anniversary of her passing. As you can imagine, I was emotional."

"So, you've been feeling emotional lately?" Leeds leans toward me. "Anyone would understand if you were. I mean, your husband drags you away from New Jersey, where you have friends, employment in the city and the opportunity to establish yourself as a real artist, and he brings you to this tiny town, and for what? So, he can carry on an affair with the mother of his illegitimate daughter? Let's face it. This is a classic, dude wants to have his cake and eat it too."

"Here's my theory." His words prick. "You're pissed at Glen. But he's six feet under. You can't bring him back to punish him. So, you take out your anger on the woman who you believe ruined your life, Lauren, his mistress. You abduct her child, Glen's child. A tit for tat. An eye for an eye. I mean, you crashed your car and lost your daughter when you found out about Glen's affair with Lauren. Am I right?"

Images shuffle in my mind. I see shattered glass on my SUV seat and blood on my dashboard. "I don't know. I don't remember. I had a concussion. The pain pills I took made me fuzzy. They affected my memory."

"Let me fill you in. According to Lauren, several hours before your accident, you read Glen and Lauren's text messages, found out about their affair and Cassie, and drove to Lauren's house. She claims you threatened her and vowed to take Cassie then. She said she wanted to go to the police, but Glen pleaded your case and convinced her not to."

"That doesn't sound like Lauren. Why would she give me a break?"

"She claims she felt sorry for you."

"She's lying," I say. "I didn't threaten her. She's the one who's always been cold and distant with me. I've never …If Lauren was so afraid of me, why did she keep Cassie in my class? Why did she hire me as Cassie's tutor? That doesn't make sense."

But Leeds doesn't seem to consider the inconsistencies. He pounds the table. "Where's Cassie? Where are you hiding her?"

"I'm not." I glance at the one-way mirror and wonder who's behind it. "Am I free to go?"

His words slap me. "I looked into your stint at the Carrier Clinic. You were hospitalized because you abducted a girl from a park."

"How did you … that information was … I didn't abduct anyone. I was protecting her."

"Are you protecting Cassie now?"

"Of course not. The situation is entirely different. That man from the park frightened that poor girl."

"That man? You mean her stepfather, her legal guardian?"

"She was screaming. I couldn't just sit back and do nothing. I took her to my car, drove to my apartment where it was safe, and called 9-1-1. She didn't want to be with him. She didn't feel comfortable being around him."

"Isn't that how you feel about Cassie? That she doesn't want to be around her mother."

"I never said that."

Leeds gestures at his notes. "You implied it. You said Lauren overshadowed her, that Cassie couldn't be herself when she was at school."

"I see what you're trying to do here, but it's not going to work. I was never arrested for kidnapping that little girl."

"Only because her stepfather dropped the charges, because your husband told him about your history with the Worm Man, and because your mother arranged for you to be treated at the clinic."

I spring to my feet. "This is insane. You shouldn't be harassing me. You should be looking for James Hoover. He's got Cassie. He didn't die in that shore house. It was his twin brother, Charles, who burned. If you don't believe me talk to James' nephew, Hollister. I just came from Dartmouth. Hollister flat-out admitted that his uncle is alive. They had lunch in Hanover at Lou's Restaurant and Bakery a couple of months ago. Check the restaurant's security camera film. And if you want even more proof, go to Reverend Shasta's farm. That's right. I saw the reverend in New Jersey, and he admitted to hiring James Hoover." My voice goes shrill. "Hoover threatened to kill Cassie. He drew an 'X' through a chalkboard drawing of her and wrote August 30th beneath her image. You've got to do something. She's only got about twenty-four hours left! You need to stop Hoover! You have to rescue Cassie!"

Leeds nods. "That's quite a story. Identical twins. An Ivy League kid. A deadly housefire. Crazy chalkboard threats and a death deadline. Sounds like something a writer would dream up. You've got the makings of a bestseller. Maybe a Netflix series. Am I to assume that you didn't come up with this all by yourself?"

"You know I've been working with Kingsley."

"And Kingsley connected you to all of these people: Hollister, Samuel, Reverend Shasta, and Emily Rose? He put the idea of them in your head, am I right?"

My heart drums. "It was my idea to talk to them, but yes, he did introduce the thought of them to me."

Leeds shakes his head. "Honestly Kate, I'm worried about you. You want my advice?"

"Sure. Okay."

"Get yourself some therapy. And start thinking for yourself. We ran a background check on Kingsley." Leeds hands me a file. "This is the report. Read it."

I skim the report. When I'm finished, I run out of the police station and to my car. I pound my steering wheel, scream, and speed to the Fairway Motel.

* * *

The Fairway Motel, a small, white complex, is located on the edge of the Lake Sunapee Golf Course, within walking distance to Liam's townhouse. I dropped Kingsley off here after our flight from the Newark Airport seventy-two hours ago. Unless Kinsley's checked out, I figure he's still chilling in his unit.

I park in the lot near the small lobby, march to room eleven, stand facing Kingsley's door, and knock. I've only just started spending time with the reporter. In essence, that makes us acquaintances. But I feel comfortable with him. I have from that first day we lunched at Tucker's. But people who play you put you at ease. That's what James Hoover did to Whitney. He chatted her up at the library, paid attention to her, and singled her out. Hoover read Whitney, sensing her desire to be seen. Is that what Kingsley is doing to me? Is he reading me? Does he know how desperately I want to be heard?

I finger my purse strap. The door to Kingsley's unit swings open, and Kingsley appears beyond the opening.

His smile is lazy, relaxed. He says, "Come inside. Check out my digs." When I don't move, he motions to the nearby fairway. "Why are you just standing there? Is it the grass thing again? 'Cause you're gonna have to get over that. It's a problem."

"It's not the grass."

He motions to his unit. "I won't bite. I swear it."

I glance back at Highway 11. No new vans. "Okay."

Kingsley steps aside and ushers me into his room. I see a queen-sized bed and a nightstand. His laptop is on the dresser. An open duffle bag filled with rumpled clothes sits on the carpet facing a mini-fridge.

He motions to an old TV hanging on a wall. "Life of a journalist. Glamorous, isn't it?" When I don't respond, he says, "Did you come here to pay me back for my Hollister intel? I'll grab my keys. I'm mighty thirsty. There's a frosty mug at the Flying Goose Pub with my name on it."

"I didn't come here to buy you a beer."

He frowns. "Okay. I'll take a rain check. So, what did Hollister say? Has he had contact with his Uncle James?"

"I don't want to talk about Hollister."

Kinsley tilts his head. "I'm confused, Kate. What gives?"

"Liam and Leeds think you're setting me up. They think you're writing about me." I make air quotes with my fingers. "The witness, how she cracks thirty years later."

"I promised you I wouldn't do that. Why would I break my word?"

"'Cause you need material. 'Cause you want to renew interest in your first book." I poke his chest with my finger. "'Cause you're not actually writing for *The Globe*. You came to that gallery show specifically to see me, didn't you?"

"Well, I—"

"It's true, isn't it? The feds checked you out. There are no Arts and Leisure assignments. There's no tyrannical editor forcing you to pet miniature horses, go on kiddy rides, or eat farm-to-table food. You got fired from *The Globe* for fabricating an anonymous source over a month ago. You got evicted from your Boston apartment. You're broke and homeless. The cops took away your driver's license and impounded your truck." My voice cracks. "Christ. I let you drive that Hertz car I rented. What if, you'd had a fender bender?"

Kingsley nods. "I was caught speeding excessively and I didn't pay my rent. That's accurate. But let's get our facts straight here. I didn't fabricate a source. My source simply panicked. Her story was important. It was about Fentanyl abuse. Not that using prescription meds is anything new, but my source was as a firefighter who treated overdoses daily. She knew how awful the stuff is. Got addicted anyway after a job-related injury. Her life spiraled out of control. Her story needed to be told. The power of opioids. People need to understand what that stuff does, even to smart educated hardworking people."

"Yeah. Yeah. Yadda. Yadda. Opioids led to that firefighter's downfall and her silence led to yours." I make a tight fist. "What an idiot I am. Leeds and Liam were right. Christ, you made me think you were working on stories for *The Globe*. What were you actually doing?"

"Working on my book. Look," he says when I gasp, "I needed to talk to you. That's why I introduced myself as a *Globe* reporter at the gallery. I didn't think you'd take me seriously if you thought I were just some washed-up schmuck without credentials." He exhales. "I admit it. I need money, the publicity, bad. But that's not why I wanted to connect with you."

I glare at him. "Did you actually even think Hoover was alive, or were you just feeding me bits of info, trying to get me to believe it?"

"I didn't need to do that. You suspected Hoover the second you heard that news report about Cassie."

"Damn you, Kinsley!" I kick his wastepaper basket, spilling its contents. "You of all people know how much I've been through. Why would you play me like that? Emily Rose's daughter was right. You're an ..."

Kingsley pulls his wallet out of his trousers. He retrieves a photo from his billfold. It's yellowing and worn. But I recognize the boy in the image. It's Kingsley. He's standing beside the Bradley Beach sign in swim trunks. His feet are in the sand.

"That's me," he says, waving the picture at me. "I'm a Jersey kid. Born and raised in Neptune City. I lived a block away from the Hoovers. I knew the Hoover boys growing up." He looks down. "I was the one who shoved Charles onto the tracks. I didn't intend to hurt him. I was just joking around. But he tripped and hit his head. Emily Rose doesn't remember me now. But I've known her my whole life. I was her paperboy. I spoke to her right after the fire too."

"Wait." My body tenses. "You knew all along how James faked his death? Why didn't you tell Leeds right away?"

"I did. That first morning he interviewed me, the morning after Cassie's abduction. Leeds said it was a load of crap. That Emily Rose was looney. That there was no record of Charles ever existing. And there isn't, so I get why he wouldn't listen to me."

"But you didn't tell me that day we met at Tucker's. I would have listened."

"Perhaps. But I figured if you heard the facts from the primary sources— Emily Rose, Samuel, Hollister, and the reverend—and you drew your own conclusion, it would carry more weight than if I spelled things out for you. I've been searching for James Hoover for a decade and I haven't found him. I was desperate. I couldn't take the risk that you wouldn't team up with me."

"But why me? It's not like I've got investigative skills, contacts."

"But you've met him. You survived him. And he's in your head, just like he's inside mine. Finding him is personal for both of us." Kingsley's lip quivers. "I messed that kid up, Kate. And Charles getting messed up made James evil." He pats his chest. "Me. I'm responsible for James being evil. You heard Emily Rose. After Charles's accident, James changed."

I stare at a piece of lint on the carpet. "You don't know that. Evil like that is complicated—genes, family environment, nature, and nurture. One incident doesn't alter a person, change them."

"Really?" Kingsley slides the photo back into his wallet. "Come on, Kate. You can't honestly stand here and tell me that watching James steal your best friend didn't change you?"

"Okay. You're right. It did. But people always have choices. They can choose to move on, to forgive."

Kingsley looks at me. "Do you forgive James Hoover?"

I don't hesitate. "I'm terrified of him, and think that what he did to Whitney and his other victims is indefensible, evil. But after hearing Emily Rose's description of James' father and James' abusive dysfunctional family and their secrets, I understand, why he is the way he is. Because of that, and because being angry with him has drained my life of so much goodness, I've decided to forgive him. Holding onto my rage, hasn't gotten me anywhere. It's practically destroyed me. So, yes. I've forgiven him."

"Seriously? But you're hunting him down. You're obsessed."

"I've forgiven him, just not..."

"What would you have done differently?"

"He looked sketchy. I should have made Whitney leave the park. I should have fought harder to save her too. Dragged her out of that car. Memorized his license plate." My voice cracks. "I should have been stronger so my parents wouldn't have felt a need to shield me from the investigation."

"You were a kid."

"So were you when you shoved Charles."

"I was, thirteen."

"Me too."

He nods. "You think if you find Hoover and save that girl, you'll be able to forgive yourself?"

"That's my hope."

He opens a dresser drawer and retrieves a manuscript. "Take a look. It's my latest project. You're in it, but only in the last thirty pages. It's a memoir. It's about my connection to the Worm Man."

I skim the working-tile *Shoving the Worm Tail.* "It's not your fault. What he did to Whitney, to those other two girls, it's not your fault."

"Not yours either." He bear-hugs me, and suddenly we're a team again. All my doubts, my reservations about his intentions, disappear.

"Who would think it?" he says, squeezing my shoulder. "We're two peas in a pod, you and me." He winks. "By the way, you look pretty."

"It's a disguise."

"It's a good one." He touches his forehead again. "Your instinct is spot-on. Hoover's alive, and he's close by. Don't let Leeds screw with your mind. He's a pro at it. He's good at pitting people against one another too."

I nod. "Too true. I'm sorry for doubting your motives."

"And I'm sorry for lying. I won't do it again. You're a strong woman, Kate Boswell. Don't ever forget that."

"And you're a good soul," I say, hugging him.

He motions to a calendar on his nightstand. "According to Reverend Shasta's blackboard, we've got a day to find Cassie."

"I know. I can't stop thinking about her. I'm going crazy." I gesture at my purse. "Hollister gave me a description of the property where his uncle is staying, and my friend's husband, Bill, who's a realtor helped me narrow down my search. Bill gave me three addresses."

Kingsley gives me a thumbs up. "Good work. Do you want to pass the info onto Leeds?"

"What would be the point? Leeds won't listen to anything Worm Man-related. He's all about pinning Cassie's disappearance on me. We've got to find Cassie and James Hoover ourselves." I gesture through the window at the surrounding trees. "The properties are local, but all three are extremely isolated."

"In other words, if things go south, no one will hear us scream."

"Exactly."

"I'm in." Kingsley touches my arm. "Hey. You sure you're up for this? Me, I can't back off. I need to do this. It's a macho thing. Besides, I don't have people relying on me, students, a hunky boyfriend." His voice softens. "Kate, just so you know. There's nothing in our Finding Cassie and The Worm Handshake Agreement that says we both have to be crazy stupid, and get ourselves killed."

"We're a team," I say. "I'm not going to bail on you."

"But the guy's a monster. When it comes to psychopaths, he's the real deal. Up until now we've just been sniffing around him. But coming face-to-face with that kind of evil, is a whole other ballgame. I know you, know that."

"I do, and I don't care. I've been dealing with Hoover for thirty years. I have to see this thing through." I motion to the window, at the darkening sky beyond the pane. "But we can't go traipsing around at night. James Hoover will see our headlights and flashlights and bolt. I can't stand waiting. I know Cassie's got to be terrified out of her mind. Christ, what if Hoover...I shudder. I'll pick you up at sunrise, around six?"

"Six it is."

I give Kingsley the addresses so he can prep on the internet. He wants to check them out on Google Maps. Kingsley closes his unit door, and I head to Glen's truck. Hoping to avoid the press, I take the backroads and service road home. As Glen's pickup rattles and jars, I think about Liam and fight the urge to call him. I wish I could resolve my issues with Liam as easily as I did with Kingsley. But the difference between the two men is vast. My relationship with Kingsley is platonic. I love Liam. Romantic love always makes things trickier.

When I see the roofline of my farmhouse, fearing the news crews might spot me, I flip off my headlights. As shadowy darkness surrounds me, I park beside the barn and remove my heeled sandals. They're impossible to run in, but practical. If need be, I can wield the shoes to fend off reporters or an irate parent.

Not wanting to make noise, I carefully press the truck door shut. Then I use the flashlight app from my cell to guide me across the overgrown lawn. The night is quiet. The grass feels slick under my bare feet. Something about its wetness and the frantic nature of my sprint reminds me of that snowy morning I bolted from the Worm Man. It doesn't matter that it's summer or that thirty years have passed, the feeling of desperation is the same.

I'm breathing hard when I reach my back landing. The hinges squeak as I open the door. My kitchen is dark. I flip on the light using the wall switch. Beside me, my faucet drips. I glance at the dirty dishes in the sink, at the sponge near the soap dish, and deadbolt the door behind me. Everything seems normal, just the way I left it.

I stand beside the stove until my eyes adjust. Without turning on any more lights, I move toward the front of the house. I don't want the news crews to notice my arrival. And if the Worm Man's here, perhaps I'll surprise him. But he isn't here. I've decided this. He's with Cassie, guarding her, watching her, making her feel both trivial and important. As I'm thinking about this, about him, Thurston calls me.

Clutching my cell, I peer through the living room window at the front lawn and the road that parallels my house.

"They're gone." I speak to Thurston as if he's beside me. "The media was camped out in front of my house earlier today. But they left. I guess they got tired of waiting for me and gave up."

Thurston sighs. "Hopefully they're off following another lead. There's a fire up north in Coos County. Quite a blaze. Could be they're covering that."

"Maybe." I flip on the living room light. "You got my messages?"

"I just did. You shouldn't have talked to Leeds without me," Thurston scolds. "You shouldn't have told him about your trip to the Jersey shore."

"I had to. He needed to know about Hoover's threat. I told you about it in my voicemail," I add when he huffs. "My point is, Leeds needs to find Cassie. She's running out of time. Jesus, why doesn't anyone get that?"

"I know how worried you about Cassie. But Kate, you have to think about yourself too. Did Leeds bring up anything new?"

I drop onto my armchair ottoman. "Just that he found Cassie's plastic shovel in my garage. It's no big deal really. I explained it all to Leeds: how Cassie left the shovel at the lake last summer, how I found it and took it home, and how I intended to return it but forgot."

"Did he believe you?"

"Probably not."

I bite my fingernail. Blood seeps from my cuticle. I don't want to tell Thurston about my time at the Carrier Clinic or the reason they admitted me. But Thurston can't help me if I don't come clean. "There's something else you should know. I should have told you earlier. I was involved in an incident before I moved to New London."

"What kind of incident?"

"It was a long time ago. I thought it was handled, gone. But evidently Leeds did some major digging." I exhale. "I was hospitalized at a treatment center outside of Princeton a decade ago."

"For your panic attacks?" Thurston asks.

"Yes. And for delusions and paranoia."

"How much time did you spend there?"

"Three weeks. It was a good thing, actually. Being there helped me. But ..." I explain how I took the girl from the park because her stepfather was yelling at her and chasing her, and how it was all a big misunderstanding that got blown out of proportion. "I wasn't kidnapping the girl. I was protecting her," I tell Thurston. "Her stepfather was abusive."

Thurston remains quiet.

"I know it doesn't look good," I say, needing for him to speak. "I should have told you sooner. But the truth is, since it has nothing to do with Cassie, I didn't think it mattered."

"It does matter. It's extremely relevant. You might not be proud of it, but it's a part of your history. It shows a pattern of behavior." Thurston clucks his tongue, and I think of Whitney, who clucked hers whenever she was worried about a test or being late for school.

"I'm almost afraid to ask," he says. "Is that it?"

"Lauren claims I threatened her prior to my car accident, the one that caused my miscarriage two years ago. But I suffered a concussion during the accident. I don't remember the days surrounding the crash."

Thurston seems to consider this. "Did Lauren file a police report?"

"No. Allegedly Glen convinced her not to." I tug at the ottoman fringe. "I got put on leave from my teaching job. My boss gave me the news yesterday."

Thurston exhales. "I'm sorry. That must really sting. I know how much teaching means to you. I should probably take a look at the contract you signed when they hired you. In general, people with mental illnesses are protected from termination via the Americans with Disabilities Act. But there's an exclusion clause. If an employee is deemed a threat to someone's safety or if they can't perform their job, he or she isn't granted that same protection. Jane could argue that she deems you a threat."

I think about the petition signed by 90 percent of the incoming third-grade parents. "Probably. Look. I'll find my contract and get it to you, but— What do we do now?"

"We wait and prepare for your arrest."

"What? Prepare for my arrest? But I didn't take Cassie."

"I know. But Leeds seems to think otherwise. And the press is reinforcing his belief." Thurston exhales. "This isn't what you want to hear. But I wouldn't be doing my job as your attorney, if I let you believe everything was going to be okay. When James Hoover murdered Whitney, Lilly and I thought the authorities would lock him up. We believed he'd be punished for taking our little girl away from us. But that didn't happen. Looking back, I know a more realistic perspective would have helped us, especially Lilly."

I shut my eyes. "How do I prepare for the worst-case scenario?"

"Put money aside. More than likely the judge will set bail for about $75,000. Ten percent of that is $7,500. They'll take your cell. Write any important numbers on your hand." A squeak sounds through the phone, as if Thurston is opening a drawer. "In the meantime, I know you're used to talking openly to the authorities because of your relationship with Liam. But just remember, Leeds isn't Liam. And though you and Liam are close and you care about him, he's still a cop. Watch your back. He's gunning for a promotion, am I right?"

"He is, but..." I'm about to tell Thurston about my conversation with Hollister, about the Worm Man potentially hiding out in a listed property, but I hear Lilly's voice in the background.

"Lilly needs you," I say. "I'll call you if Leeds or any of his men contact me."

"Kate," he says, clearing his throat, "whatever you do, stay away from Lauren Rossi."

Chapter 15

*A*round late-night comic hour, after I've cleaned out my voicemail mailbox, Liam calls me. We haven't spoken since our fight. I'm angry with him, but I still love him, so I take his call. "How you doing?" he asks when I answer.

"Not great." I tell him about my possible arrest.

"Don't get yourself worked up. Sometimes cops and agents act like they have a solid case against you when they don't. It's a tactic. They think if you get upset, you'll confess."

"I have nothing to confess."

"I know that. I'm telling you, it could be a bluff on his end."

"Do you think it's a bluff?" I ask.

He hesitates. "Don't know."

I cradle the phone in my palm. Despite the serious tone of our conversation, it feels good to hear his voice. But like grime on a windowpane or dust on the wood of a chair arm, the tension between us is still there. I could say something apologetic to wipe it clean. I could admit that he was partially right, that Kingsley was lying and is writing about me, but I don't.

I wait for Liam to say that he believes Hoover is alive and that he values my judgment. But he doesn't. I consider telling him Kingsley's very personal reason for capturing the Worm Man, but the story isn't mine to share.

Liam's voice jars me. "Hey. I'm working, but why don't you stay at my place? I've got close neighbors. It's safer. The possibility of someone trespassing and vandalizing your property again, worries me."

"No one's going to bother me," I say. "Everyone thinks I'm a crazy."

"Not everyone. Not the people who know and love you. Not me."

"Thanks for being Team Kate," I say. "But honestly, if I'm gonna be hauled off in handcuffs, which seems like a definite possibility, I want to sleep in my own bed tonight. I'll be fine really. I've got my cell."

"You sure? I've got paperwork to finish. There was an accident on 89. But I can come over to your house if—"

"Don't." I stifle a sob. "It's best if I'm alone."

"Don't do this, Kate. Don't punish yourself, or me. So, what if we don't see eye to eye on everything. I want to be with you. I love you. Even if it's just for a few hours, I want to hold you."

My eyes mist. I allowed Glen to steal little pieces of me by accepting our differences for the sake of our marriage. This time around, I won't compromise. I'm going to be true to myself and my beliefs. If Liam loves me unconditionally, he'll respect this and me. Also, if we're together come morning, he might keep me from searching for Cassie and Hoover in Newbury. With my arrest looming, I can't have anyone getting in the way of my search, even Liam. Finding Cassie is too important.

"I want you to hold me too. But being alone now, is what I need," I say. "Please respect that."

I tell him goodbye and end the call before he can argue with me. As I'm checking my door locks and alarms, Randi calls. My gut tells me Liam texted her, telling her I'm being stubborn.

"So, what happened with Leeds? Bill said he was out in the parking lot waiting for you when you left his office."

"Same drill. Just more questions. The guy doesn't let up. Keeps going down the same path."

"Do you want me to come over? Bill can watch the boys. Or you can come here."

"Thanks, but I'm fine."

Randi's voice gets raspy. "Look, if you're not here, I'll worry about you. Kate, it's okay to need help. We all need help, get off-kilter, from time to time."

"I know that. I'll call you if I need to talk or if I change my mind."

"Or just come over. We're not going anywhere."

When the call ends, my cell dings. It's a text from Mom. Her connecting flight was canceled. She's arriving tomorrow night. I haven't heard from Reverend Shasta or Hollister, not that I expected to. My only hope is finding Hoover and Cassie at one of the addresses Bill gave me. But it's too late, too dark, to go anywhere now. I'll have to kill time until daylight, until I meet up with Kingsley.

I put my cell on vibrate, open the blinds, and gaze through the kitchen window and into the night. As Jimmy Fallon's voice seeps from the den TV, I draw Lauren, Cassie, Oscar, and Glen. I sketch Hollister, Reverend Shasta, Thurston, Lilly, Randi, Bill, Kingsley, Evelyn, Leeds, Maria, and Emily Rose. I draw them together, interacting, like at a cocktail party. Then I draw them separate, each posing on the bandstand stage facing Main Street and looking at the town green. I draw for hours. I draw both standing and seated. As the sky brightens, I draw Cassie and Glen on Bucklin Beach making a sandcastle. The Cassie in my sketch grips her red plastic shovel. The Glen I create kneels beside her, as he puts a flag leaf in the sandcastle turret. Smiles crease their penciled lips.

When the sun creeps across the field, I watch the Rossi's news conference on YouTube. My eyes watery, I grab the MLS sheet Bill gave me. Bill's words echo in my mind. *My money's on Proctor Road.* I circle the Proctor Road address, check my cell, and notice a voicemail from Kingsley.

Sorry, Kate. Can't meet as planned. Leeds and his minions showed up at my motel about an hour ago. The fools dragged me down to the station.

I told Leeds I had to take a piss. I'm in the John. Anyhow, Leeds' is threatening to arrest me because I didn't show on my court date for that speeding ticket thing. He says he's gonna lock me up for six months if I don't

tell him where you're keeping Cassie. I gave him the three addresses you gave me and told him the Worm Man's in one of them.

Kate, he said his men already checked out those properties and found nothing suspicious. I don't know. Maybe Hollister's description was wrong. Could be Uncle James was messing with his nephew. Just...I don't want you to get your hopes up.

Someone's here! Gotta go.

Heads up. The feds are coming to arrest you, like now! You need to hightail it out of there ASAP!

My heart drumming, I grab my sketchbook and quickly collect the supplies I need for hunting James Hoover. Trembling, I slip out the back door, jump in my Subaru, and zoom out of my driveway onto the road fronting my farmhouse.

I'm confused, thrown off. We had a plan. Kingsley and I were going to find Hoover and Cassie in one of the vacant properties and contact Leeds. Yesterday, when I was with Kingsley, I was certain Hoover was in that Newbury house on Proctor Road. I was sure of this, almost positive. But now, I'm driving toward town, just driving, and I'm alone.

I take the curve by Gene's orchard too sharply. Thurston's words, echo in my mind. *Stay away from Lauren Rossi.*

"Sorry Thurston," I say, "But, no can do."

I swerve, hit Main Street, and turn left onto Pressey Court, Lauren's street. Halfway down the block, I ease to the curb, park, and climb out of my Subaru. Though I've never been inside Lauren's house, I recognize her Cape Cod with the yellow shutters. Karen, the third-grade teacher and Lauren's neighbor, hosted a brunch earlier in the summer. Karen pointed out the Rossi's home.

I glance past the sidewalk. The street is empty. Oddly, despite the Rossi's recent news conference, the reporters seem to have moved on. If it weren't for the collection of candles, balloons, teddy bears, and wilting flowers on the curb, no one would know that a missing child lives here. The only sign of the Rossi's family crisis is Ian's Big Wheel. It sits beside the hedge in the front yard. Its plastic wheels tilt skyward.

It's not appropriate, and potentially even dangerous for me to be here, given my run-in with Oscar. But I don't care. I take the front path, step onto the Rossi's landing, and knock. Slippers patter, the door swings open, and Lauren appears in the foyer, looking sleepy and beautiful. She's wearing a bathrobe, a fuzzy blue one. Ian's balanced on her hip. His nose is red, runny.

"Oscar," she says, her focus entirely on Ian, "I knew you'd be back. You forgot Ian's ..."

In her hand, she grasps a prescription, most likely for antibiotics. Her head swings my way. She drops her prescription onto the foyer floor mat, a braided rug that resembles a giant potholder.

I make a peace sign with my fingers. "I realize it's ungodly early. But..."

Lauren's cell sits on the entryway table. As she attempts to grab it, Ian wiggles and squirms. She gives up on her quest for the phone and presses him against her chest.

I wave the drawing of Cassie and Glen. "Don't freak. I just wanted you to have this."

She frowns. She's likely thinking, *Why now? At six thirty on a Wednesday morning?*

I stammer, "I didn't want to put off giving it to you. You see, I drew it last night."

I'm not making sense. Drawings don't have a shelf life, like milk or eggs. But in my mind this particular drawing does. Today is August 29th. I still believe Cassie's alive. I want to give this drawing to Lauren while hope flows through me.

I finger the drawing. When Lauren doesn't lean in and grab it, I kneel and place it on the landing. I don't dare enter her home. I know better. I'm not welcome here, never was.

I say, "Glen loved Cassie. I want you to have something tangible to remind you of that love."

Lauren glances at the image of Glen and Cassie. The drawing is riveting, my best work ever. She can't help but be moved by its raw simplicity, by the unconcealed love in Glen's eyes.

Her lip quivers. She has yet to speak. And when she does, she shouts, "What the hell did you do with my daughter?"

As Ian wails, I merely shake my head. My words mean nothing to her. She's made up her mind about me. In truth, our relationship was doomed from the start. Glen doomed us when he chose to sleep with us both.

I back away from her and retreat down the landing steps. This time she manages to juggle Ian and grab her phone. As I turn, she presses her cell against her cheek. I figure she's calling Oscar, Leeds, or maybe the police. As her shrill voice echoes across the driveway, I sprint past Ian's Big Wheel and the makeshift memorial and jump into my SUV. I drive south toward Newbury.

* * *

I'm parked on the shoulder of Proctor Road. The road's narrow and windy, with not many houses, just trees. A rusty mailbox is positioned by my bumper. A red reflector rests beside the roadside ditch. I shut my SUV door. The sound echoes like a gunshot, and I jump.

"Relax," I say, rubbing my forearms.

I'm here, at this property, even though Leeds told Kingsley that James Hoover and Cassie aren't inside, because Bill said it was my best bet.

My heart drums. I need to get moving. It's only a matter of time before Leeds comes looking for me.

As a cool wind sweeps off Mount Kearsarge, I scan my treed surroundings and stand tall in my hiking boots. My tote-sized purse contains a steak knife, a boat horn, a screwdriver, and pepper spray.

My plan remains the same. I'm going to confirm my hunch that James Hoover is holding Cassie captive on this property. Once I spot him, I'll call Liam. I'm not going to attempt to rescue Cassie; nor will I confront Hoover. I know my limits. I'm not trained. I dip my hand into my jacket pocket. After my nightly drawing marathon, out of habit, I tucked a drawing pencil inside.

Squeezing the pencil, I step onto the driveway blanketed with pine needles and leaves. If I hear a car motor, I'll dart into the woods. Trembling, I walk down the driveway, away from Proctor Road. Claw and bite marks mar the trunk of an oak several yards ahead of me.

Bears. Don't think about the bears, I tell myself, but of course I do.

It's still early, a half past seven now. I wonder if Oscar has returned from the twenty-four-hour pharmacy and if Ian has gone back to bed. I picture Ian's runny nose. In my mind, I see Lauren's quivering lip. I think about Kingsley and wonder if he's still in the interrogation room. I walk for about a half-mile. Something small and furry scampers into a bush, a squirrel or a chipmunk. The creature looks harmless enough. Still, I pick up my pace. My hiking boots make this squeaking noise. They're wet from the dew. I stomp on some loose dirt, and the sound goes away.

I walk for five more minutes. As the sun's rays brighten the sky, I reach an overgrown lawn. I'm sweaty, not from exertion, but from fear. In front of me, the old colonial looms. Despite its poor condition, it's majestic. A three-season porch overlooks the approach. Its faded white exterior paint is peeling and makes me think of dry sunburnt skin. The porch's muted colors match the morning clouds.

I glance down. The grass surrounding the driveway is flattened. Beside the flattened grass is a creek. If there's a seasonal lake view, it's blocked by pines. I recall Hollister's description. *Isolated. Needs work. A creek. Winter view.* My blood ices. I peer through the colonial's windows. I don't see any signs of life—no lights, no curtains moving, and no dogs barking or voices. I quietly and cautiously circle the exterior. The house looks abandoned. No hoses or gardening tools are outside. No towels are on the clothesline. The window curtains are all closed.

The truth is, I don't want to go inside. It's risky, dangerous. *But necessary,* I decide. Either I go in or go to prison. It's that simple. If I'm locked up and Leeds jails Kingsley, the chances of anyone finding Cassie before James Hoover kills her are low. I finger my screwdriver, ascend the porch steps, enter the enclosed area via a screen door, and walk forward about eight feet. A lockbox hangs on the entryway door. I study the windows separating the enclosed porch from the main house.

This is nuts, I tell myself. *You can't just break in. Call Bill and get the access code. No,* I counter. *Bill and Randi don't really believe Hoover's alive. They'll drive you back to their house, give you a sedative, and call Liam. Leeds will arrest you.*

Okay. So, I can't call Bill and Randi. But knocking and ringing the doorbell don't make sense either. The homeowner is deceased. The heirs are in Colorado. No one is supposed to be inside. If the Worm Man's in the house, knocking will alert him. He'll hide or grab a weapon. He might hurt or bolt with Cassie.

I eyeball the windows. They all appear locked. But one looks rickety. I slide my screwdriver between the frame and the pane. When the glass pops out, I lower the pane onto the wicker table and peek into the interior room.

A couch, two wing-back chairs, and a coffee table rest on a beige rug. I see a fireplace with candles, but no people. I don't hear any sounds. As I slide through the opening I created and enter the house, my heart drums against my chest. The urge to flee is powerful. But I can't run. For thirty years I've second-guessed myself, wishing I'd stopped the Worm Man from stealing Whitney. This is my chance to better things, not to fix them, because there's no bringing Whitney back, but I can do my part to help Cassie. She deserves that. If I don't save her, I won't recover this time around. I know this. You can't fail two girls and stay sane.

I step gingerly onto a window seat and lower myself onto the living room floor. The air surrounding me is dusty and stale. I scan the space, note the realtors' cards stacked on the coffee table, and drop my screwdriver into my tote. Clutching my knife, I move toward the foyer. The floor squeaks, and I halt. The place is staged. A vase containing artificial roses sits on the mantle. I turn away from the fireplace and tiptoe into the kitchen. The kitchen is where life reveals itself the most.

I look in the fridge. There's no food, just bottled water. I peer in the trash. An old cookie tin sits in the trash bin, most likely from an open house. I open drawers, but see no utensils. My gaze shifts to the pantry. It's empty. No supplies. Emotions tumble through me and twist. The idea of being in the same house with Hoover terrifies me. But the alternative, not finding him here, is worse. But he's here. I know it. I can smell him and taste his fowl presence.

I search the dining room and tiptoe upstairs. By the time I reach the second-story hallway, I can barely breathe. Fear tightens my muscles. The floors creak beneath me. I look in the first bedroom. It's sparsely furnished, just a bed and a dresser. I fling open a closet door and spring back. There's nothing—no hangers, no clothes, no James, and no Cassie. I search the other three bedrooms but come up empty.

"He's not up here," I say, gazing up into the attic, void of furniture and clutter. "He's not anywhere in this house unless he's in the basement."

Not likely, I think. *New Hampshire basements are damp and moldy and fill with water when it rains. Besides, there's no food in the kitchen. There are no toiletries or clothes in the drawers or closets. But James hid in Emily Rose's basement*, I tell myself. This detail propels me to the first floor. As I enter the hallway, I hear a ding. *Air in the pipes?* I have to be sure. I open the cellar door, which is located off the kitchen, flip the light switch, and descend slowly and cautiously, one step at a time.

When I reach it, the cement floor feels bone-hard beneath my boots. I do a quick visual sweep. Except for two lawn chairs, the basement is practically empty. A washer and dryer are hooked up beside wooden shelves, and a large cabinet sits along one wall. But that's it. Like a rat, I move deeper into the cellar, toward the furnace.

Upstairs, a door slams. *Leeds? The Worm Man?* My blood goes cold. Panic hits me, panic like I've never felt before. I dart toward the hatch door leading to the yard and push. The door is locked. My heart thumps. *Shit. Shit.* Footsteps thud above me.

I scan the walls, looking for a place to hide. That's when I spot the steel door leading to the fallout shelter by the large cabinet and the scrape-marked floor. My mind churns. *What if the feds didn't notice the fallout shelter when they searched the property because the cabinet was blocking the door? What if Cassie's inside the shelter now?* I attempt to turn the heavy latch, but it sticks. I kick the latch and the door swings opens.

"Cassie," I say. "Cassie, are you here?"

As footfalls thud above me and the ceiling light blinks, I quickly survey the fallout shelter space. A small cot sits on the floor, complete with blankets and pillows. Beside the cot are a tool chest, a portable radio, and a shower caddie containing toiletries. A stack of books and notebooks rests against a far wall. Beside the books is a duffle bag. A man's shirt and jeans lay on the cot. Boxes containing canned food, dry goods, water bottles, dishes, and utensils fill the far corner. A small card table sits beside a folding chair. There's a fridge too. What's missing is evidence of Cassie's presence here. No girl-sized clothes or shoes here. No ropes or chains to bind her with. I don't see any blood either.

She's not here. Cassie isn't here. She's dead. Reverend Shasta was right! Hoover already killed her! He chopped her up. I want to drop to the floor, curl into a ball, and sob. But I can't. Someone is upstairs. And they're looking for me!

I pull the steel door shut, lock it, and fumble for my cell. *No bars.* Trembling, I slide my phone into my shorts pocket.

I've got two choices: hide or attack. Hiding seems difficult, given the size of the space. Using pepper spray and attacking if the door opens is the better option. I clutch my spray and wait. Five minutes pass. Ten and then twenty. I don't hear any noises, but this means nothing. The fallout shelter walls are thick, solid. I stare at the door latch. I've decided that it's James who's inside the house with me. If Leeds were here with his men, he'd announce his presence and call out to me. But why isn't James opening the fallout shelter door? I left the cellar door ajar. The windowpane is on the table. My Subaru is parked on the road. He has to know I'm in the house. Perhaps he's checking the other rooms.

Five more minutes tick by. My chest tightens. The air seems thinner, though I'm guessing this is anxiety, not reality. *Maybe he'll go away. Maybe I can wait this out. Maybe Leeds will come and rescue me.* Sweat drips off me. Too hot,

I open the fridge door. That's when I see them. The worms. There are hundreds of them, wiggling and squirming amongst the compost and food scraps inside the refrigerator. As I stare at their tube-like bodies, I picture worms crawling on Whitney's dismembered body parts. I gag. Fear zips up my spine. I can't stay in the small space a minute longer.

I slam the fridge door, charge out of the fallout shelter, and run like hell toward the cellar stairs. Out of the corner of my eye, I see a man beside the lawn furniture, ready to pounce. When I aim my pepper spray at him, he leaps at me. As the spray stream misses my attacker and the bottle falls from my grasp, my attacker tackles me. He yelps, as if the physical contact gives him joy, some kind of release. I hit the cement hard, face-first. As pain dazes me, my pepper spray, knife, and purse slide across the floor. My attacker is like an MMA competitor. He's on top of me, squeezing the life out of me, handling me. He's all stubble and sweat, boozy, and calloused.

"I knew you'd come out eventually, little lady," he whispers.

It's him, James Hoover, the Worm Man, the monster from my nightmares. I don't have to see his face and his severed finger to know this. I don't even have to look into his steely grey eyes. The knowing is instinctual. Did Whitney just know he planned to kill her that snowy morning in Lawrenceville? Because that's what I'm sensing now. He wants me dead. James licks my cheek, tasting me.

"Where is she?" I yell, recoiling. "Where is Cassie? Did you kill her?"

His weight shifts onto my tailbone. Putting his hand onto the back of my neck, he presses my cheek into the floor. "Who?" he growls.

"Cassie!" I shout the name. I want him to hear it. "Cassie Rossi. The New London girl you abducted."

"Goldilocks?" He spits when he says "locks." Saliva sprays onto the nape of my neck.

"Yes," I say, squirming and kicking.

"Don't have her. Never did. But I heard about that cutie on the news. I heard about you too. They were talking about you on the car radio, at the convenience store this morning. You're wanted, a fugitive. Guess that makes you and me the same."

"Polar opposites. You're guilty. I'm not."

He laughs. "Oh, honey. You got evil in you just like I do. That evil spilled out all over that drawing you did. You can't take it back. It don't work like that." He yanks my hair. "I remember your friend, quite a treat that one. Blonde, just like Goldilocks. Had a mouth on her. I usually like that. I don't like it when they just sit there and take it."

I twist and ram him with my elbow.

He moans. "Yeah. Keep doing that. It's more fun that way, makes it last longer."

I pat the floor and feel around. Pain pierces my shoulder. I flinch. *Did he just stab me with a knife? WTF?* Blood trickles down my arm. It puddles on the floor. I thrash. "What'd you do with Cassie?"

He bites my neck, vampire-like. "Come on, Katie. You know me. When I get down to business, the world knows it. If I'd grabbed and murdered that New London girl, she'd be chopped up, dumped, and enjoying the company of worms and the whiz of the I-93 traffic. I take credit where credit is due."

He seems to relax some. The weight pressing down on my spine lessons. *Keep talking,* I tell myself. *Keep asking questions. If nothing else, it'll buy you time. Maybe Leeds will show up.*

My gaze shoots to my purse. Its contents have scattered. I see my SUV keys and my pepper spray near the washer and dryer. My knife and screwdriver are by the furnace. I say, "If you didn't grab her, then why are you in Newbury? You came because of my drawing, right? The drawing I exhibited at the gallery?"

"That pic of my hand? Not my best feature." He leans over me and presses his fingers against my mouth. One of them is missing. "I wanted to squeeze the breath out of you when my brother showed me that pic in *The Herald*," he says.

When I gasp for air, he laughs. "I don't like it here much. It's boring. In a month, it'll be cold as Alaska. And now cause some stupid fuck took Goldilocks, I have to be extra careful. Can't watch the kids playing in the park. Can't count the sun freckles on their butt cheeks as they prance around the lake. I can't even offer to buy them ice cream or watch their eyes widen when I run into them on the trail. Dullsville. But now you've come to entertain me."

As he rams his knife into my thigh, I scream.

He laughs. "Little lady, you're going to be playing with Whitney real soon. It's what you want, isn't it? You've missed her. And we both know what comes before that." He pricks my arm with his knife blade. "Your fingers, you're gonna lose them. Then I'm gonna watch you feebly attempt to draw my male anatomy with your stubs."

He pounds me with his fist. He could fatally stab me, but he chooses not to. It's a game to him. He knows where to cut me, which arteries to avoid. The torture, the prolonging of the death, is all part of it. I twist. That's when I feel the drawing pencil in my pocket, the one I fingered earlier on the driveway. If I can get my hand free, I'll grab it and use it.

I say, "You're an ass ... a fucking worm's tail."

He flips me over. "What the f ... did you say to me? What'd you call me?"

"A fucking worm's tail. No, wait. Pardon me. I'm wrong. That was your brother, Charles. The twin you burned and murdered. That's right, I said, 'murdered.' You've got respiratory problems," I say, recalling Reverend Shasta's account of James' breathing issues. "That fire was no accident. You don't smoke. You can barely handle being in a smokey room. You intentionally fried your twin. What would your poor sweet mother say? You killed her Bambino?"

The shifting of his body weight is all I need. I grab the pencil from my pocket and jam the point into his eye. He howls and claws at his face. I push him off me and bolt up the cellar stairs.

Cursing, he tears through the house after me. I tumble out the front door and sprint down the driveway. I don't have my SUV keys or my purse, so I simply run toward the road. I'm thrashing and breathing. Behind me, I hear footfalls, movement. Silence follows. I hear a click.

"Stop!" he yells. "If you don't, I'll shoot you."

I turn and freeze. He's aiming a gun at me. My body goes numb.

"Get over here," he says, stomping his booted foot. "Now!"

When I don't move, he walks toward me. Though blood drips from his eye, he doesn't seem to care. Adrenaline makes him like a wild animal. He points the gun at my chest. Desperate, I charge at him. We collide. The gun falls from his grasp. It drops, hits the driveway, fires. As the bullet ricochets off a tree, I shove him off me and kick him in the groin. When he staggers, I scoop the gun off the driveway and aim it at his torso.

He laughs. "You're not going to fire that thing. You don't have the balls. You didn't have the stuff to save your friend back in Jersey. You don't have what it takes to save yourself now."

"Tell me where Cassie is."

"Never had her."

He lunges at me. An image of Whitney lying unconscious in Hoover's Chevy flashes in my mind. I pull the trigger. Bang! James falls to the ground, lifeless.

I finger the gun and stare at his chest. When it doesn't rise or fall, I wrap my arms around my body. There's blood on my shirt and shorts from where he cut me. But from what I can tell the wounds are superficial, part of his game, his foreplay. Still, when the wind lifts the cotton fabric of my top, my flesh stings. I'm okay with the pain. It means I'm alive, that I've survived. I should feel better. I won this time, but I don't feel victorious. Even if I hated James Hoover, and many people would say he deserved to die, I still took a life. Besides, I haven't found Cassie.

I vomit and rock. I fumble for and find my cell in my shorts pocket. I've got reception again. I should call Liam or Leeds. I should call Thurston and tell him what I've done. Instead, I call Samuel. His number's in my cell. I don't want Samuel to hear about James' death on the news, the way I found out about Whitney.

Samuel picks up.

"Are you driving?" My voice sounds distant, foreign.

"I'm sitting on my couch. Why?"

"I just shot James. Killed him. I'm sorry. I didn't mean to."

"Sure, you did."

I swallow and taste blood.

"If you expect me to thank you, it's not happening."

"I … I …" My wails come out, loud and primal.

"Shut up and listen," Samuel says. "I meant to tell you. Someone picked up the blue carry-on at baggage claim, the one with the backpack inside. The attendant told me it was a guy in his fifties or sixties. What I'm saying is, you were right. James was messing with you. More than likely, my brother took that girl, like you said. What you did just now—well, in my book—it's justified. Before, on the bus, I didn't think he was involved. James told me he came to New Hampshire to be near me and Hollister. Plus, James usually liked things messy, dirty. The backpack had this sweet odor. Nice. Pleasant. It made me think it wasn't James who grabbed the girl. But I guess he decided to mix things up. Weird. The gear in that bag oozed lilac."

My heart pounds. "Lilac?"

"Yeah. My lady, Helena wears lilac. I know the scent."

"You're sure?"

"Positive."

My head spins. The day of the bus ride, I'd had an allergy attack and couldn't smell anything. I look at Hoover's lifeless body. *What did I do? Lilac. Lilly wears lilac.*

Samuel rambles. "After you and I chatted, James and I talked again about why he was in New Hampshire. He swore being here wasn't about you. Don't know why I believed him? Stupid on my part. We were raised in our grandpa's bait and tackle shop." Samuel laughs. "Hell, fishermen always obsess over the one that got away."

"I've gotta go. I need to call the feds. I'm sorry about your loss. Regardless of everything he did, James was still your brother."

I end the call and cover my face with my hands. *What if James was telling the truth? What if he never had Cassie? What if the Bays only pretended to forgive Mom, Dad, and me? What if my drawing of Hoover's bloody hand set them in a tailspin?*

I picture the mangled birch tree, and my thoughts race. *Lilly understands the tree's significance. Lilly also knows that "Straight up" was Whitney's favorite song. She knows where I worked. She could have snuck into my classroom and planted Cassie's sneaker in my closet. And she knows Reverend Shasta. She's been to his farm. She could have drawn on his chalkboard. She said that Sunday school kids satisfied her grandchild fix, but is that really true? Thurston seems normal. But it's almost as if he's been intentionally avoiding my urgent calls.*

Not wanting to be tracked, I toss my cell into the trees. I collect my purse and keys off the basement floor, climb into my Subaru, fumble in my wallet for Thurston's business card and contact info, and program the Bay's Vermont address into my GPS. It's stupid and likely a crucial mistake, but I leave the gun on the ground beside James' body. I've already killed one person. I don't want to be tempted to shoot another.

Chapter 16

It takes nearly two hours to get from Newbury to Stowe. I don't want to call attention to myself, so I drive the speed limit and use the right lane. It's still relatively early, late morning-ish. But the sun is stronger now. Its rays seep through my windshield and make me squint. The day's brightness makes the reality of what I'm doing—fleeing from a murder scene—tough to ignore.

Despite the intensity of James' attack, my injuries all seem relatively superficial—cuts, bruises, just the one deep gash in my thigh, and the small knife wounds on my shoulder and arm. I focus on finding Cassie and ignore my pain. I pass exit signs for towns and villages and try to imagine the inhabitants living their lives, but can't. This is worse than after Glen's death. My thoughts race, and I fear they'll never slow again, that I'll never be at peace.

I'm almost halfway to Stowe, near South Royalton, when the cop pulls up beside me. I keep my eyes glued to the road in front of me and pray he doesn't look at my license plate.

As my knees bounce, I count, "One Mississippi, Two Mississippi. Three Mississippi."

When the cop hovers for two whole minutes, my body goes stiff. The traffic is practically nonexistent in front of me, just a minivan a baseball pitch away. I grip my steering wheel and stare straight ahead. I don't dare look at the cruiser. I refuse to take the bait.

I've been holding my breath and have to exhale. Out of the corner of my eye, I see the red blinking light on top of the cruiser. I look at my fingers. Dried blood coats my knuckles. Fresh blood oozes through my T-shirt near my collarbone. I feel blood dripping down my back.

How are you going to explain your injuries? I ask myself.

Oh, who are you kidding, Kate? I counter. *If he's pulling you over, he knows exactly who you are and what you've done. What matters now is getting him to believe that Cassie being at the Bay's is a definite possibility.*

The cruiser speeds up. He's going to cut me off, box me in. I glance in my rearview mirror, expecting to see another cop car behind me. But the road is empty. The cop zips up behind the minivan driving ahead of me and motions to the driver.

As I zoom by them, relief expels from me like gas. I feel it physically in my gut. I spot the van's broken taillight. I fight the urge to flip on the radio. If I hear a news bulletin about me, it'll psyche me out, and I'll turn myself in. If I hadn't tossed my phone, I'd use it to call Mom, Liam, and Randi. I want to tell them all I love them, that I'm sorry for making them worry and for causing them pain. I think of Kingsley. I want to tell him I consider him a true friend.

My gas tank is nearly empty, and I'm shivering when I hit Stowe's Main Street. I pass arts and craft shops and an old inn and glimpse a white church steeple. People, likely residents and summer tourists, use the sidewalk. Ahead of me, a little girl walks beside a woman in a tennis skirt. The girl has brown hair, and her chin is too square, but I study her anyway to be certain, to be sure. *No, I tell myself. It can't be. That would be a miracle. It's too easy. No way would Cassie be skipping around in broad daylight.*

As I mentally dismiss the girl, my GPS cues me, and I turn off Main Street. The side street is paved at first, but after a mile or so, dirt crunches beneath my wheels. Like me, the Bays live on the outskirts of town. I get their need for solitude. When someone in your life is murdered, you can go to therapy, join support groups, and attempt to rebuild your life. You can fake being a Normal Joe or Joanne, but you'll always be an outsider. You remain on the cusp. Being the loved one of a murder-victim indelibly separates you from normal society, for sure.

I turn the steering wheel. Pain shoots down my shoulder. The dirt road curves and arches, serpent-like. I pass trees and driveways. The homes are few and far between and set back from the road. They're invisible, camouflaged by woods and distance. I peer at my GPS. I've only been here once before, with Glen two Easters ago. The Bays normally host holiday dinners in Brooklyn. Glen missed the driveway that Easter. I don't want to miss it now.

I glance in my rearview mirror. As if by magic, a blue sedan appears behind me. It must have come from one of the driveways, but I can't be certain. A man is driving. He's nondescript. He's in his forties with no facial hair. I wonder if he's one of Leeds' agents. *Relax*, I tell myself. *He's just a guy, a resident.* Still, I auto-lock my doors and accelerate. The GPS alerts me. "Destination," it says. The Bay's driveway comes at me fast. I turn too quickly and barely miss a reflector. The sedan swerves and speeds by me.

"Thank you, God," I murmur as the whoosh of the passing sedan lingers.

I straighten out my Subaru, pull farther down the driveway, and put my gearshift in park. Trembling, I rest my forehead against my steering wheel. A bead of something liquid slides down my nose. I wipe it off. A mix of perspiration and blood soils my fingers. If I'm going to turn around, this is the time to do it. Once I make contact with the Bays, my life as I know it will change. It has too. If Cassie's not here and my instincts are wrong, I'll never trust my gut again. I'll have to accept the fact that I'm delusional, paranoid, and mentally ill. I'll go to a psychiatric prison for hunting down James Hoover and killing him. And if Cassie is here, there will likely be a showdown. The Bays aren't going to allow me to just take her and leave. There's too much at stake for them. They'll go to prison. They'll lose everything.

My muscles go rigid. I suddenly feel very tired, as if I've lived too long, as if I'm ancient. Yet at the same time, it's like I'm falling forward. Momentum dictates my course of action. I have to do this. I can't stop now. I put my SUV in drive and head toward the Bay's house. The driveway's just as long as the entrance to Proctor Road. But the pines surrounding me now are even thicker. They crowd and darken the sky, so much so that rain seems imminent. But then the road curves, the trees thin, and sunlight spills out of a blue sky. The Bays' farmhouse appears on the hill, white and stark. No parked cars are in view. A random thought drops from my brain. *A lodge or A-framed cabin would suit the site better.*

I park facing the porch, check my face in the visor mirror, and use antibacterial wet wipes from my glove compartment to clean off the blood on my knuckles and nose. I tie a bandana around the stab wound on my thigh. The wound is trickling, but not gushing. I tell myself that I'm stable and not going into shock, though this is debatable.

I grab my purse off the passenger seat, march up the wooden stairs, and ring the Bay's doorbell.

Footsteps follow, and Lilly answers. Her eyes widen when she sees me, which makes sense. I'm bloody. And I've just killed a man and left the murder scene. She likely knows this. Samuel had to have called the authorities. My mug has to be on TV and on the internet. Probably the radio stations are broadcasting news bulletins about me too. I'm a fugitive, a killer. I'm almost surprised the cops aren't here.

"I came to see Thurston," I say when Lilly doesn't speak or ask me in. "Please," I beg. "I need his legal advice."

Lilly tugs at her cardigan. She looks normal, not like a kidnapper, not like someone who'd frame me for a crime she committed. She points toward the road. "Thurston's out getting gas."

I fidget and rub my palms together. Blood drips from my wrist and dots the landing I'm standing on. Lilly looks at the dime-sized blood blotches on the slate.

She motions to the door. "Oh, come on in, Kate. You're hurt." She frowns at me. "Thurston and I have been so worried about you, honey."

Guilt, doubt, and confusion wash over me. I don't know up from down. *What am I doing here? What was I thinking? This is Lilly, Lilly and Thurston. They don't have Cassie. If they ever blamed me for Whitney's death like Mom said, they don't anymore.*

Like a zombie, I follow Lilly into her two-story home. She motions to a sitting area off the foyer, and I sink onto an accent chair. The home, decorated with country-style furniture, is tidy. No signs of a young girl—no sneakers, hairbrushes, or Harry Potter books. My eyes drift to the foyer. Suitcases sit in front of the coat closet, two large black ones and a blue carry-on.

I stare at the blue carry-on. Samuel's words drop from my brain. *Someone picked up the blue carry-on. The attendant said it was a guy in his fifties or sixties.*

I think about how I spoke to Thurston prior to my bus ride and told him I planned to confront Samuel. My heart pounds. A sense of certainty fills me. *Thurston and Lilly really are framing me! They really do have Cassie!* I want to grab Lilly, shake her, and knock her to the floor. But I can't, not until I've found Cassie, not until I know she's safe.

"You look pale. I'm going to get you some juice," Lilly says as I tremble.

"I see suitcases," I blurt out. "Are you going on a trip?"

"Mexico. Just for a few days. Our flight's this evening. We bought the tickets before you asked Thurston to represent you." She motions to the blood on my hands. "But clearly what we're dealing with here is pressing. Don't worry," she adds, hurrying into the kitchen. "Thurston won't abandon you. He can communicate with you via cell, email, or Skype. Call in a temporary backup attorney. We'll figure something out."

Dishes clank. I hear the soft thud of the refrigerator shutting and her footsteps. A thump sounds from the second floor. Lilly's words, *Thurston's out getting gas,* fill my mind. A minute later, Lilly reappears carrying a glass of juice. Lilac wafts off her skin.

"Drink," she says, handing me a glass of apple juice. "You'll feel better. You're bleeding. You need electrolytes."

I sip the juice. It tastes too sweet. But I need to get her out of here to look for Cassie, so I force it down. "May I have another glass? Maybe something to eat. Toast? I'm weak."

"Sure." She takes the empty glass from me. As she scurries back into the kitchen, I tiptoe up the staircase. All the doors I encounter are open except for one. I rap softly on the locked door.

"Cassie! Are you in there? It's Miss Kate."

I listen. Silence follows. My thoughts tumble. *She's not here. You're imagining things. The thud, the lilac, and the blue carry-on, it's like what Liam said that day you heard the Paula Abdul song? You're looking for signs. Everyone's right. You've truly lost it.*

I stare at the locked door and knock one last time. Nothing.

As I turn, Cassie's muffled voice seeps through the transom above me. "Help! Help! Miss Kate! Miss Kate!"

I twist the doorknob and bang on the door. My focus is on Cassie, nothing and no one else. The floor creaks behind me. I whirl about. Lilly is standing in front of the linen closet, a carving knife in her hand.

I point to the bedroom door, the one imprisoning Cassie, and eye the knife in Lilly's grasp. "Lilly, please. You're not going to use that. Put down that knife."

Lilly shakes her head. "Can't. Whitney would still be alive if it weren't for you. If you'd been brave enough to tell the cops about Hoover's missing finger, if your parents had dragged you down to that lineup, she'd still be here." She cocks her chin at the locked door. "She's a sweet girl, a bit active and high-spirited, but she'll calm down. That's what I keep telling Thurston. He gets so impatient with her. But it's only because he knows how important she is to me. He knows I don't want anyone taking her away from us."

Thurston, I think. *Thurston will see reason. He might be angry with you, but he isn't off his rocker. You can talk to him.*

"You know I have to kill you," Lilly says, stepping toward me. "Not with this knife. Too messy. Too much work. I'm gonna tie you up and leave you in the woods. No one comes out here. The bears will eat you. Should you manage to beat them off, you'll starve to death or freeze." She smiles. "Weather's supposed to turn any day now."

Turn. Turn. Turn. The room spins. I lean against the wall. *What's wrong with me?* A fuzzy image of the apple juice I downed pops into my head.

"The juice," I say. "You put something in it."

As my knees buckle and I slide to the floor, Lilly nods. "Valium. I crushed it up and mixed it in," she explains stepping around me. "Cassandra!" she says, "Let's get ready for Cozumel, sweetie."

I open my mouth to call out to Cassie, but no words come out. My eyelids feel rock-heavy. I can't stay awake. Everything goes black.

* * *

The scent of sap curdles my stomach. As the wind blows, pine needles fall and hit my shoulders. I want to brush them off, but can't. My wrists are tied together. I'm on my butt, knees bent to my chest, and hugging a pine tree trunk.

"She drugged me. Lilly actually drugged me," I say.

My voice sounds weak and hollow to my ears. My mouth tastes like cotton, not that I've ever eaten cotton. But I'd chow down on something if it would keep me awake, because I have to stay awake. Time matters. Darkness comes early in the forest, and with the darkness comes bears. I squint at a patch of graying sky peeking through the trees.

"If I had to guess, I'd say it's after six," I say, needing to hear the sound of my own voice. If I can hear myself, that means I'm alive. "You got to Stowe around noon. Lilly put the pill in your juice at around twelve thirty." I bite my lip and taste blood and dirt. "How long do the effects of Valium last? Four to six hours?" I surmise.

Shivering, I glance at my upper arms. They're bruised. The pain in my thighs and calves tells me that my legs are scratched, but not deeply. The wounds on my thigh, arm, and shoulder seem to have stopped bleeding. I don't feel them dripping. I attempt to stand, but my muscles refuse to hold me. The position I'm in is pretzel-like. A branch snaps. I twist. That's when I see her. She's standing amongst the trees, a tennis serve away from me.

"Lilly? What are you doing here? Don't you have a flight?" It's a ridiculous thing to say, given the circumstances. But I can't equate the Lilly I know, have known for three decades, with the Lilly who drugged me and tied me to a tree trunk. The Lilly I know isn't violent. But obviously she's snapped. As she moves toward me, my eyes shoot to her feet. Lilly is wearing a navy ensemble and slip-on flats.

She follows my gaze and motions to her shoes. "Easy to take these off in the airport security line. Oh, our flight's at nine. We still have time. I've been busy in the kitchen." She gestures a grocery bag in her grasp. I didn't see it until now. She pulls out its contents, a plastic food storage bag filled with bacon. "I fried up the whole package," she says, tossing pieces at me and around the wheelbarrow.

When the storage bag is empty, she puts it back into her grocery bag. She retrieves a can of dog food from the same bag, pulls off the lid, and, using a fork, dumps the mixture on the ground. As I violently shake my head, she smears the goop on my cheeks and chin.

"You came all the way out here to do that? I thought you said the bears were hungry, that they'd eat anything."

"Oh, they will," she assures me. "They're gearing up for hibernation. But I wanted to make sure that you were nice and tasty for them. I didn't want to disappoint." She turns to leave but hesitates. Her eyebrows arch. "Oh, I've lost something. I wanted to find it before my flight. I thought perhaps you had it. Actually, it's Thurston's, but I borrowed it the other day. Anyhow, I was certain I put it back, but it's not there now. So maybe I didn't. Or maybe you took it."

Her eyes hone in on me. What the hell? She misplaced a book, a charger, or one of those neck pillows people use on long flights. But if she'd done that, why would she be hounding me? I decide that the lost thing is important, that it matters. It's a driver's license, a passport, or something she needs to board the plane and leave the country with Cassie, because that's what she's doing.

I'm still loopy. I have to keep reminding myself that Lilly is the enemy, that she dragged me out here, tied me to a tree, and is using me as bear bait. I picture the second-story hallway. How did I even get here? Did she roll me down the stairs like a tennis ball or push me down like a laundry basket? Did she manhandle me onto a tarp and drag me out here? In my mind, I hear my bones, thumping down each step and clanking across the hard ground. I swallow. *Focus, Kate. Focus.*

I ask, "Took what? What did you lose, Lilly? What is Thurston missing?"

"His Glock. I borrowed it to spook a raccoon. The bugger was in my garden." Lilly makes a gun sign with her hand and aims it at me. "Bang."

When I jump, she laughs.

"Clearly, I don't have it on me, and I didn't hide it anywhere either. You can check my SUV, if you want." More than likely she already has. I no longer have my purse. This means I don't have my keys or my phone. Pain shoots through my forehead. *How the hell am I going to get out of here? How am I going to save Cassie?*

Lilly moves closer to me. She circles me like a dog circles soil before it shits. "I think you hid it," she says. "I think you heard me coming up the stairs and hid it."

I frown. "But I didn't even know it existed."

"Don't lie to me. Where is it?" she says.

She's in my face. Her breath is hot. It reeks of vodka. I recoil. It shocks me to think of her drinking. It shocks me back in time. I'm thirteen again. Whitney and I are almost at the Lawrenceville park. We're singing the Paula Abdul song and it's snowing.

So glad Mom's not here, Whitney mutters.

The Whitney in my mind, presses her first against her lips and tilts her head back like she's guzzling something.

The revelation hits me. Whitney wasn't copying a Paula Abdul's dance arm move. She was pretending to drink booze.

"You drank when Whitney was alive," I say.

Lilly flinches, like I've slapped her.

"You did drink when she was alive, didn't you?" I say, "That's why Whitney didn't want you at the park with us that morning. You were hungover. You were probably drinking when went to the library on Tuesdays. You wanted everyone out of the house so you could drink. You're a drunk. That's why Whitney never wanted to be home alone with you. You were a bad mom to Whitney. You feel guilty. That's really why you snatched Cassie. You wanted a do-over."

"Lies," she says. "It's not going to work. You're not going to distract me with your lies."

But she is distracted. I can tell by her lined expression. "Is that why you're not sure about the gun? Were you drinking the other day when you had it? You're not certain you put it back, are you?"

"I did," she says. "I did put it back. It's you who took it and hid it."

I eyeball her. She eyeballs me. I don't understand why finding the gun matters so much. I'm tied up. It's not like I can attack her. And in a few hours, she'll be on a plane with Thurston and Cassie to Mexico. They'll be starting a new life. The chances of someone finding me before the bears get to me are slim. Kingsley and Leeds know that I was going to the listed properties in New London and Newbury, but I didn't tell anyone I was going to Stowe.

"I don't need my gun," Lilly says suddenly. She wiggles her fingers. "I've got these."

She walks behind me. I feel her hands wrap around my neck. Her fingers are sweaty and warm, and smell of bacon and Purina. She squeezes hard. I thrash, kick my legs, whip my head, and elbow her. I'm not going quietly. I want her to remember this. Remember me. If it's one thing James Hoover has taught me, it's this: you have to own what you do. The Worm Man owned his crimes. I'm going to own my death. *Remember me, Lilly. Remember what you did to me, bitch.*

My chest tightens. Dizziness overwhelms me.

"I'm going to make it super easy for the bears," she whispers.

Bang!

Lilly topples to the ground. Gasping for breath, I turn toward the bang. Cassie is standing several yards away from us, from me. She's holding a gun. I take in Lilly's lifeless body and understand. Finding the Glock mattered to Lilly because she feared Cassie had taken it. Lilly wanted Cassie to love her. Cassie's theft, her disloyalty, proved that she didn't care about Lilly and likely never would.

Cassie lowers the gun to the ground. As she runs to me, I keep my eyes on Lilly. Blood pools on the leaves beside her still body. As I exhale, Cassie barrels into me and presses her forehead against mine.

"You're alive! I've missed you so much. We've all been so worried," I murmur.

I stare into her teary sky-blue eyes, Glen's eyes. As Cassie squeals, I rake my fingers through her white-blonde hair. I want to soak in this reunion, celebrate her being alive, finding her. But the forest is darkening, the bears are hungry, I'm covered with dog food, and I don't know where Thurston is.

I nudge Cassie. "Untie me. We've got to get out of here."

Cassie's focus shifts to Lilly's lifeless body. She goes stiff. "I killed her! She's dead! Miss Lilly's dead!" She shakes and flops to the ground, rag doll-like. "The man at the range said I needed to be careful. That I should only shoot at targets, not people! I killed her! I killed Miss Lilly!"

"Cassie," I say, pulling on the rope encircling my wrists, "if you hadn't shot her, she would have killed me. You're brave and strong. You did the right thing."

She pulls her knees to her chest and sways.

"Listen, I know you're scared. But I need you to be brave just a little bit longer. Cassie, look at me," I say in my teacher voice. "You had to shoot her. No one is going to be angry with you. You're not in trouble."

Cassie peers up. I've gotten her attention. "Why did she take me?" she sobs. "What did I do wrong?"

"Nothing. You did everything right. She was angry and sad. She thought loving you would make her feel better."

"But I didn't love her back," she says, her lip quivering. That's why I climbed through that window with the broken lock. I want to go home.

"I know. You miss your parents and brother. You'll see them soon. But we have to get out of here, which is why I need you to untie me."

"Can't," she wails. "My fingers are too shaky."

"You can. It's just the same as untying a shoelace. Just a few more knots." I picture her pink Converse sneakers, the one from the slide and the other in the supply closet. "It's just like untying those pretty pink sneakers you're always wearing. Piece of cake. You can do this," I say when she shudders. "I know you can. Don't look at Miss Lilly. Look at me."

Our gazes lock. "Untie it like my pink sneakers?" she whispers.

"Yes. Exactly like those sneakers."

Nodding, she positions herself behind me. I feel the bindings on my wrist tighten. I can tell she's working the knots.

"I can't do it," she whines. "The rope is too tight. Slippery. I can't see anything. It's too dark. I can't untie the knots."

"You can. Concentrate. Do one knot at a time. You've got this, Cassie. You built a sandcastle in the rain. I saw you. You've made dozens of birdhouses out of pinewood. That's super hard too. And you mastered your times tables. You thought you'd never do that. What's nine times seven?"

"Sixty-three!"

The rope around my wrists loosens. "Got one!" she says.

"That's great," I tell her. "Now move onto the next one."

The rope twitches. "Got it!"

"Excellent. How many more to go?"

"Just one," Cassie says.

I hear gravel crunching.

Cassie squeals, "It's him! Mr. Thurston! It's the man who lives with Miss Lilly!"

"Don't worry about Mr. Thurston." I squint in the direction of the driveway. All I see are pines. *What if it's not Thurston? What if it's a bear?* "Keep working on that knot," I tell her. "You've got time. Loosen it. Don't think about anyone or anything else. Just the knot. Focus on untying it." The rope slides off my wrist. "You did it," I whisper. "You're my hero."

I hug Cassie, retrieve the gun off the ground, and steer her behind a spruce. I want to tell her how I failed to save Whitney and how I hated myself for not doing enough to rescue her, that she shouldn't feel guilty about saving herself and fighting for her life and mine. But someone or some animal is stomping on those pine needles and getting closer. I finger the Glock in my grasp. I told myself I wasn't going to shoot another living thing. But I'm going to protect Cassie, no matter what. I'm not going to lose her like I lost Whitney. I'll do whatever it takes to save her. I step away from Cassie, aim at the movement in the trees, and finger the trigger.

"Kate!" a male voice shouts.

"Cassie!" a second male voice hollers.

It's Liam and Kingsley. I lower the gun.

"Over here!" I yell. "We're over here!" I grip Cassie's hand. "It's okay," I murmur. "They're friends of mine. We're safe now."

A flashlight beam sweeps the forest floor. Cassie and I run toward it, and I fall into Liam's embrace. Kingsley scoops Cassie up into his arms.

"How did you know where to find Cassie?" I ask.

"Thurston," Liam says, hugging me. "He turned himself in. He told Leeds that Lilly abducted Cassie to punish you, that he was afraid Lilly would harm herself or Cassie if he went to the authorities, so he kept quiet. Samuel Hoover called the precinct too. He said his brother was hiding in a house in Newbury. That he attacked you, and you shot him with his gun." He cocks his chin at the road. "The ambulance and Leeds' team will be here any second. I should have believed you, Kate. I'm sorry. So sorry." He touches my bloody shirt, the dog food on my cheek. "Are you okay?"

"I will be. Cassie's alive. That's what matters." I peer at Cassie. I can't stop staring at her. I see only the best parts of Glen in her, his tenacity and his bravery. I squeeze her girl-sized hand. Kingsley, who's been abnormally quiet, lowers Cassie to the ground, and kneels beside us.

"Leeds let you go?" I say Kingsley.

Kingsley nods. "He was only holding me to get to you. Once Thurston came forward, Leeds released me." Kingsley drapes a blanket over Cassie's shoulders and winks at me. "Gotta hand it to you, Kate. You did just what you said you'd do. You got the bad guys and saved the little girl to boot. Impressive. You make a great secondary character. It's a hell of an ending."

My eyes mist. Still clutching Cassie's fingers, I cling to Liam. "It's not just an ending. It's a beginning."

Kingsley smiles at us. "I stand corrected. It's that too."

Epilogue

*E*velyn hurries across the gallery floor. "Here, let me take that from you, Kate." As she collects the package in my grasp, my heart beats fast. Beneath the brown wrapping paper is the bloody snowball hand drawing Liam purchased at the gallery show. Evelyn found a new buyer, an art collector from Dubai. Liam doubled his money.

Evelyn holds the package and fingers a piece of loose tape. "This drawing is mesmerizing, Kate. You sure you don't want to take one last peek?"

I frown. "Absolutely not. I'll be back in when I've completed my series for the spring show."

"I'll be waiting." Evelyn smiles. "Hey, Randi told me you're teaching art classes for kids at the library now. Any prodigies?"

I picture Cassie, a drawing pencil in her grasp. Lauren and I aren't friends, not even close, but for Cassie's sake we've called an awkward truce. Cassie's enrolled in my Portrait Drawing for Kids Class. She's still my favorite student. My heart swells every time I see that dimpled cheek of hers. "All my students are perfectly imperfect," I say.

Evelyn grins. "And Liam?"

I flash my engagement ring.

Evelyn claps. "I knew it!"

"My mother and Randi are helping me plan the wedding," I tell her. "The ceremony is going to be the first Saturday in May. We're waiting for Kingsley to return from his book tour. May 4ᵗʰ! Save the date."

"You couldn't pay me to stay away," Evelyn says, hugging me. "I'll be there with bells on."

As she waves, I exit the gallery, and button my coat. I've got a crime victim support group to speak at, a painting class to prepare for, and a Christmas tree to decorate. But instead of driving away, I sit idle in my SUV.

Five minutes pass. A man, who appears to be of Arab descent, cruises into the lot. He parks beside me and enters the Wyndham Gallery. I watch him through the gallery window as he and Evelyn shake hands. The man gives Evelyn what I assume is a cashier's check. He exits with my wrapped drawing, slides the piece onto the backseat of his Tesla, zooms onto Main Street, and heads west toward the interstate and the airport.

"It's over," I murmur. "It's finally over."

As the sun's rays pierce the December clouds, a wave of lightness washes over me. I leave the parking lot, drive two blocks to a tiny blue house, pull into the home's driveway, and smile. The house is old, and the trim needs painting, but the place is amazing mostly because it's mine. Correction, "ours." Liam is moving in after the wedding. With Bill's help, I sold Glen's farmhouse. I didn't have to. I wanted to. It was simply time to let go of Glen and my past.

Humming, I climb out of my SUV. Shoulders back and chin up, I amble across the leaf-covered lawn, clinking my house keys. When I near my front porch, I glance down. An icy puddle has formed on the bricks by the gutter downspout. An earthworm wiggles in the partially frozen rainwater.

I stare at the worm. My muscles stiffen. It's cold, just above freezing. The worm should be hibernating.

As "Straight Up" the Paula Abdul tune echoes in my mind, I stomp on the worm, and march up the front steps and toward my future.

About the Author

*M*ary Frances Hill, received her MA in counseling psychology from Rider University. Like many of her protagonists, she's infatuated with New England and its picturesque towns filled with history. When MF isn't writing, she's walking her dalmadoodle, watching HGTV, and spending time with her husband and adult children. She currently lives in Southern California. The Worm Man is her first novel.

Made in United States
North Haven, CT
16 August 2022

22787837R00114